poached

Also by Stuart Gibbs

Belly Up

Spy School

Spy Camp

Evil Spy School

The Last Musketeer

Space Case

STUART GIBBS

poached

A funjungle NOVEL

Simon & Schuster Books for Young Readers

New York   London   Toronto   Sydney   New Delhi

For the Sterns: David, Tara, Marni, and Kira

And the Heisens: Christopher, Laura, Aaron, and

Emmett

And Adam Zarembok

SIMON & SCHUSTER BOOKS FOR YOUNG READERS
An imprint of Simon & Schuster Children's Publishing Division
1230 Avenue of the Americas, New York, New York 10020
For information about special discounts for bulk purchases, please contact Simon & Schuster Special Sales at 1-866-506-1949 or business@simonandschuster.com.
The Simon & Schuster Speakers Bureau can bring authors to your live event. For more information or to book an event, contact the Simon & Schuster Speakers Bureau at 1-866-248-3049 or visit our website at www.simonspeakers.com.
Also available in a Simon & Schuster Books for Young Readers hardcover edition
Book design and cover illustration by Lucy Ruth Cummins
Map illustration by Ryan Thompson
The text for this book is set in Adobe Garamond.
Manufactured in the United States of America
0321 OFF
First Simon & Schuster Books for Young Readers paperback edition April 2015
12
The Library of Congress has cataloged the hardcover edition as follows:
Gibbs, Stuart, 1969–
Poached / Stuart Gibbs. — First edition.
pages cm
Summary: Twelve-year-old Teddy Fitzroy is the prime suspect when FunJungle's newly acquired koala goes missing, thanks to a prank staged by middle school bully Vance Jessup.
ISBN 978-1-4424-6777-4 (hardcover) — ISBN 978-1-4424-6779-8 (eBook)
[1. Mystery and detective stories. 2. Zoos—Fiction. 3. Zoo animals—Fiction.
4. Bullies—Fiction. 5. Family life—Texas—Fiction. 6. Texas—Fiction.] I. Title.
PZ7.G339236Po 2014
[Fic]—dc23
2013000539
ISBN 978-1-4424-6778-1 (pbk)

acknowledgments

I'd like to thank Jason Jacobs at the Los Angeles Zoo for answering all of my koala questions, no matter how strange they probably seemed to him at the time.

Thanks to David Stern, who has helped me with so many jokes over the years, like the "Baron Wasteland" one in this book.

I'd also like to give a very special thanks to my children, who are now getting old enough to influence the tales I tell. My son Dashiell's fascination with sharks (particularly bull sharks) inspired many of the scenes in this book. And my daughter, Violet, who loves the zoo as much as I do, was always thrilled to join me on research trips to visit the koalas. (Of course, I was always equally thrilled to have her along as well.) I love you both more than words can say.

THE PRANK

I would never have been accused of stealing the koala if Vance Jessup hadn't made me drop a human arm in the shark tank.

It wasn't a *real* human arm. It was a plastic one Vance had stolen from a department-store mannequin. But it *looked* real enough through the glass of the tank, which was how all the trouble started.

Vance was the toughest, meanest kid at my middle school. He was in the eighth grade, but he'd been held back. Twice. Which made him a fifteen-year-old eighth grader. Plus, he was big for his age, nearly six feet tall with biceps as thick as Burmese pythons. Every other kid looked like a dwarf next to him.

There was a very long list of things I didn't like about

Lyndon B. Johnson Middle School, but Vance was at the top of it. He'd been bullying me since my first day of seventh grade—and it was now mid-December. I didn't know what he had against me. Maybe it was because I was new at the school and thus fresh meat. Or maybe it was that, having spent most of my childhood in the Congo, I was different from all the other kids. Whatever the case, Vance homed in on me like he was a lion and I was the weakest wildebeest in the herd.

Vance stole my lunch. He gave me wedgies. He flushed my homework down the toilet. I reported these incidents to my parents, who angrily informed the school principal, Mr. Dillnut. Unfortunately, Mr. Dillnut was afraid of Vance himself. So he merely threatened Vance with detention— and then ratted me out as the kid who'd squealed. If anything, this made Vance even *more* determined to harass me. And now he warned that if I ever got him sent to the principal again, he'd hurt me.

So I fought back the only way I knew how: I played pranks on him. Covertly, of course. I filled his locker with aerosol cheese. I submerged a dead roach in his chocolate pudding. I caught a king snake and hid it in his gym bag. That one worked out the best. Vance was changing in the boys' locker room when the snake popped out and scared him silly. Vance shrieked like a girl and fled into the gym, forgetting that he was only in his underwear until he found himself face-to-face with the entire cheerleading squad.

Unfortunately, the snake tipped my hand. I'd kept my identity as the prankster secret until that point, but I was well-known at school for being good with animals. My mother was a world-famous primatologist, my father was a world-famous wildlife photographer, and I lived with both of them at FunJungle, the world's largest zoo. Vance quickly deduced that I'd planted the snake and came looking for payback.

He found me in the cafeteria on Monday, having lunch with Xavier Gonzalez. Xavier was my best friend at school. In fact he was my only friend at school. He was an outsider too, a smart kid who'd once made the terrible social error of admitting that he actually enjoyed his classes. Before I'd come along, Xavier had been Vance's favorite target.

There was a distinct hierarchy to the seating in the school cafeteria. The coolest kids, known as the Royals, sat in the center, where they could be seen and admired. These were the eighth-grade jocks and cheerleaders, plus a few rich kids. They were surrounded by the Lower Royals: the younger jocks, cheerleaders, and rich kids who would assume the throne someday. Then came almost everyone else: the normal kids who hoped to be popular, but knew it would probably never happen. At the very corners sat the lowest of the low, whom even the normal kids looked down on: the losers, loners, and freaks who hadn't mastered how to fit in.

I had spent every lunch so far in one of the corners with Xavier. So it wasn't hard for Vance to find me.

As usual, Xavier and I were talking about FunJungle. Most of my fellow students liked FunJungle—after all, it was the biggest tourist attraction in all of Central Texas—but Xavier was a FunJungle fanatic. He had more than twenty different FunJungle T-shirts (not to mention sweatshirts, caps, pins, and other assorted merchandise) and claimed that the day the park had opened was the greatest day of his life. He wanted to be a field biologist when he grew up and idolized my mother the way other kids revered rock stars. He'd read everything he could find about her, so he knew all about me before I'd even set foot in the school. He'd sought me out on my first day at Lyndon B. Johnson, wanting to know if I could introduce him to Mom.

Xavier generally spent every lunch peppering me with questions about FunJungle. The day that Vance came after me, we happened to be talking about Shark Odyssey, which was one of the more popular exhibits. It was a huge aquarium with a glass tunnel running through it, from which guests could watch sharks swimming all around them.

"Doesn't that drive the sharks crazy?" Xavier wanted to

know. "It must be like waving red meat in front of a bear."

"Sharks don't really eat humans," I told him. "In fact, most attacks seem to be accidents. The sharks usually spit the humans back out after biting them."

"I know," Xavier said. "But still, they're hunters, right? And now all these humans are moving right through their habitat. It must trigger some sort of primal instinct."

I shook my head. "No. In the first place, the glass tunnel is lined with some kind of reflective surface, so the sharks can't see the humans from inside. And even if they could, sharks don't really hunt by sight. They hunt by smell— and by sensing vibrations in the water. You could drop a whole mannequin in the shark tank and the sharks probably wouldn't even give it a second look."

"I bet it'd freak the guests out, though," Xavier laughed.

"Yeah," I agreed. "It would be pretty funny."

Xavier stopped laughing at that point, which I should have taken as a sign that something was wrong, but I was too caught up thinking about the prank. I kept rambling on, unaware that Vance Jessup was bearing down on me. "Know what would *really* freak the guests out? If you only put *part* of a mannequin in the tank. Like just an arm. So it'd look like the sharks had already eaten the rest. *That* would be hilarious."

Now, Vance decided to make his presence known. He grabbed my chair and spun me around to face him. "What would be hilarious?" he demanded. "Are you planning another prank on me?"

I gulped, terrified, and did my best to lie to Vance's face. "What are you talking about? I've never played *any* pranks on you."

"I know you put that snake in my gym bag, Monkey Boy. And you're gonna pay for it." Vance held up a clenched fist the size of a grapefruit.

I recoiled, aware this wasn't an idle threat. Vance got in fights almost every day—and usually won. He was covered with bruises, scratches, and scrapes, though his opponents generally looked far worse. He was currently sporting a half dozen Band-Aids dappled with blood that was probably someone else's.

Meanwhile, I'd never been in a fight in my life. I wouldn't stand a chance against Vance.

"Teddy wasn't talking about playing a prank on *you*," Xavier said quickly, trying to bail me out. "He was talking about playing a prank at FunJungle. Dropping a fake human arm into the shark tank to make all the guests freak out."

Vance lowered his fist. His sneer faded and he made a strange noise. At first I thought he was choking—but then realized he was laughing. "That *would* be funny," he said. "When are you going to do it?"

"Er . . . never," I said. "I only meant it would be funny *in theory*. I would never really do something like that. It might start a panic—"

"Exactly," Vance said, and then laughed again. "Let's do it after school tomorrow."

I shook my head and tried to come up with a believable excuse. "Sorry, but it's not possible. There's a ton of security at FunJungle. They'd catch us if we tried to sneak the arm inside."

"No, they'd catch *me* if I tried to sneak the arm inside," Vance corrected. "Not you. You don't have to go through the main entrance."

I winced. I hadn't expected Vance to know that. I struggled to come up with something else. "We don't have a fake arm, either . . ."

"Leave that to me," Vance said. "I can steal one from the department store in town."

"You know, now that I think about it," I said, "I don't think this would be that good a prank at all. But I'll tell you what might be a lot more fun. Maybe I could get you a backstage tour of the shark exhibit. It's pretty fascinating. . . ."

Vance's eyes narrowed in anger. "I don't want a tour of some dumb shark tank."

"Oh, it's not dumb," Xavier put in, trying to be helpful. "It's actually quite amazing. In fact, it's the largest shark tank in the world, housing over thirty different species—"

"Shut up," Vance told him.

"Okay," Xavier said, backing down.

Vance clamped a hand on my shoulder. "I want to play this prank," he informed me. "And I need your help to do it. So you're going to help me, right?"

I wished I'd had the nerve to stand up to Vance right then and there and tell him what I really thought of him. But my shoulder was already in terrible pain, and Vance wasn't even squeezing that hard yet. I got the sense that if he wanted to, he could snap me like a twig. And yet I still hesitated before giving Vance an answer.

That didn't please him at all. "Trust me on this," he said. "You don't want to be my enemy. Before I heard about this shark-tank thing, I was about to pound your face in. I'd still be happy to do that."

"No!" I said desperately, wanting to keep my face the way it was. "I'll do it!"

"Okay, then." Vance released me and flashed a cruel smile. "See you tomorrow afternoon."

So that's how I ended up dropping fake body parts into Shark Odyssey.

Vance cornered me right after school the next day. True to his word, he'd obtained the arm of a mannequin—and a foot as well. "The more body parts the better," he explained. Just in case I'd managed to work up the nerve to say no to him—which I'd been working on for the past twenty-four hours—he'd brought along two bullies-in-training: Jim and Tim Barksdale. The Barksdales were identical twins in the eighth grade. They were so dumb and mean that everyone, even their parents, had trouble telling them apart. Since they were rarely without each other, everyone simply called them TimJim.

Vance had hidden the mannequin parts in a large backpack, which he insisted I take with me on the school bus. "Don't even go home," he threatened. "Take it right to the sharks. We'll be waiting for you there. If you try to chicken out—or tip off security—we'll come find you."

"And then maybe we'll feed *you* to the sharks," either Tim or Jim said.

The boys all laughed at this.

I felt like throwing up, but I didn't really see that I had a choice. So I left my regular backpack in my locker, took my homework and Vance's backpack, and hopped onto the school bus. Xavier, who rode the same bus as me, volunteered to come to Shark Odyssey as moral support—although I suspected he was actually more interested in getting to sneak into FunJungle the back way with me. "Thanks," I told him, "but I should probably do this alone. Maybe I can trick Vance into doing it himself and get him busted for it."

"I wouldn't do that," Xavier warned. "If Vance catches on, it'll only make him angrier at you."

"He won't catch on," I said. "He's a moron. The guy's flunked eighth grade twice."

Xavier shook his head. "Vance didn't flunk because he's stupid. He flunked because he's lazy. In fact, Vance is smarter than most people realize. If he put as much thought into studying as he does into being cruel and mean, he'd be graduating college by now."

I thought back to my many nasty encounters with Vance and realized Xavier was right. Vance was actually quite clever; he just used his gifts for evil. For example, he knew how to make his own cherry bombs with chemicals he'd pilfered from the science lab. "So what should I do?" I asked.

"Pull the prank as fast as possible," Xavier advised, "and pray you don't get caught."

My bus stop was the last one, as FunJungle was located several miles from town. Technically it wasn't located in *any* school district; a special exemption had been made for me, the only child living there, to attend Lyndon B. Johnson.

FunJungle was so big it actually qualified as its own city. The park had been built by J.J. McCracken, a local billionaire. He claimed he'd done it for his daughter, Summer—but the fact that 175 million people visited zoos in America every year had certainly influenced him as well. FunJungle was officially a zoo—the world's biggest, by far—though, to attract tourists, it was also part theme park. There were thrill rides, stage shows, themed hotels, and plenty of innovative exhibits, like a massive African habitat where you could go on a safari and several pools where you could swim with dolphins. Despite the gimmicks, however, FunJungle was committed to providing top-quality care for its animals. J.J. had hired lots of distinguished biologists (like my mother) and had shelled out big bucks to make the animal exhibits state-of-the-art. The whole park was nearly ten miles square, with its own police department, fire station, and hospital. (Technically it was an *animal* hospital, but it was nicer than most human hospitals and had a physician on staff for any FunJungle employees who got sick.)

I didn't really live at FunJungle per se. There was a trailer park behind the safari area that served as free housing for the distinguished biologists and their families. As Vance had ordered, I didn't go home once the bus dropped me off. But then I never did. There was no point in sitting in our trailer all by myself. Not when Mom's office was nice and cozy and had windows that looked into the gorilla exhibit. Many days I went straight there to do my homework, but if anything interesting was happening at FunJungle—and there often was—I'd go there instead. Thus Mom didn't really expect me to show up at any specific time. And as for Dad, he was generally roaming the park taking pictures—if he was even at the park. His contract allowed him to accept freelance jobs as well. He'd just returned from photographing anacondas in the Amazon for *National Geographic* a few days earlier.

I entered the park through the rear employee entry booth, which was next to the employee parking lot and the trailer park. Darlene, the guard posted inside, barely gave me a glance as I entered. She was watching a downloaded movie on her iPhone, which was probably a violation of sixteen different security directives, but on that day I didn't care. I didn't want any scrutiny.

The entry booth wasn't much bigger than a storage closet. On one side a door led in from employee parking. On the other side a door led into FunJungle. Darlene sat between them next to a metal detector. "Hey, Teddy, how was school?" she asked.

"Same as usual." I set the backpack down by Darlene, passed through the metal detector, and grabbed the pack again without giving her the chance to rifle through it. Not that she tried. Darlene hadn't examined my things once in the last six months. However, she did stare at the pack a little bit longer than usual.

"That new?" she asked.

"Yeah. Mom just got it for me."

"It's awful big."

"They give lots of homework at my school," I explained.

"Yuck." Darlene made a face of disgust, then returned to her movie.

I exited into FunJungle and made a beeline for Shark Odyssey.

The rear employee entrance was on the opposite side of the park from the main gates, hidden behind a thicket of trees so that tourists wouldn't notice it. A narrow path brought me out onto Adventure Road, the main route through the park, right between Carnivore Canyon and the Land Down Under.

The park was eerily empty. During the summer, capacity crowds had come every day and Adventure Road had been as crowded as a Manhattan sidewalk. But now the tourists were few and far between. The reason, everyone claimed, was the weather, which had been far worse that year than anyone had expected.

The main reason J.J. McCracken had built FunJungle in the Texas Hill Country was that it was supposed to be warm all the time. This would be good for the animals, most of which came from warm climates, and better for the tourists, who would theoretically flock there year-round. (This was the same reason that Disney and Universal Studios had built their theme parks in Southern California and Florida.) Unfortunately, this particular winter had been the nastiest anyone could remember. Ever since mid-November, a freak cold front had stalled over the Hill Country, pelting the park with an incredible array of horrible weather. There had been hail, freezing rain, record cold temperatures, and even a few tornadoes. (Thankfully, these had all been quite small and done little damage, although one had uprooted a jungle gym in the Play Zone and flung it into the World of Reptiles.)

Thousands of guests who'd booked for Thanksgiving and the Christmas holidays had canceled their FunJungle travel plans. This was terrible luck for the park, which had finally rebounded from its previous crisis, the murder of its mascot, Henry the Hippo, that summer. If anything, this was worse. Henry's death had at least sparked interest in the park; tourists had streamed in to see the notorious murder site. But few people had any interest in spending their vacations shivering in a sleet storm, staring at animal paddocks that were empty because the animals themselves had had the sense to go inside.

The stretch between Thanksgiving and Christmas should have been a low-tourism time anyhow, but now it was far worse than expected. So J.J. McCracken had resorted to a few desperate moves to lure people to the park. The first was to drastically slash ticket prices.

The biggest deal FunJungle now offered was on annual passes. For only five dollars more than the cost of one visit, people could upgrade their FunJungle FunPass and come for free all year-round. McCracken's idea was that the park could make back the money by gouging repeat visitors for expensive food and park merchandise—although most people quickly caught on to this and started smuggling in their own lunches. However, virtually everyone within a fifty-mile radius had bought the passes. FunJungle, no matter what the weather, was still the most exciting thing to happen in that area in decades, and the discount deal was simply too good to pass up.

Vance Jessup and TimJim had annual passes. And at fifteen, Vance had his learner's driving permit. This meant he was only supposed to drive with an adult in the car, but he drove himself all the time anyhow—and since he looked like an adult, the police never stopped him. The boys had all come to FunJungle directly from school and were waiting inside Shark Odyssey for me.

Normally, Shark Odyssey was one of the most crowded exhibits at FunJungle. In the summer there had often been hour-long waits to get inside. Now almost no one was there. It wasn't hard to spot Vance and TimJim in the sparse crowd.

Shark Odyssey was designed to display its inhabitants from many different angles. You began at the top of the massive three-story tank, from which you could look down into the water and watch the sharks from above. From there you moved down a long ramp that spiraled around the tank, allowing you to see the sharks from the side. And finally you ended up in the big glass tube with sharks swimming all around you.

Vance and TimJim were at the first viewpoint, above the surface of the tank. Vance checked his watch as I approached. "Took you long enough," he groused. "I figured you'd chickened out. We were about to come looking for you."

"I got here as fast as I could," I said. "The bus has a lot of stops to make before mine."

"Whatever," Vance said dismissively, as if this explanation didn't make sense. "We've waited long enough. Security's already started to pay attention to us."

"How so?" I asked, trying to hide my concern.

"Some big woman guard with a ton of attitude's been giving us the stink eye," Vance explained.

Large Marge, I thought. *Of course.* Marge had been a constant thorn in my side since I'd come to FunJungle; she'd always been far more concerned with busting me rather than catching any park guests disobeying the rules. Originally this had been a mere annoyance, as Marge was only a grunt in the security force, but after she'd helped catch Henry the Hippo's murderer, she'd been promoted to head of park security. In truth, *I'd* done almost all the work catching the killer, with some help from Summer McCracken. I'd found all the leads, taken all the risks, and finally solved the crime. All Marge had done was punch the bad guy as he was trying to escape. But she'd done that right in front of J.J. McCracken, who'd been impressed and promoted her. Now Marge had an entire security force she could order to keep an eye on me—although she still preferred to try to catch me red-handed herself.

"Where is she now?" I asked.

"I don't know," Vance admitted. "She came over a few minutes ago and warned us not to cause any trouble, but then someone called her on her radio and she took off."

"Why'd she think you were going to cause trouble?" I asked.

"What do I look like, a mind reader?" Vance demanded. "She was just being a jerk."

"Yeah," either Tim or Jim muttered. "All we did was spit in the shark tank."

I turned on Vance, unable to control my annoyance. "You spit in the shark tank?"

"What's it matter?" Vance asked. "It's not like it'll hurt the sharks or anything. They live in water—and that's all spit is."

I tamped down the urge to call Vince a moron. Spit *isn't* just water. It carries all sorts of diseases, which could be spread to the sharks, for which reason there were dozens of signs posted around the shark tank telling people not to spit into it. The boys had blatantly broken park rules, getting Marge's attention.

"We can't do the prank now," I said. "I know Marge. She wouldn't just let you guys off with a warning. She's probably still lurking around here somewhere."

I started for the doors, but Vance seized my arm and squeezed it hard. Even through my heavy winter jacket it hurt. "You're not weaseling out of this," he told me. "Just do it. And put some of this on the body parts before you drop them in." He yanked something out of his pocket and slapped it into my hand.

It was a squirt bottle of ketchup he'd filched from one of the FunJungle restaurants.

"What's this for?" I asked.

"To look like blood. Duh," Vance said, like *I* was an idiot. "If there's no blood, everyone will know the body parts are fake."

"It's not going to look like blood," I argued. "It's going to look like ketchup. And we really shouldn't put food that isn't for sharks in their tank. It's not healthy for them."

"Know what's not healthy for you?" Vance jabbed me in the chest with a thick finger. "Talking back to me. Wait thirty seconds for us to get down to the tube and then do the deed, okay?"

"Hold on," I said. "You're not doing it with me?"

"And take the fall if you get busted?" Vance asked. "No, thanks. Security's already got an eye on us. But you're the prince of this place. Your pal Xavier's always going on about how you helped find Henry's killer. So you've got immunity."

I frowned. Xavier had been right; Vance was more clever than I'd realized. He'd figured out how to see the prank and still keep his hands clean. He was completely wrong about my immunity, though. In fact I was number one on Marge's hit list. But I knew it'd be pointless to argue this. Vance wouldn't believe me anyhow.

I glanced around the exhibit. There was no sign of Marge or any other security, and most of the tourists had headed down the ramp toward the viewing tube. If I was going to drop the body parts in, this was probably the best time to do it. "Okay," I said. "Let's go."

"That's the spirit!" Vance hustled toward the viewing tube with TimJim, all of them actually giggling with excitement.

I peeked into the tank and watched the sharks' dorsal fins slicing through the surface below me. Although sharks provoke fear in most people, only a handful of the 360 different species are dangerous to humans. And even then they're generally not hunting us. In the entire world, sharks kill fewer than ten people a year, while coconuts falling from trees take out 150. (Meanwhile, we humans slaughter sharks by the millions, mostly to make shark fin soup, which I've heard doesn't even taste that good.) The tourists still want to see man-eaters, though, but they are notoriously difficult to keep in captivity. Aquariums have tried time and again to feature them—especially great whites—but have inevitably had to set them free. However, FunJungle had recently had some success with one man-eater: the bull shark.

Bulls aren't nearly as renowned as great whites, but they've actually attacked far more humans, in part because they're the only sharks that can survive in freshwater. They've been found as far up the Mississippi River as Indiana. FunJungle's bull was a seven-foot-long male named Taurus who'd been caught in the San Jacinto River disturbingly close to downtown Houston. Taurus had only been in Shark Odyssey for a few weeks, but he seemed to be doing all right. Ironically, while the "man-eater" was a decent draw, most tourists couldn't even pick him out. There were many bigger and far more ominous-looking sharks in the exhibit that were often mistaken for the bull.

I could see Taurus now, though. The torpedo-shaped fish skimmed below the surface right beneath me. A pair of nurse sharks, although significantly larger, split apart to give him a wide berth.

I figured thirty seconds had passed. Vance and TimJim would be in the glass tube by now. All the tourists were a good distance away from me, although I could hear a fresh batch outside the exhibit, approaching the entrance. If I didn't do the deed now, I'd probably never do it, and eventually Vance would get tired of waiting and decide to pound my face in.

I unzipped the backpack, whipped out the fake arm, and dropped it over the railing. Then I tossed in the foot. I decided to pass on the ketchup, though. I was quite sure the sharks would ignore the plastic body parts, but one might accidentally inhale the condiment. If Vance wanted to beat me up for this transgression, then he was probably just looking for an excuse to beat me up anyhow.

The fake body parts didn't make much n ... s they hit the water. All the tourists were too distracted by the sharks to notice them. I figured I'd done my duty and decided to get out while I could. I slung the backpack over my shoulder and doubled back toward the entrance, as the exit was a long distance away. The doors flew open as I approached.

I ducked my head down, not wanting any of the tourists to get a good look at my face, just in case things went bad.

Only it wasn't a group of tourists at all. It was a group of five security guards. And Large Marge was leading them.

THE ESCAPE

Marge hadn't forgotten about Vance and TimJim at all. In fact she'd been so concerned about them she'd gone off to round up the cavalry. "The boys are right this way," she was telling the other guards. "I guarantee you they're up to no good."

I was right out in the open. There was nowhere for me to hide. The moment Marge saw me, her gaze hardened. "Teddy!" she snarled. "I should have known you'd be involved in this!"

"Involved in what?" I asked innocently. "I just dropped by to see the sharks."

I started to back away, but Marge snagged the hood of my winter jacket. "Where are your pals?" she demanded.

I tried to sound as convincing as possible. "I don't know what you mean. I'm here by myself."

"Don't give me that," Marge snapped. "There were three suspicious teenagers loitering in here a few minutes ago. When I asked what they were doing, they said they were waiting for a friend. And now you're here. It doesn't take a genius to figure out the connection."

"Obviously not," I agreed. "You did it."

It was the wrong thing to say, but I couldn't help myself. Behind Marge, two of her deputies snickered.

Marge's brow furrowed angrily. "What are you hoodlums up to?" she demanded.

"Nothing," I said. "I'm not here with anyone else. I'm on my way to my mom's office to do my homework and I just stopped in here for a minute. I swear that's the truth."

I sold the lie pretty well. The other security guards, who didn't share Marge's innate distrust of me, seemed willing to give me the benefit of the doubt. Even Marge wavered slightly.

"Look around," I continued. "Whoever those teenagers were, they're not here anymore. If they were up to something, you obviously scared them off."

Marge cased the exhibit. A slight smile crossed her lips. "Yeah," she said proudly. "I suppose I did."

"So can I go, then?" I asked.

Marge took another look around Shark Odyssey. Nothing bad was happening. "All right," she said, letting go of my jacket. "But I'm still gonna keep an eye on you."

At which point a tourist gave a bloodcurdling scream. "There's an arm in the tank!" she shrieked. "A human arm!"

The security guards reacted with alarm, but Marge instantly suspected the truth. "Teddy!" she roared, and lunged for me again.

I sidestepped her with an inch to spare. The security guards blocked my escape, though. I had no choice but to spin around and race into the exhibit.

Marge launched herself after me. "Get him!" she ordered, and her guards dutifully obeyed, falling in behind. And as if five security guards weren't enough, Marge whipped out her radio and called for backup. "We have a red alert at Shark Odyssey!" she announced, so gravely that one might have thought she'd caught some terrorists armed with a nuclear weapon. "Teddy Fitzroy has really done it this time. I need all available personnel to report here ASAP."

I raced past the woman who had sounded the alarm. She was with her family, pointing in horror at the center of the tank, where the fake arm now bobbed amongst the dorsal fins. Her husband had gone green with disgust. Their three children, meanwhile, were thrilled, clambering up on the railing to see if they could spot any other body parts.

"I think I'm going to faint," the mother gasped.

"Just stay calm," her husband said. "It can't really be an arm. It must be some debris that simply *looks* like an arm. . . ."

"There's a foot, too!" his daughter shouted[...]
see a foot!"

The mother made a weak little noise and p[...]

I continued down the ramp, circling the shark tank. Other guests, alerted by the family's cries, now spotted the body parts too. The plastic arm and foot had taken on water and were sinking slowly through the center of the tank. If anyone had really taken the time to look closely at them, they could have easily realized they were fake. For one thing, both body parts ended in perfectly straight lines, whereas if a shark had truly wrenched them off a human, they would have ended in torn flesh and shards of bone. But no one was taking the time to look closely. Instead they were gasping in dismay or slapping their hands over their children's eyes or bolting for the bathroom to throw up. As usual when there was a crisis, many guests' immediate reaction was to record the event on their phones; thus, instead of watching everything clearly unfolding right before their eyes, they were watching it on miniature screens with poor resolution.

Marge and the security guards pounded down the ramp after me. I had hoped that at least one of them, faced with a potential shark attack, would have thought to look for the victim. Instead they were blindly following orders and chasing me.

Normally, Marge, who was easily a hundred pounds

overweight, would have been trailing the pack. But since we were heading downward, she had inertia working for her. Not only was Marge leading the attack, but she was actually gaining speed and closing the gap on me. Even more frightening, she wasn't in complete control of her body. She was in more of a barely controlled fall, her legs racing to keep up with the rest of her as she hurtled down the ramp. I began to worry that instead of catching me, she'd trample me flat.

Meanwhile, inside the tank, the sharks still hadn't even noticed the body parts. They continued swimming about without so much as a glance at them, exactly as I'd guessed they would.

Except for Taurus, who lightly nudged the fake arm with his nose. I don't know if the bull actively homed in on the arm or accidentally swam into it, but whatever the case, the panicked tourists immediately assumed he had just taken another nibble of human flesh. The air was suddenly filled with screams and shrieks, mingled with a few distinct wet splats: the telltale sounds of vomit hitting the ground.

I was quickly closing in on the glass tube. This was always the most crowded part of the exhibit, and today was no exception. Even on a slow day the tube was jammed with guests. Most were staring in shock at the descending body parts or riveted to their phone's camera screens. As promised, Vance and TimJim had stationed themselves here for the show. They were laughing hysterically at all the displays of disgust and horror around them.

Large Marge was right behind me, her legs pinwheeling madly. In the reflection of the aquarium glass I saw her out-stretched hands closing in on my neck.

There was a very large patch of fresh vomit at the bottom of the ramp, right at the tube's entrance. I leaped over it, but Marge wasn't quite so agile. She planted her foot in it and skidded, out of control, into the tube. The tourists were all so focused on the events in the shark tank that even Marge's yelps of fear didn't grab their attention until it was too late. Marge caromed off the safety rail and bowled over a dozen tourists like tenpins. They all went down in a huge, groaning pile of humanity.

Fortunately, this blocked the tube behind me. The other security guards had to gingerly maneuver around the sprawled-out tourists, which slowed them down long enough for me to get some distance on them. I wove through the crowded tube and slipped past Vance and TimJim.

Marge, struggling to worm her way out from under the pile of tourists, howled when she spotted the bullies. "There's his friends!" she shouted to her underlings. "Get them! Get them all!"

Vance and TimJim gulped in alarm, then raced after me. Despite all the chaos around them, a great number of tourists in the tube were still watching the shark tank. As luck would have it, the disembodied arm had drifted right toward the tube and now settled atop it with a resounding thunk, which provoked another round of gasps, shrieks, and puking.

I shoved my way to the end of the tube and bolted for the exit. I'd gained ground on the guards, but now I had Vance and TimJim after me.

"You idiot!" Vance barked. "You led the cops right to us!"

"They were already coming for you!" I shot back. "They knew you were up to something!"

"If we get busted for this, I'm gonna kill you," Vance threatened.

We burst through the exit doors, only to find a phalanx of security guards racing toward Shark Odyssey, responding to Marge's call for backup. As the only kid who lived at Fun-Jungle, I was well-known enough for all of them to recognize me at once.

"There he is!" one guard shouted, and everyone veered toward me.

Vance immediately showed his true colors and sacrificed me to save his own skin. He lashed out a leg and sent me sprawling. "We're not with him!" Vance declared. "He's the one who did it!"

His ploy might have worked if TimJim had been intelligent enough to play along. But instead of stopping to help implicate me, they kept running.

The guards immediately suspected something was up. "Don't believe them! They're all in cahoots!" the leader yelled, and part of the group split off after them. Vance had no choice but to flee as well. The bullies all raced toward the entrance of the park.

As the remainder of the guards bore down on me, I scrambled to my feet, dodged a few hands, and sprinted away.

Large Marge and the other guards emerged from Shark Odyssey just in time to take up the chase as well. Marge was now quite rumpled from her tumble in the shark tube—and there was a huge splotch of someone else's vomit covering the front of her uniform. She was as angry as I'd ever seen her. I half expected fire to burst from her eyes. "Whoever catches that kid gets a raise!" she bellowed.

I ran as fast as I could down Adventure Road, heading for the rear gate. I shot past the swim-with-the-dolphins area (temporarily closed due to frigid weather) and the Amazing Skyway boarding station.

It was getting near to closing time, and with night coming, most park guests were heading the opposite direction, toward the front gates. I zigzagged through them, topping a small rise, and the Land Down Under came into view.

Ahead of me another group of guards blocked the way to the rear exit. For a few frightening moments I thought I was trapped—but then a new plan to escape the security squad came to me. I veered toward Australia.

For most of FunJungle's existence, the Land Down Under had been the least-visited part of the park. Like the real Australia, it was remote and filled with animals people had never heard of. Creatures like bettongs, bandicoots, numbats, and quokkas. True, there were also a lot of kangaroos, which people liked well enough, but after walking for miles around the rest of the park, few guests felt like taking a fifteen-minute detour to see them. However, in the last few weeks the Land Down Under had become the most popular part of FunJungle, thanks to another of J.J. McCracken's schemes to boost attendance.

FunJungle had acquired a koala.

Although zoos and aquariums are popular throughout the world, there are very few animals that can draw big crowds on their own. Giant pandas are probably the most notable for this, but koalas are a close second. For one thing, they're adorable—they're basically living teddy bears—and for another, they're quite rare to see. Australia is very protective of its koalas and doesn't allow many to be taken out of the country, so only a few zoos have them.

J.J. McCracken, however, was rich and influential enough

to get anything he wanted. He owned several businesses in Australia and was friends with a lot of politicians there. So he twisted a few arms, dashed off a five-million-dollar check for koala conservation (tax-deductible, of course)—and within less than a week a koala was on its way to FunJungle.

There was only one catch: The Australians hadn't sold the koala to the park; they'd merely lent the koala for six months as a "goodwill ambassador." In truth this wasn't unusual. Every giant panda in the United States has technically only been lent out by China. Australia had done it plenty of times for koalas. However, J.J. was fine with this. He figured that having the koala for a limited time made its arrival more of an event. And so FunJungle's mighty marketing machine swung into action.

The very first thing was to change the koala's name. The koala had originally been christened Goongiwarri, which was an Aboriginal Australian word for "swamp," but J.J. McCracken claimed it sounded "like an elephant passing gas." Thousands of dollars worth of marketing research indicated that park goers preferred animal names that were short, cute, and alliterative—and thus Goongiwarri was rechristened Kazoo.

Next a deluge of press releases went out. Within a day the story was all over the national news. In FunJungle-mad Texas, it was the lead story in every major market.

A large section of the Land Down Under suddenly became KoalaVille, the center of which was a temporary koala exhibit built in just three days. (Luckily, koalas don't need much room, so the exhibit didn't have to be very big.) But Kazoo's habitat was puny compared to the most significant part of KoalaVille: the Kazoo merchandise area. A huge tent, designed to look like it was part of some exotic bazaar (never mind that bazaars were Middle Eastern, not Australian) was erected and filled with anything you could slap a koala's photo on: T-shirts, sweat-shirts, coffee mugs, backpacks, license plate frames, beach towels, posters, pennants, jigsaw puzzles, plates, napkins, and of course commemorative boomerangs. (The photo on the items wasn't even Kazoo. It was just some random photo that Pete Thwacker, the head of PR, had found on the Internet, but as Pete explained, "No one will notice. All koalas look exactly the same.") The bazaar covered an entire acre. There were four aisles of Kazoo the Koala plush toys alone.

The marketing push worked. People who'd canceled their Christmas trips to FunJungle now rebooked. And attendance numbers, which had been dismal, rebounded a bit. People who lived within a day's drive of FunJungle streamed back to see the new arrival and snapped up plenty of koala mer-chandise to boot. Given the time of year, the crowds weren't massive, but attendance predictions for the next few months were beginning to look up, thanks to Kazoo.

Therefore, as closing time approached, lots of people were streaming out of KoalaVille. It seemed as though half that day's visitors were there. I plunged in, fighting my way against the tide of humanity like a salmon swimming upstream. The security guards quickly lost sight of me amongst all the tourists.

I ducked into the bazaar, veered down an aisle of T-shirts, and slipped around the back of Kazoo's exhibit. There was a door marked with a sign that read AUTHORIZED KOALA PERSONNEL ONLY. I pounded on the door but got no answer.

Instead of a standard keyhole, the door had a coded entry keypad. Every door at FunJungle was like this. Each had a different code, which was changed almost every day for security purposes. However, there was also one secret code that worked on every door: J.J. McCracken's personal code. He'd shared it with Summer, who had shared it with me in a moment of crisis. I hadn't used it since, figuring it was only for emergencies, but at the moment this seemed to qualify. I could hear Large Marge storming through the bazaar close by.

I typed in J.J.'s code, hoping it hadn't been changed in the last six months.

The door clicked open.

I stepped through it into the koala keepers' office.

The room wasn't very big. The koala exhibit had been built so quickly that FunJungle had almost forgotten to add the keepers' office in the first place. There was a tiny desk and a folding chair, but the space was mostly used for storage. Jugs of water were stacked against one wall. Sheaves of eucalyptus lined another. The desk was piled with books and magazines. A door on the other side of the office led into Kazoo's habitat.

The door had a window in it, and I peered through this. Kazoo's room wasn't a whole lot larger than the office— about twelve feet square. The rest of the exhibit was taken up by the viewing area, which arced around Kazoo's habitat like a horseshoe. Kazoo's habitat was filled with eucalyptus trees. I spotted the koala in the central one, asleep as usual. Beyond him, through the foliage, I could see through the glass into the viewing area.

Guests were lined up at the glass, pressing their noses against it for a glimpse of Kazoo. Beyond them I could see the keeper on duty.

It was Kristi Sullivan.

I heaved a sigh of relief. Kristi was one of my favorite keepers at FunJungle. She'd only been hired a few weeks before, as part of the new staff for Kazoo. She was his main keeper, meaning she was on duty most days, but since koalas don't do a whole lot, much of her job involved standing at a podium in the viewing area and dispensing fascinating koala facts over a loudspeaker. As Kristi was young, pretty, and extremely perky, a lot of the guests ended up watching her more than the koala. (Especially the male guests, Mom liked to point out.) Kristi had always been nice to me. I was hoping she wouldn't have to get involved in my current crisis, but if she did, I was sure she'd back me rather than Marge.

At the moment it was four forty-five, and Kristi was trying to herd the tourists out of the viewing area. Kazoo's habitat was actually supposed to close at four thirty, a half hour before most other exhibits, because it was a long way to the park gate. (In the winter, FunJungle closed two hours earlier than it did in summer, on account of darkness.) However, Kristi never had the heart to just kick the tourists out, so it generally took her fifteen minutes to gently coax everyone out the door. "Go on now," I could hear her teasing the stragglers. "If you folks don't get out of here, I'll have to lock you in for the night."

Behind me, outside the keepers' office, I could hear the far less sweet sound of Large Marge shouting at her underlings. "He must be around here somewhere, you morons! Just find him!"

Kristi shooed the last tourists out of the viewing area and then slipped out after them.

There was no lock on the door that led into Kazoo's habitat; the one on the office door was assumed to be security enough. I slipped inside the exhibit.

The room was extremely warm and smelled like cough drops. The heat was jacked up to simulate the hot, dry climate Kazoo was used to—and eucalyptus is a main ingredient in lozenges. Since koalas eat nothing but eucalyptus, they tend to smell a bit like cough drops too.

Kazoo didn't flinch at the sound of my entry. This wasn't a surprise, though. If there's one thing koalas are good at, it's sleeping. Even sloths are more active than koalas.

This is because koalas have a really lousy diet. Eucalyptus leaves are chock-full of chemicals that are toxic to other animals. For a long time many scientists suspected that koalas were so lethargic because the compounds that make eucalyptus a good medicine also kept the cute little marsupials in a drugged-out haze their whole lives. But more recent research has shown that the leaves are simply so low in nutrients that koalas have almost no energy. Therefore they tend to move as little as possible—and when they do move, they often look as though they're in slow motion. (They *can* move quickly when they need to, however.) They rest sixteen to eighteen hours a day and spend most of that unconscious. In fact koalas spend so little time thinking, their brains actually appear to have shrunk over the last few centuries; the koala is the only known animal whose brain only fills half of its skull.

The FunJungle keepers who cared for far more active

animals always marveled at how something as sluggish as a koala could attract such crowds. Tourists would walk right past exhibits full of playful monkeys, antelope, or otters so they could crowd ten deep at Kazoo's windows and watch him sleep. And more often than not he was tucked far back in the eucalyptus trees, so the guests couldn't even see him well. All most people got was a glimpse of gray fur hidden among the leaves.

"They might as well be looking at lint," a carnivore keeper had groused to me one day. "Koalas aren't animals. They're statues with fur."

At the moment, however, I was perfectly fine with Kazoo being such a sound sleeper. I was never supposed to enter any animal's habitat without permission, and I certainly didn't need Kazoo making a racket. (Kristi had told me that koalas have a startlingly loud cry when they're upset, though I'd never heard Kazoo make a sound.) I gave Kazoo a wide berth and tried to be as quiet as possible. I took off my backpack and hid behind a thick clump of eucalyptus.

No sooner had I done this than Large Marge burst into the viewing area. Kristi Sullivan was right on her heels.

"I told you he's not in here," Kristi said.

"I'd prefer to see that for myself," Marge replied. She then stormed from one end of the viewing area to the other. The only place for me to hide out there would have been under the bench that ran along the back wall of the room, where guests could sit after getting bored of watching Kazoo sleep. Marge checked under every inch of it.

"Are you satisfied now?" Kristi asked.

Marge fixed her with a suspicious glare. "Why are you in such a hurry to get rid of me?"

Kristi sighed. "Because it's closing time and I want to go home."

Marge kept her gaze locked on the keeper. "You're friends with Teddy, aren't you?"

"Teddy is ten years younger than I am," Kristi replied coldly. "I'm not friends with any twelve-year-olds. But if you're asking do I like the kid? Then yes, I do."

"Just as I thought," Marge said. "I'll need to see in your office as well."

Kristi rolled her eyes. "You're wasting your time. He couldn't possibly be in there."

"I'll decide what's a waste of my time and what isn't." Marge started out the door, then paused and stared through the glass into Kazoo's exhibit.

I held my breath, hoping I was far back enough in the leaves to be hidden from her view.

Marge stayed frozen for several seconds. Then she raised a fist and banged on the glass. "Hey!" she shouted. "Kazoo! Wake up!"

I heaved a sigh of relief. Marge had been looking at the koala, not me.

"Stop that!" Kristi ordered. "You're not supposed to tap on the glass! No one is!"

"Oh, pipe down," Marge said. "Kazoo didn't even notice. The lazy thing's been here two weeks and I've never seen it awake."

She stormed out of the viewing area. Thirty seconds later I heard her and Kristi enter the keepers' office. Marge took her time casing that room as well, even though it was small enough to reach across. Finally I heard her warn Kristi, "If you see any sign of Teddy Fitzroy—and I mean *any* sign— you'd best report it to me right away. That boy caused some serious trouble today. People could've been hurt. And if I hear you've protected him, by gum, I will come down on you like a sledgehammer. Understand?"

"Sure," Kristi said. "I understand."

I heard Marge leave.

Then, after the door clicked shut, I heard Kristi say, "What a psycho."

A minute later she entered the koala habitat. As her shift was almost over, it was time for her to do a final check on Kazoo. She moved quietly, doing her best not to wake the koala.

I thought about saying hello, but I couldn't figure out

how to do it without scaring the daylights out of her. After all, Kristi had no reason to suspect that I—or anyone—would be hidden in Kazoo's exhibit. If I suddenly popped out of the eucalyptus, I'd probably give her a heart attack. Or she'd scream so loud that she'd give Kazoo a heart attack. And then I'd really be in trouble.

So I held still. Kristi's rounds didn't take very long anyhow. She spent less than a minute in the habitat. She simply filled a bowl with fresh drinking water, then whispered, "Nighty-night, Kazoo," dimmed the lights, and slipped back out the door.

I listened to Kristi collecting her things in the office, planning to wait a few minutes after she left to make sure the coast was clear before going myself. However, I was wiped out from my race across FunJungle, the koala habitat was warm and cozy, and all the eucalyptus fumes made me drowsy. Before I knew it, I'd nodded off. I wasn't even aware of it happening.

When I snapped awake again, it was almost pitch-black in the exhibit. Night had fallen. For a moment I had no idea where I was. Then everything came back to me. I checked my watch and saw it was five thirty in the evening. I'd been asleep for half an hour.

I couldn't hear Kristi in the office anymore, and I figured that even Large Marge would have called off the hunt for me after thirty minutes. The exhibit was so dark I could barely see my own hands, let alone Kazoo.

Not wanting to disturb him, I quietly got to my feet, slipped my backpack on, and tiptoed out of the exhibit. Outside, FunJungle was dark, cold, and eerily deserted. I hurried off toward Monkey Mountain, figuring Mom would still be in her office there. There was no sign of Marge or any of the other security guards.

I couldn't help but smile as I crossed the park, proud of myself for outwitting security and eluding capture—at least for the time being.

I had no idea that my troubles were just beginning.

RUDE AWAKENING

That night, at dinner in our trailer, I told my par-ents everything that had happened. There was no point in lying to them. They would have found out anyhow, so it was better that they heard the truth right up front from me.

Although they weren't pleased that I had participated in the prank, they were far angrier at Vance and TimJim for forcing me into it—and at Marge and the security guards for blindly assuming I was involved. I think Dad actually found the whole thing pretty funny, though he didn't admit it in front of Mom. When I told about Marge slipping in the vomit and taking out all the tourists, Dad had to leave the room. He claimed he had to blow his nose, but I'm 99 percent sure he was laughing.

The only thing my parents were *really* upset at me for was hiding in the koala exhibit. "You know you are never, ever to enter a habitat without a keeper," Mom scolded. "Kazoo could have been hurt."

"He didn't even know I was there," I said. "He slept through the whole thing. I didn't go anywhere near him."

"Even so," Mom chided. "I don't want you thinking that's ever okay." There was no one more protective of the animals' welfare than my mother.

"It was an emergency," I explained. "It's not like I did it for fun."

"I understand that," Mom said. "But the next time you're in trouble—not that I expect it to happen again—come to me or your father. We can handle Marge and her minions."

I lowered my eyes, feeling ashamed. "Everything happened so fast. I didn't have enough time to think things through."

"How'd you even know the security code to get inside?" Dad asked.

"Summer gave it to me," I admitted. "It works on all the exhibits."

Dad looked at me curiously. "And you never told us about it?"

"Summer told me not to. She said it was for emergencies only. I forgot I even knew it until this afternoon."

"If you ever use it again, you'll be in big trouble," Mom warned.

"Okay," I said.

Mom started to say something else, but Dad put a hand on hers and said, "I'm sure Teddy understands. He was in a tough spot tonight, and frankly, I think he handled himself rather well overall."

Mom nodded and gave me an apologetic smile. "I suppose you did, given the circumstances. It's those bullies who put you in this situation that I really ought to be talking to." She pounded the kitchen table angrily. "I ought to call their parents right now."

"No!" I said, a little too quickly. "That will only make them angrier at me."

Mom frowned at this but realized I was right. "Well, we have to do *something*. This has to stop. And your principal was obviously completely ineffectual against these boys."

"I think Mr. Dillnut got me in *more* trouble with them," I said.

Mom sighed. "It's times like this when I feel a bit too removed from society. After all those years in the bush, I keep thinking humans will behave as nicely toward one another as gorillas do. But they don't, do they?"

"No," I admitted.

"So what do we do now?" Mom looked to Dad for help.

"You could put itching powder in those guys' shorts," he suggested.

"Jack!" Mom cried, then gave Dad a playful smack on the shoulder. "Don't go putting bad ideas in Teddy's head."

"Too late," I said. "I already tried pranking Vance. In fact that's why he was so mad at me this time."

"What'd you do?" Dad asked.

"I put a snake in his gym bag."

Dad stared at me for a moment, then grinned. "That's my boy," he said.

We all went to bed without solving the bully problem. I had a lot of trouble going to sleep, plagued by thoughts of Vance or Large Marge coming after me the next day. Plus, my bedroom was as cold as a meat locker.

The perk of free housing at FunJungle had sounded great on paper, but in reality it hadn't turned out so well. We'd known we were only going to live in trailers, but I, at least, had assumed they'd actually be nice trailers. Instead J.J. (who lived in a sprawling, twenty-four-room ranch house) had simply bought a bunch of cheap trailers in bulk. The walls were paper thin, the electricity tended to conk out, and the heaters were so weak that I could often see my breath inside. Despite this, no one ever complained. This was partly because the employees were so committed to their animals that they were usually at FunJungle during all their waking hours—and partly because field biologists have very low standards for living conditions. In the Congo my family had spent more than a decade living in a tent, so for us, simply having a roof counted as a luxury.

It seemed as though I had just finally fallen asleep when an intermittent buzzing woke me.

It took me a few seconds to figure out it was my phone. According to my clock it was five thirty in the morning. I sat up groggily, annoyed at whatever jerk had the nerve to call so early, then I checked the caller ID.

It was Summer McCracken.

All my aggravation vanished in an instant. In fact I was suddenly thrilled.

I hadn't spoken to Summer in months. Unlike me, she didn't have to attend the closest public school. Being the thirteen-year-old daughter of J.J. McCracken, she attended an elite girls' prep school in Connecticut.

Summer was the first friend I'd made in Texas. We'd bonded while investigating Henry the Hippo's murder. We'd hung out a bit after that, so I'd expected—perhaps a bit naively—that we'd stay in close touch once the school year began. However, once Summer left town, it quickly became evident that she had plenty of other friends to distract her. I had only received the occasional e-mail or text message from her since. And while we'd planned to get together for lunch over Thanksgiving break, that had been derailed when her parents had suddenly decided to take her skiing in Aspen. Not that I could blame her for going.

I tried not to text Summer too much, wanting her to think I was quite busy myself, even though I wasn't. On occasion I actually found myself hoping another animal would die under mysterious circumstances so that we'd have an excuse to talk again.

Given that, I probably should have been more suspicious about *why* Summer was calling at such a ridiculously early hour. But all I could think about was how nice it would be to hear her voice again.

"Hey," I said, trying to sound like I hadn't just woken up.

"Where are you right now?" she asked.

"Where do you think? I'm in bed. It's five thirty in the morning."

"Well, get up and get dressed. Fast. You need to get out of there."

I stayed where I was, thinking Summer was joking. "This isn't funny."

"No, it's not. Large Marge is coming to arrest you right now. And she's got some cop from juvenile services with her."

I leaped to my feet. "Why? Because I put a plastic arm in the shark tank? That's not really a crime, is it?"

"An arm in the shark tank?" Summer suddenly seemed to realize she knew far more than I did about my current situation. "Teddy, they think you stole the koala."

Summer might as well have slapped me across the face. I was completely stunned, a hundred questions tumbling around in my head at once. Without even realizing I was doing it, I started yanking clothes on. "Somebody stole Kazoo?"

"Yes! Last night!"

"Well, it wasn't me."

"If I thought you'd done it, would I be calling you right now?"

"No, but . . ." I shook my head, trying to clear the last cobwebs of sleep from my brain. "Why do they think it was me?"

"Apparently, they have security footage of you going in and out."

I winced. There were security cameras everywhere around FunJungle. Thousands of them. "But they couldn't possibly show me with the koala. I didn't take him."

"They show you with a backpack, I think. Something big enough to put the koala in. And now the koala's gone—and no one entered the exhibit last night besides you."

I did my best to remain calm, though it wasn't easy. "You're sure about that?"

"That's what my dad says."

I was now dressed. My clothes, which I'd simply grabbed

off the floor, were completely mismatched. I jammed my feet into a pair of sneakers, grabbed my winter jacket, and exited my bedroom. Our trailer only had four rooms: my bedroom, my parents', the bathroom, and the kitchen/family room/ living room/everything else. Mom and Dad emerged from their bedroom as I came out of mine, obviously roused by my phone call. I hadn't thought to keep my voice down. Both my parents wore pajamas but were surprisingly alert, given the time.

"What's going on?" Dad asked. "Is something wrong?"

The room suddenly lit up as a pair of headlight beams slashed across our windows. I glanced outside and saw two official vehicles approaching in the distance.

"Very much so," I said.

"Who is that?" Mom asked, worry in her voice.

"The police," I told her. "Large Marge is bringing them to arrest me. She thinks I stole Kazoo."

My parents both gasped at the very thought of this.

"Summer just told me," I explained. "I have to get out of here. I'll stay close, though."

Before either Mom or Dad could protest, I banged out the door.

We lived on the very fringe of civilization. Beyond our front door there was a small patch of grass and then miles of uninterrupted woodland. A herd of white-tailed deer was gathered on the grass. They'd frozen like statues, staring at the approaching cars, but at the sound of my exit they scattered, darting about frantically before melting into the darkness.

I followed them, ducking into the woods before the headlights could catch me.

It was freezing outside. My breath clouded the air in front of my face. I pushed deeper into the trees, putting distance between myself and the police. "You still there?" I asked into the phone.

"Yes," Summer said. "Sounds like you're taking my advice."

"Marge is practically here," I told her. "Thanks for the warning."

"What would you do without me?" Summer asked, only half teasing.

A thought suddenly occurred to me. "How'd you even know the police were coming right now?"

"Because you got me involved."

"How?"

"You used my secret code to break into the koala exhibit."

I winced again. I'd forgotten something like that could be tracked. "Oh. Sorry."

"You should be. Daddy didn't know I'd given that to you."

I figured I'd run far enough. I scrambled up a cedar tree and peered back through the woods, just in time to see the police vehicles stop in front of our trailer. I tried to tell Summer to be quiet for a moment, but when Summer wanted to tell you something, it was impossible to get a word in.

"They didn't realize the koala was missing until about an hour ago," she was saying. "Some night watchman noticed. He freaked out and called Marge, and then she declared a full-on red alert."

Since there weren't any streetlights around the trailer, the police left their headlights on so they could see the way to our door. I saw four of them silhouetted in the high beams. Marge was easy to pick out, given her girth. A man built like a linebacker with a ten-gallon hat walked beside her, while two humans of slighter build—I couldn't tell if they were male or female in the dark—hung back by the cars.

Luckily, I was far enough away that they couldn't hear Summer on the phone. To be safe, though, I turned the volume down so she was barely audible.

"The first thing they did was call Daddy," Summer went on. "He's in Germany on business. Of course, he flipped when he heard the news. When they told him which code had been used to enter the exhibit, he recognized it and called me."

Marge pounded on the door of our trailer. Her fist on the metal rang out like gunshots in the still night air.

"I didn't answer right away, seeing as it was crazy early in the a.m. and I had my phone off," Summer continued. "But I checked my calls when I got up and there were like a hundred from him, so I called back, and by that time park security had looked at the tapes and seen you on them. Daddy said they'd have to arrest you—"

"Even *he* thinks I did it?" I asked, worried.

"He doesn't *want* to," Summer explained. "But he also says video doesn't lie."

My parents opened the trailer door. I couldn't quite tell from the distance, but it looked like they were pretending that Marge had woken them.

"Hold on for a bit," I told Summer. "Marge is with my parents. I want to listen."

"Gotcha," she said.

Even though there were a dozen trailers near ours housing sleeping FunJungle employees, Marge made no attempt to be quiet. In fact she seemed to be speaking louder than usual, as though she wanted everyone within earshot to know what her business was there. "Good morning, Mr. and Mrs. Fitzroy," she announced, then nodded to the giant man beside her. "This is Officer Bubba Stackhouse from the Juvenile Services Division of the Kendall County Sheriff's Office. He's here to take Teddy into custody for the kidnapping of Kazoo the Koala."

My parents were illuminated by the headlights, so I could

see them do a solid job of feigning surprise, followed by indignation. "You're making a mistake," Mom told Marge. "Teddy didn't do any such thing."

"Oh, he did it all right," Marge said. "We've got it all on video. Caught your boy red-handed. Now, you have thirty seconds to produce your son or we will take him by force."

"Teddy's not here," Dad said. "He's having a sleepover at a friend's house."

Marge snorted with disdain. She sounded like a hippo coming up for air. "I don't believe that for a second. Step aside. We're coming in."

Dad and Mom quickly blocked the doorway with their bodies. "You can't do that!" Mom protested. "Not without a warrant. This is our private property."

"Actually, it's not." Marge sounded as though she was enjoying this. "You haven't paid one red cent for this place. It is officially the property of FunJungle—and as the chief security officer of said park, I have the right to enter any structure I choose whenever I choose. So step aside—or I'll have Officer Stackhouse here arrest the both of you as well."

If I'd actually been in the trailer, Mom and Dad probably would have put up more of a fight, but as it was, they stepped back from the door. "J.J. McCracken is going to hear about this," Mom warned.

"Oh, he already knows all about it," Marge chuckled. She shoved past my parents into the trailer and called out tauntingly, "Teddy! Come out, come out wherever you are!"

Bubba Stackhouse followed her inside. The trailer groaned under his and Marge's weight. The other two police officers remained outside. My parents stayed by the door.

"What's going on?" Summer asked me.

"Marge is searching our trailer," I reported. "Did your father send her?"

Summer waited a bit too long before answering. "I don't think so. He likes you, Teddy."

"Can you get him to call Marge off, then?"

"I'll see what I can do. It's just that . . ." Summer trailed off.

"What?"

"Well, from what I understand, the evidence against you is awfully strong. And you have a history of causing trouble at the park."

"I only play pranks!" I snapped. "I've never broken the law! In fact, I *caught* someone who was breaking the law here. Doesn't that count for anything?"

"It should, but you and I both know Marge has a serious bone to pick with you. If all the evidence points to you, she won't be very motivated to look anywhere else."

In the trailer, Marge roared in frustration. Our home was so small she and Bubba had already searched every corner.

She stormed back to the door, glaring at my parents. "Where is he?"

"We told you," Mom said. "He's sleeping at a friend's."

"Where?" Marge demanded.

When Mom and Dad hesitated, Marge told them, "I can have Officer Stackhouse run you in for impeding a police investigation, you know."

"I think we have the address somewhere around here," Dad said. He disappeared into the trailer for a few moments, then came back jotting something on a scrap of paper. "Here you go."

Marge greedily snatched the note out of his hand. "If you hear so much as a peep out of Teddy, you'd best report it to me. Otherwise I'll consider that you've aided and abetted a felon."

"He's only *accused* of being a felon," Mom shot back. "You haven't shown us one shred of proof yet."

"Oh, there's plenty of proof, all right," Marge said cheerfully. "I'll be happy to show it to you once we have your son in custody." She then hurried toward her car, excited to find and arrest me.

Officer Stackhouse tipped his hat to my parents, then returned to his vehicle as well. If he'd said anything to them, he'd spoken too softly for me to hear it. The other two officers followed him to the cars.

Marge had caused a big enough commotion to rouse our neighbors. In every other trailer the lights had come on. Ken Parker, the polar bear expert who lived next door to us, and Mike Matthews, an elephant researcher who lived on the other side, were both on their way over in bathrobes and slippers to see what was going on.

I waited until Marge and the police were back in their cars and driving away before speaking to Summer again. "So since this crime occurred at FunJungle, Marge is the one in charge of the investigation?"

"That's right. FunJungle is technically its own incorporated municipality."

"And since she's convinced that I'm the thief, she probably won't look for the real one."

"Exactly," Summer agreed. "You know what this means, Teddy?"

"Yeah," I said sadly. "I do."

"If you want to prove you're innocent, you're gonna have to find the bad guy yourself."

FRAMED

"Absolutely not," Mom told me. **"You are not** investigating any more crimes."

"But if I don't, no one else will," I protested. "Marge is the law here, and all she wants to do is bust *me*."

It was only a few minutes after Marge and the police had driven away. Dad had lied to our neighbors about what Marge had wanted and sent them all home. He'd also lied to Marge: He'd given her a fake address in town where I'd supposedly spent the night, one he'd simply picked at random out of the phone book. We figured it would take half an hour for Marge to discover this and another half hour to get back. In the meantime our trailer would be safe. Dad and I were seated at the kitchen table. Mom was making us breakfast, although I didn't think I could eat it. My stomach was churning with anxiety.

"Marge will come around," Mom said, cracking eggs into a bowl. "J.J. McCracken will force her to. He needs her to find that koala as soon as possible, not waste time with you."

"But Summer says all the evidence points toward me," I protested. "What if that convinces J.J. McCracken, too? What if everyone really thinks I'm the thief?"

"That's ridiculous," Mom said. "We know you didn't do it."

"You're my parents," I argued. "You're *supposed* to think I didn't do it. I'm going to need more proof than that to get Marge off my case."

Dad nodded. "I think you're right."

"Jack!" Mom snapped at him.

"I mean about Marge," Dad told her, then turned to me. "Though I agree with your mother that you shouldn't take this on yourself. . . ."

"Why not?" I pleaded.

"Because the last time you investigated a crime here, you nearly got yourself killed a couple times over," Dad said.

I sat back in my chair sullenly, aware he had a point.

"In fact," Dad went on, "this time, I suspect whoever kidnapped Kazoo knows you all too well, Teddy."

Mom froze in the midst of scrambling the eggs. "What do you mean?"

"It seems Teddy has been framed," Dad explained. "And

to do that, the kidnapper must have been keeping an eye on him." He turned back to me. "What's this evidence Marge has on you?"

"Video from the security cameras," I said. "Summer says they have footage of me entering the koala exhibit and leaving it last night."

"But no footage of you inside?" Mom asked.

I thought back to my phone conversation. "Summer didn't mention anything about that."

Mom started scrambling the eggs again. "Aren't there cameras inside the koala exhibit?"

"I'd assume so," Dad replied. "There are cameras everywhere else in this park."

"Then there ought to be footage from inside the exhibit proving that Teddy didn't take Kazoo," Mom said.

"Maybe not." Dad sipped his coffee thoughtfully. "If that footage existed, Marge would have seen it, wouldn't she? And more importantly, there should be footage showing who actually *did* steal Kazoo. Someone else entering and leaving the exhibit besides Teddy. So where is that?"

None of us had an answer. I could only shrug.

Mom began to soak slices of bread in the eggs, then drop them on the griddle. "Do you think someone tampered with the footage?" she asked.

"Maybe," Dad said. "Sadly, we know from experience

that people in FunJungle security can corrupt the cameras when they want to." (During Henry's murder investigation, we'd learned his killer knew how to turn off the security systems in some exhibits.) Dad grabbed a pad of paper and a pencil and started to make notes for himself. "I know one of the guys who works with the security system. I'll see if he can show me what they've got. Maybe somewhere in all that footage there'll be video of the *real* thief—or something else that proves Teddy's innocence."

Mom nodded approval.

"So you think whoever stole Kazoo was watching me last night?" I asked.

"They must have been," Dad said. "It's the only way to make the crime work. They saw you go in and out and knew you'd been recorded. Then they went in and took Kazoo."

"How?" I asked.

"That's the million-dollar question," Dad admitted. "Either they knew how to get in and out without being recorded—or they were recorded and knew how to erase the footage."

"I don't think there's any way to get in and out of that exhibit without being filmed," Mom said. "You can't go anywhere in this park without being filmed."

"Then that would mean someone in security stole Kazoo, right?" I asked. "Who else knows how to erase the recordings?"

"J.J. McCracken might," Dad said.

"Why would J.J. steal his own koala?" Mom asked.

"I don't know," Dad admitted. "I'm just spitballing here."

"J.J.'s in Germany," I informed them. "He couldn't have done it. But Marge could have. She was already angry at me last night. She slipped in a bunch of puke because of me. Then she followed me to KoalaVille. Maybe she actually saw me inside the exhibit. And then, after I left, she came back and took Kazoo, knowing she could frame me for the crime."

Mom and Dad chewed on that for a while. "I suppose it makes sense," Mom said. "Only I have a hard time believing Marge would do all that just to get you in trouble."

"Why not?" I asked. "She's said I ought to be shipped off to juvenile hall plenty of times. Now she's found a way to make it happen."

Mom and Dad shared a look. "It makes as much sense as anything else we've got," Dad said. "Though it also brings up the main issue we haven't discussed yet: Why would someone want to steal Kazoo?"

"Marge called it a kidnapping." Mom slid plates full of French toast in front of us and uncapped a bottle of syrup.

"If it's a kidnapping, where's the ransom note?" Dad asked.

"Maybe it hasn't been delivered yet," Mom replied. "It's still awfully early in the morning."

"I thought kidnappers always left the note at the crime scene," Dad said.

"Since when are you an expert on kidnapping?" Mom teased.

"I'm not," Dad told her. "But I know as much about koala-napping as anyone else, seeing as this is probably the first case there's ever been."

"There's also the possibility that there won't be a ransom note at all," Mom suggested. "Someone might simply want a koala."

"You mean, as a pet?" I asked.

"Yes," Mom said. "You're not eating your French toast."

"I want to," I said. "But my stomach's all jumpy."

Mom gave me a sad smile and tousled my hair. "I understand, given the circumstances. If I'd been unfairly accused of a crime, my stomach would be jumpy too."

"Who would want a pet koala?" I asked.

"Lots of people probably *think* they do," Mom said. "Look at the crowds who have come to see Kazoo. To most of those people, koalas probably look like the perfect pet. They're adorable, and yet they just sleep all day."

"But they're not easy to take care of," I countered.

"Not at all," Mom agreed. "But not everyone knows that."

"And even if they do, they still might want one," Dad put in. "There are far more owners of exotic pets than anyone realizes. Especially around here. Did you know there are more tigers in captivity in Texas than wild tigers in the entire world?"

I looked to him, surprised. "As pets?"

Dad nodded. "And that's just tigers. People also have lions, leopards, bears, chimps, zebras, and who knows what else. Maybe one of those collectors was dying to have a koala."

"Is there anyone like that around here?" I asked.

"I think there is," Mom said thoughtfully.

"I remember hearing that too." Dad jotted down another note to himself. "I ought to find out the name."

"Of course, you wouldn't necessarily have to be a collector to want to steal a koala," Mom said. "Back when I worked at the Bronx Zoo, regular people occasionally broke in and tried to steal the animals. No one ever succeeded, but they tried. It wasn't common, but it wasn't that rare, either. Now, that zoo is right in the middle of New York City. There are a couple million people living around it, so you'd expect that sooner or later a few of them are going to do something stupid. I'd hoped that, being out here in the sticks, we'd have a bit less crime, but we all know that hasn't been the case so far. The sad fact is, there are probably a lot of people out there dumb enough to try to steal a koala."

"But the person who did this *wasn't* dumb, were they?" I asked. "I mean, they figured out how to get around all the cameras and frame me."

"True," Mom admitted. "The person who stole Kazoo was clever. I just meant that the motive itself was dumb." She shook her head sadly, as she often did when she talked about how badly people could behave. Then she looked at my plate. "Still not hungry?"

I still hadn't touched my French toast. "Sorry. It smells great, but . . ."

Mom put a comforting hand on mine. "No need to apologize. I get it."

"No need for it to go to waste." Dad reached across the table, speared a slab of my French toast with his fork, then moved it to his plate and dug in.

A thought suddenly occurred to me. "What if Kazoo wasn't stolen at all? Is there any chance he could have just escaped?"

Mom considered that for a moment, then shook her head. "Koalas don't like the cold, and it was freezing last night. Kazoo's exhibit is nice and warm, and he had plenty of food and water there. Even if someone left the door to his exhibit wide open, I'd doubt he would have ventured outside."

"Plus, koalas aren't exactly the most adventurous creatures," Dad added. "I've never heard of one escaping from anywhere before. And from what I can tell, that exhibit was built pretty well. I don't think there's any way Kazoo could have gotten out on his own."

"You're sure about that?" I asked.

"Not completely." Dad made another note on his pad. "I could check it out, though I'm pretty sure it's a dead end."

Mom glanced at her watch, trying not to look nervous. "It won't be long before Marge and the police realize they've been had. Then they'll probably come right back here, and I doubt they'll be happy."

Dad turned to me and spoke with his mouth full of French toast. "That means you'd best not be here, kiddo."

"Well, I've got school," I said.

Mom and Dad shared a look, then both shook their heads. "Not today you don't," Dad said. "After here, that's the next place they'll look for you."

I failed to stifle a smile. "Guess there's one good thing about being framed for a crime."

"This is only temporary," Mom told me. "And if I felt we could trust Marge to lay off you and hunt for the real thief, we wouldn't even be doing it. But Marge has a real bug up her bottom where you're concerned. So for now you're going into hiding."

"Where?" I asked.

"The one place they'll never think to look for you," Dad said.

5

SCENE OF THE CRIME

I spent the day hiding out at FunJungle.

That might seem odd, seeing as I was a wanted criminal there, but I knew FunJungle from end to end, better than any of the security guards did. Plus, I didn't really have anywhere else to go.

My parents hadn't put roots down in Texas. They had no family there, and all of their friends worked at the park. My only close friend was Xavier Gonzalez, and I still didn't know his family well enough to ask if they could help me lie low from the police. (I'd only met them twice.) If it had been a bit warmer, I could have hung out in the woods near our trailer all day, but it was frigid and windy, and Mom said she didn't want me to die of pneumonia.

So FunJungle it was. We had to take some precautions,

though. For example, I couldn't go in through the back gate as usual. That was staffed by FunJungle security, and Marge had put out an all points bulletin for me.

Instead I walked right in through the main entrance. There were security personnel posted there, but they just searched through guests' bags to make sure no one was bringing anything dangerous into the park, like weapons or fireworks. They weren't really part of Marge's platoon of guards, and they were so focused on everyone's belongings they rarely looked at anybody's face.

Marge hadn't posted anyone at the front entrance to keep an eye out for me. Most likely she assumed that I wouldn't come through the front gates because you needed a ticket to get through them—and tickets were expensive. However, all park employees got a few free passes every year. (Technically, these counted as bonus pay, although Dad always grumbled about them. "In the first place, they don't cost J.J. McCracken a thing to give away," he'd say, "so it's not like he's giving us money. And second, what good is a free pass to a place that we work at anyhow?") The passes were ostensibly for us to give to family and friends, but none of our family had visited yet, so we had a wad of them sitting unused in a kitchen drawer.

It was more than two miles to loop around the park to the front gates. Dad went with me, though we split up in the main parking lot. Dad went through the front employee entrance, while I fell in with a group of schoolkids. Another part of J.J. McCracken's plan to increase attendance at Fun-Jungle was to offer big discounts to schools (which also allowed the PR department to claim FunJungle was "a major supporter of education"). On this particular morning, there were a dozen yellow buses discharging students at the front gates. Given the cold weather, half the kids had pulled the hoods of their jackets up over their heads, so I did the same. Since I didn't have a bag with me, the bag checkers waved me past without even a glance. I was through the front gates in less than a minute.

I kept the hood on and joined back up with Dad by the FunJungle Friends Theater. (This had been the Henry and Pals Theater back when Henry the Hippo had still been alive, but FunJungle had renamed it, for obvious reasons.) Dad had hoped to leave me with Mom in her office all day, but when we got close to Monkey Mountain, we saw several of Marge's minions posted by the doors.

"Looks like the heat is on," Dad sighed. "Marge must have realized by now that we sent her on a wild-goose chase. Guess you're spending the day with me."

"I can't," I said. "You have to see your friend about the security recordings, and that's inside the administration building. Admin has more security than any other building at FunJungle."

Dad frowned. "I can't just leave you alone."

"I'll be fine," I said. "Besides, I'm probably easier to spot with you than without."

"How's that?"

"This place is crawling with schoolkids today," I explained. "If I stay close to a school group, no one will look twice at me. But if I'm only with you, we'll stand out. If security knows to look for me, they'll probably be looking for you, too."

Dad waffled a few moments, but he ultimately realized I was right. "Your mother's probably going to kill me for this," he sighed. "Be careful. This is a big park. It shouldn't be too hard for you to keep some distance from the guards. And you're right about the schoolkids. Try to blend in with them if you can." He pointed toward a large, rowdy crowd of students my age gathered close by.

"Will do," I said.

"I'll be in touch the moment I'm done," Dad told me. "It shouldn't be too long."

We split up, although Dad kept looking back to make sure I was okay. It was kind of silly, but I appreciated it anyhow.

I dropped in at the rear of the school group. No one noticed I didn't belong. The parent chaperones and teachers had their hands full with the rest of the class. The students were so excited to be at FunJungle that groups of them kept racing off to see different animals. The adults were so busy trying to wrangle the rogues that they were thrilled to see anyone actually staying with the group.

Eventually, after several demands that everyone settle down and a few threats ("If anyone else wanders off, they will spend the rest of the day on the bus!"), the class headed into the park.

"What should we see first?" a teacher asked.

"The koala!" almost everyone shouted at once.

A few boys tried to argue for either Carnivore Canyon or World of Reptiles, but they were quickly overruled. The teachers and chaperones seemed just as eager to see Kazoo as the kids did. The class eagerly veered toward the Land Down Under.

I stayed with them. I knew my parents wouldn't have been pleased I was heading back to the scene of the crime, but I had a couple of reasons for sticking with the school group besides safety in numbers.

First, something strange was going on. If the entire field trip was so excited to go see Kazoo, that meant no one knew Kazoo wasn't on display. Kazoo's kidnapping should have been the top story on the local news. FunJungle dominated the press in Central Texas; when the park so much as considered changing the ticket prices, it would make the front page of the paper. It seemed unlikely that a whole class—including teachers and chaperones—could have missed the news. The only way no one could have known Kazoo was missing was if FunJungle hadn't revealed it. However, I couldn't imagine how anyone at FunJungle thought they could get away with that.

Second, I wanted to do some snooping myself. Summer's words kept coming back to me: If I didn't try to find Kazoo's kidnapper, no one would. Perhaps J.J. McCracken could get Marge to back off me for a bit, but if Marge truly believed I was the culprit, she wasn't going to look anywhere else.

As proof of this, there wasn't a single security guard anywhere near KoalaVille. If there had been, I would have kept my distance. In fact there didn't seem to be *anything* to indicate Kazoo's habitat was a crime scene. To my surprise, the exhibit looked exactly the same as it always did. There was no crime tape blocking it off—or, more to FunJungle's PR-minded style, signs claiming that the exhibit was CLOSED FOR RENOVATIONS TO ENHANCE YOUR FUNJUNGLE EXPERI-ENCE. Instead there was actually a line of tourists snaking out the door.

It was all rather eerie. For a moment I found myself wondering if I had merely dreamed the whole thing about Kazoo being stolen.

"My class" excitedly headed toward the koala exhibit. But as they did, Freddie Malloy leaped into their path.

Freddie was the closest thing we had to a human celebrity at FunJungle—which wasn't saying much. He'd started out as an actor in the *FunJungle Friends Revue* playing the evil land developer, Baron Wasteland, who was the villain of the show. However, he'd aspired to more and had eventually convinced the administration to let him host a show he'd cooked up called *The World's Most Deadly Animals*. According to my father, the show might have worked out if Freddie had done what he'd promised, which was to present a few dangerous animals—like tigers, cobras, and Komodo dragons—and teach the audience about them. But Freddie had been far more interested in promoting *himself*, hoping to attract a TV network and score his own reality show. Therefore he kept provoking the animals so they'd be more exciting. He never hurt them, but he'd invade their personal space, make direct eye contact, and do other things they found threatening. Then they'd lunge or snap at him and Freddie would leap away and the audience would gasp in excitement. In theory. Unfortunately, Freddie sometimes lost his focus on the animals—which resulted in him losing other things, like fingers. (A gelada baboon had bitten one off, while the Komodo dragon was responsible for the other.) He'd also lost an earlobe (thanks to an ocelot) and a toe (Nile crocodile) and the tip of his nose (golden eagle). Each time, Freddie had managed to be surprisingly calm for a man who'd just lost a body part, but many audience members had freaked out. They had fainted, vomited, and stampeded for the exits—and those were the adults. (Most of the kids had thought seeing a man lose a finger was pretty cool, but many parents had threatened lawsuits against FunJungle anyhow, claiming their children had been traumatized.)

FunJungle had shut *The World's Most Deadly Animals* down and sent Freddie back to being Baron Wasteland. Freddie was devastated by the demotion. Ever since, he'd been ambushing tourist groups in the hopes of being recognized.

"Hey, kids!" he shouted to the school group. "How's everyone doing today?"

Not a single kid responded, although the teacher gasped in fright at the sight of Freddie. Close up, the patchwork of scars on his face could be a bit disconcerting.

Freddie was obviously disappointed, but he soldiered on valiantly. "I can understand your reserve. It's not every day you get to meet a real celebrity. But you don't all have to be so shy around me. I don't bite. Although some of the animals I work with do!" At this, Freddie held up the hand that was missing two fingers.

The joke had never been that good when Freddie used it onstage. Here it was worse. The sudden reveal that his hand was maimed made several kids scream in terror.

One boy now actually recognized Freddie, however.

"Hey!" he exclaimed. "You're that crazy guy who gets attacked by animals all the time!"

"Er, yes," Freddie said, then whipped out some glossy photographs of himself. "Would you like an autograph?"

"No," the boy said. "I want to see Kazoo."

The rest of the class eagerly echoed this, and the teacher quickly led us past Freddie, who sagged with disappointment. I almost felt bad for the guy. But then I remembered my father saying that FunJungle had done Freddie a favor by closing his show. If they hadn't, he would probably have provoked an animal into biting his head off by now.

The school group hurried into the koala line. From inside the exhibit I could hear the standard thrum of excited tourists, as well as Kristi Sullivan dispensing her standard koala facts over the loudspeaker. ("A newborn koala is only the size of a jelly bean!") Though I was desperate to get in and see what on earth was going on with Kazoo, I stayed at the rear of the class. A dozen kids were arguing over who got to be first, drawing the attention of all the chaperones, and I figured it was safer to remain off their radar.

An excited young couple in matching Kazoo T-shirts joined the line right behind me. They seemed to be in their midtwenties and were so excited they couldn't stand still.

"Are you here to see the koala?" the woman asked me.

As if there might have been another reason I was standing in the koala line.

"Yes," I said.

"Us too!" the man exclaimed, as if this were the most incredible coincidence. "We're so excited. We've never seen a koala before."

"Except on TV," the woman added. "We just love them, though. They're so adorable. We came all the way from Oklahoma City."

"Just to see Kazoo?" I asked.

"And the rest of FunJungle, of course," the man said. "But Kazoo was the kicker. It's our honeymoon!"

"Wow," I said. "Congratulations."

"Thanks!" the bride chirped. "We really wanted to go to Australia to see wild koalas, but the plane tickets there are crazy expensive. And then FunJungle got Kazoo and started offering all these deals . . ."

"We're staying at the FunJungle Caribbean Resort for half price," the husband told me. "It's just like being in the *real* Caribbean, only closer!"

That was actually the promotional line from the resort's commercials.

"It just seemed like fate," the bride told me. "So we drove down right after our wedding. We only got here last night. The resort even gave us a free bottle of champagne on account of our just getting hitched. And now we're about to see Kazoo. Our first real koala! I'm so excited!"

I didn't know what to say. These two amped-up newly-weds were going to be devastated to learn that Kazoo was gone. Their honeymoon would be ruined.

There was a FunJungle employee stationed at the door of the exhibit. His job was to wave people in once there was room for them so that the viewing area didn't get too crowded. He was only a teenager, probably just out of high school, but people still paid attention to him. He waved my class inside.

All the students filed in ahead of me. I cringed reflexively, expecting to hear them scream.

Instead I heard them all gasp with delight.

I entered and gasped myself. Only I was doing it in surprise.

There was a koala in the exhibit.

It was difficult to see, since it was tucked into a crook of one of the eucalyptus trees in the back. And, as usual, it was asleep. I couldn't even see its face, as its head was tucked down between its arms, like a student who'd fallen asleep at his desk in math class. Its big, fuzzy ears poked out, however, which was enough to trigger squeals of delight from the schoolgirls.

The kids all crowded around the viewing windows, pressing their noses against the glass. "Aw nuts, he's sleeping," one boy groused, and many other kids echoed his disappointment.

"Let's wake him!" another boy suggested, and then, despite the PLEASE DO NOT BANG ON GLASS sign posted right over his head, he began to bang on the glass.

Thankfully, a teacher swooped in and grabbed the kid's wrist after only a few seconds. "Roscoe, if you can't behave yourself, you'll have to wait outside," she hissed.

"So what?" Roscoe asked. "The koala's not doing anything anyhow."

Kazoo hadn't so much as flinched at the sound of his glass being banged on, but that wasn't unusual. A bomb could have gone off in the room and Kazoo probably would have slept through it.

Kristi Sullivan was in her usual spot, perched at the small podium, rattling off facts as though nothing were unusual. "The baby koala begins its life by consuming only its mother's milk," she was saying, "But after a few months it begins to eat pap, which is actually a special form of the mother's feces."

Several of the kids squealed with disgust.

"I know it sounds terrible," Kristi told them, "but it's really a wonderful way for the mother to pass on the microorganisms that will allow her baby to digest eucalyptus leaves."

I kept my jacket hood up and my back to Kristi so that she wouldn't recognize me. Then I pressed my own nose against the glass, staring at the koala, wondering how he could possibly still be there . . . and if he was, how I could be in trouble for stealing him. I stared at the white tufts of Kazoo's ears, trying to make sense of everything.

And then, suddenly, I realized exactly what was going on.

Someone shrieked behind me. I spun around, startled, to find it was only the new bride. She and her husband had just been allowed into the viewing area, and she couldn't control her excitement. "It's him!" she screamed. "It's Kazoo! Get a picture, honey!"

"I'm already on it!" the groom replied. He had his digital camera out and was firing away.

"He's so cute!" the bride crooned. "Isn't he the most adorable thing ever? I want one!"

"Me too!" her husband agreed. "A pet koala! How awesome would that be?"

I started to turn back to the glass, but I wasn't fast enough. The bride spotted me and rushed over. "Could you take a picture of us and Kazoo?" she asked.

I considered saying no, as I didn't want to attract any attention—and the bride and groom were magnets for it. (Since the koala wasn't doing anything, lots of people were now watching the newlyweds, amused by their over-the-top enthusiasm.) But the bride looked so excited; I couldn't bring myself to turn her down. "All right," I said.

"Thanks so much!" the bride sang. "That is soooo nice of you."

The groom handed me his camera and quickly showed me how to work it while his bride kept expounding on how absolutely adorable Kazoo was. "Look at those ears! And that nose! He's so cute I just want to eat him up!"

This drew Kristi's attention, and she swiveled our way. "You're not alone in finding him lovable," she said. "Humans have a natural tendency to consider certain physical traits appealing: things like large eyes, large ears, and large noses. We find our own human babies cute because they have these features—and koalas have them too."

Kristi kept looking our way, so I kept the camera to my eye, hiding my face from her. "Let me get a couple pictures," I said, so I'd have an excuse to keep the camera up. "To make sure I get a good one."

"Why, thank you!" the bride said. "What a chivalrous young gentleman!"

"This attraction to cuteness is actually a very important human trait," Kristi went on. "When we think something is cute, we have an innate desire to take care of it. And as we all know, babies need a great deal of care. So when you find a koala adorable, in a way, you're actually feeling the genetic drive that makes humans such great parents."

I had now snapped more than a dozen pictures. The groom was beginning to get suspicious, as though he thought I might be plotting to make off with his camera. "Okay," he said, reaching for it. "I think that's enough."

I glanced over at Kristi. She had finally turned away and was now correcting some tourists who mistakenly believed that koalas were from Austria rather than Australia.

I handed the camera back to the groom. "Have a great honeymoon," I told him, and then hurried for the exit. I'd seen all I needed to. Now I needed to get out of Koala-Ville while I could. I scurried past Kristi's podium, where she was explaining, "Australia is a warm continent in the South Pacific, with plenty of eucalyptus for koalas to eat. Whereas Austria is a cold, mountainous country in central Europe."

Unfortunately, the exit was blocked. A tourist family was trying to drag their daughter out, but she was digging her heels in. "I don't want to go!" she cried. "Kazoo hasn't done anything yet."

"We've been watching him for an hour!" her frazzled father pleaded. "He's sleeping. Please, let's go see some animals that actually move."

"Like monkeys!" her desperate mother added. "You love monkeys! And they move all the time."

"No," the little girl demanded. "I want to stay here. Kazoo's going to wake up soon. I know it."

I wouldn't bet on it, I thought.

"We'll come back later," her father said. "I promise. But for Pete's sake, let's leave KoalaVille."

He tried to pull his daughter away, but she clamped on to the door frame with both hands and wouldn't let go.

I squeezed past them and finally got outside again. After the heat and the crush of humanity inside the exhibit, the chill air and empty walkways felt wonderful.

Before I could take another step, however, someone grabbed my jacket from behind. The hood came off my head, revealing me to the world.

"Not so fast, Teddy," Kristi Sullivan said. "We need to talk."

THE EMERGENCY BACKUP KOALA

Kristi dragged me into her tiny office. Since there was only one chair, she steered me into it. Then she shoved aside a stack of fashion magazines and perched on her desk.

"I didn't steal Kazoo," I said quickly.

Kristi laughed. "If I thought you had, Teddy, I would have called security."

It took me a moment to process that. "So . . . you already know it wasn't me?"

"No, I don't know anything for sure," Kristi admitted. "I just don't *think* you did it. You might be a handful, but you're not stupid. However, I *would* like to know what you were doing in the exhibit last night."

I explained everything. How Vance Jessup had forced me to play the prank at the shark tank, how Marge had caught us, and how I'd taken refuge in the exhibit. Kristi listened intently to it all. She even laughed a few times.

When I finished, she stared at me thoughtfully, then said, "You picked the wrong night to hide out here, Teddy. You're in some serious trouble."

"I know," I said, then asked, "Why's there a toy koala in the exhibit?"

Kristi reacted with surprise, but quickly broke into a smile. "I knew you were smart," she said. "It's there because we don't have a real koala anymore."

I was annoyed at myself for not realizing the Kazoo on display was a fake right away. After all, the toy koalas for sale in the gift shop looked almost exactly like the real thing; they would look even more real hidden behind a bunch of eucalyptus branches. What had kept me from putting it all together right away was denial: Even though FunJungle had done some sneaky things before, I still couldn't believe that the park would try to pass off a fake koala as a real one.

"I know *why* you're using a toy," I said. "What I meant was, why hasn't the public been told Kazoo is gone?"

Kristi raised her hands in a gesture of innocence. "I had nothing to do with this. In fact I think it's terrible. But . . . well, you see, when the kidnapper took Kazoo last night, they put the fake one in the tree to cover their tracks."

I sat forward, intrigued. "Really? Did it work?"

Kristi looked embarrassed. "For a few hours, I guess. No one's quite sure when Kazoo was taken last night. But the fake was discovered around four thirty this morning."

"Who noticed?"

"Someone in security. I forgot his name. Apparently, the toy koala fell out of the tree. At first, the guard thought it was really Kazoo and that he'd died. He called the vet on night duty, who determined it was a fake."

"And so the park decided to just put it right back on exhibit?"

"Like I said, I don't agree with this. The decision was made by the head of PR."

"Pete Thwacker." I wasn't surprised.

Kristi's eyebrows raised slightly. "You know him?"

"Unfortunately." I'd run into Pete a few times while investigating Henry the Hippo's death. He was a vain, cheesy man who knew very little about animals and a great deal about how to manipulate the public. I'd even considered him a suspect in Henry's murder for a while.

"I've been trying to reach him all morning . . ." Kristi was interrupted by the ringing of her office phone. She glanced at the caller ID, then groaned. "Speak of the devil." She signaled me to be quiet, then put on the speakerphone. "Kristi Sullivan."

"Hi, Kristi. This is Pete Thwacker. I understand you've

called my office a few times. Is something wrong over there?" Pete's phone voice was extremely dramatic; it was probably a habit from being interviewed on TV all the time.

"Yes," Kristi said. "I'd say that lying to the public is wrong."

Pete hesitated upon realizing what all this was about, but when he spoke again, he sounded as confident as ever. "Kristi, we're not lying to the public. We're merely delaying the reveal of the truth until a more opportune time."

"And when might that be?"

"Hopefully never. I've been assured that FunJungle security knows the identity of the perpetrator and is currently engaged in a full-scale manhunt. If they can find him and return Kazoo quickly, then what's the point of upsetting people with the fact that the koala was ever gone?"

Kristi sighed, exasperated. "This isn't right. You can't pass a toy koala off as the real thing."

"First of all, Kristi, it's not a toy. It's an emergency backup koala—"

"It's a toy. From our very own gift shop."

"Second, have any of the guests noticed?"

Kristi frowned. "No," she admitted.

"Well, there you go!" Pete cried. "No harm done! I'm not saying that we here at FunJungle aren't concerned about the welfare of our animals. We are. In fact that's our primary directive. But our secondary directive is to provide our guests with a day of wholesome family fun. Frankly, I don't see how informing them of Kazoo's disappearance fits into that scenario. Instead it will merely distress them. And to what end? Isn't it better for all these people—many of whom have come from quite far away to see a koala—to *think* they've seen one? Would you rather they came all this way only to be disappointed?"

"No," Kristi said, sounding less sure of herself now. I couldn't really blame her. Pete was surprisingly convincing. Even though I was sure his plan was morally wrong, there was a certain bizarre sense to it. "But what if our security doesn't find Kazoo right away?" Kristi asked. "Or what if they never find him?"

"I think that's unlikely," Pete said. "I have every confidence in our security here."

"I don't," Kristi told him. "Marge is a lunatic. So let's suppose she fails. Won't FunJungle look worse for covering this up?"

"Only if the public finds out we *have* covered it up, which they won't," Pete said. "As you've observed yourself, the emergency backup koala is working perfectly well. And I certainly hope you're not thinking of spilling the beans." As Pete said this, his voice gained an unsettling edge of menace.

"Of course not," Kristi said.

"Good," Pete replied. "Because doing so would be a violation of park policy, which is a fireable offense."

Kristi swallowed, looking a little frightened. "And what if one of the guests notices on their own that the emergency backup koala is just a toy?"

"They won't—as long as you take the proper steps to prevent such a scenario: Position the koala as far from the viewing windows and behind as much foliage as possible. And shift its location every evening so that it appears to have moved during the night. Frankly, I don't see that you have anything to complain about. This seems considerably easier than taking care of a *real* koala."

"I *like* the real koala," Kristi protested.

Pete didn't seem to hear her. "In fact," he said, "it almost makes you wonder why we bother having real animals here at all."

"What?" Kristi asked, aghast.

Pete either didn't notice the horror in her voice, or he was too consumed with his own idea to hear it. "It'd be a significant financial savings for us," he mused. "After all, fake animals don't require expensive food or medical care—and they don't poop, pee, or smell bad. Plus, it's much easier to acquire a fake panda or rhinoceros than a live one."

"You have to be kidding me," Kristi said. "Tell me you're not seriously considering this."

"What's so wrong with it?" Pete asked.

"*Everything*," Kristi replied. "People don't come to a zoo to see fake animals."

"We have fake dinosaurs," Pete countered.

"Because dinosaurs are extinct, you moron."

Even this didn't faze Pete. "I understand why you're upset," he said. "You're worried that you'd lose your job if there weren't animals to tend to. True, fake animals would certainly require fewer staff to care for them—at a further savings to the company, I might add—but we'd still need some people such as yourself to maintenance the creatures and sell the idea that they're real. This is quite a ground-breaking concept, if I do say so myself. If you'll excuse me, I need to go work up an action plan. It's been a pleasure talking to you, Kristi."

Kristi tried to say something else, but it was too late. Pete had hung up.

The koala keeper returned her attention to me. "See what I'm dealing with here?"

"Pete's an idiot," I said.

"Unfortunately, he's an idiot with power." Kristi sighed. "I'm just scared this whole thing's going to blow up in our faces. And you know who's going to look bad then? *Me.* Not Pete Thwacker. His whole plan hinges upon FunJungle security finding Kazoo quickly, and frankly, I don't have much faith in them. They're not even trying to find the real thief. They're trying to find *you*."

I nodded sadly, and then thought to ask, "Do you have any idea who the real thief is?"

"Sure," Kristi said. "I have plenty of ideas. Only I can't get Marge or any of her stooges to listen to one of them."

I straightened up, intrigued. "*I'm* listening."

Kristi gave me a doubtful look, then seemed to think better of it. "Okay. You're the one who figured out who killed Henry, right? I think Freddie Malloy is a possibility."

"The actor?" I asked. "Why would he want to steal Kazoo?"

"Because he thinks Kazoo ruined his career," Kristi replied.

"How? If anyone ruined Freddie's career, it was Freddie."

"Well, let's face it, Freddie's a bit delusional. I mean, the guy thought that provoking dangerous animals on stage would be a good career move. He believes FunJungle canceled his show because they wanted to focus on Kazoo instead."

"But then he ought to be angry at FunJungle, right?" I asked. "Not the koala."

"Yes, if he were a rational human being," Kristi replied. "But he's not. He *hates* Kazoo. I saw him skulking around here all the time—and once, I heard him say he wanted to throw Kazoo into the crocodile pit."

I gulped. I'd always thought Freddie wasn't playing with a full deck, but this was worse than I realized. I thought back to my encounter with the actor that morning, how he was still skulking around KoalaVille, desperate to be noticed. If he'd gotten rid of Kazoo, it must have been driving him insane that a fake koala was still attracting more attention than he was. "And you told security about him?" I asked.

"I *tried* to. But Marge is so sure you're the culprit here, she won't listen to anything else." Kristi rolled her eyes. "I probably should have reported the threat when Freddie first made it, but at the time I thought it was all just talk."

"How long ago was that?"

Kristi shrugged. "Two weeks or so. Not long after Kazoo arrived here."

"Who else do you think the kidnapper might be?" I asked.

"Charlie Connor," Kristi replied. "He's one of the guys who dress up in animal costumes here—"

"Oh, I know who Charlie is," I told her. "He was a suspect in Henry's murder."

Kristi reacted with surprise. "Really?"

I nodded. Charlie was a dwarf ex-con who had become a clown after serving time in prison. He had briefly been at the same poorly run circus as Henry, where the hippo had attacked him one day. (Charlie had chalked this up to the hippo having an inexplicable hatred of little people.) Eventually, both of them had ended up at FunJungle. Charlie played a character named Larry the Lizard, which merely involved wearing a reptile costume and standing still so that tourists could take pictures with him. There were a lot of characters like this at FunJungle: Eleanor Elephant, Zelda Zebra, Uncle O-Rang—although Henry the Hippo had been the most popular by far. Until his alter ego had ended up dead. After that, fake Henry had been cut from the mascot squad.

"I'm surprised Charlie's still working here," I said. "He hates being a lizard."

"He's not a lizard anymore," Kristi said. "He's a koala."

Now it was my turn to be surprised. "Since when?"

"Since Kazoo got here. FunJungle took everyone who used to play Larry the Lizard and switched them to playing Kazoo."

"Then what happened to Larry the Lizard?"

"FunJungle surreptitiously retired him. I don't think many people ever liked Larry. He wasn't that interesting a character, and frankly, he looked like a mutant frog to me."

I thought back to all the times I'd seen someone dressed as Kazoo at FunJungle. There were probably too many to count. To my surprise, I realized that someone in a Kazoo costume had been stationed near KoalaVille almost all the time during regular park hours. I'd simply stopped noticing.

This happened a lot at FunJungle. You tended to forget that the characters were merely costumes with real people inside them and started to think of them as scenery. I wasn't the only person who'd done this. The actors had plenty of stories about tourists discussing everything from crimes they'd committed to their secret ATM codes right in front of the mascots.

I had probably walked right past Charlie Connor a dozen times, if not more, without having any idea he was inside the Kazoo suit. This was a bit unsettling, as Charlie didn't like me much. During the investigation into Henry's death, Charlie had secretly given me some information, but park security had forced me to cough up his name, and Charlie had felt I'd betrayed him. Now that I thought about it, there were at least two times when Kazoo had tried to trip me as I'd passed. At the time I'd figured it was all in my head, but now I was quite sure it was Charlie Connor lashing out at me.

"Why was he angry at Kazoo?" I asked.

"He wasn't," Kristi told me. "He's angry at FunJungle. He claims he was badly hurt here as a result of criminal negligence by the park."

"How?"

"Large Marge fell on him."

"Oh. I actually saw that happen."

"You did?"

"Yeah. Large Marge was chasing me at the time. I was racing to tell J.J. McCracken that my parents had been framed for Henry's death. Marge tried to stop me—and Charlie got in the way. She squashed him like a pancake."

Kristi laughed, then seemed to feel bad about it. "Well, Charlie claimed he was suffering from chronic back pain as a result. He said he could barely walk and wanted a couple million dollars to settle. But the park hired a private detective who caught him dancing at a nightclub, and the case was bounced out of court."

"How do you know all this?" I asked.

"Charlie told me," Kristi said. "He talks to me a lot. He's also asked me out a bunch of times."

"What'd you say?"

"No, of course. Not because he's a little person or anything, though. Because he's a criminal. The guy admitted to trying to bilk a couple million dollars out of FunJungle—and then thought I'd go on a date with him? Forget it."

"So how does Kazoo fit into all of this?" I asked.

"Charlie claimed he'd come up with a way to take FunJungle for even more money than he would have made through his insurance scam. He never told me what it was, but ransoming Kazoo fits the bill. Or selling him to some rich collector like Flora Hancock."

"Who's that?"

"This crazy lady who collects wild animals," Kristi told me. "Her husband made a ton of money in oil, and now she's got her own private menagerie: lions, tigers, monkeys, bears. Some folks say she even has an elephant. She lives all the way up by Waco, but she's already been here five times to see Kazoo. One of the other keepers pointed her out to me. She's hard to miss. She's the only person I've ever seen who comes here in designer clothes and high heels."

"My parents said a collector might have wanted Kazoo," I said. "Did you ever hear her say anything about that?"

"Oh yeah. She came right up to me here one day and asked about it." Kristi stuck her nose in the air and spoke in a deep Texas accent. "'Child, you must tell me. How did J.J. evah get himself a koala beah?'"

The impression was funny enough to make me laugh. "What'd you say?"

"That Kazoo didn't belong to J.J. He belonged to Australia. And that no private collector can get themselves a koala. Australia would never allow it."

"And what'd she say to that?"

Kristi shifted back into her Flora Hancock impression again. "'Oh, they might, sugah. They just might.'"

"You think she looked into it?" I asked.

"She seemed very determined," Kristi said. "And once

she discovered there was no legal way to get a koala, maybe she started looking for an illegal way."

"Like Charlie Connor," I concluded.

"Exactly. I'm sure he saw her here. Maybe he overheard her talking about wanting a koala at some point and then approached her with a plan. If anyone could have made off with Kazoo, it's him. He probably knows KoalaVille better than anyone. All he does is lurk around here in that koala suit eight hours a day."

"And because he's a criminal, he probably knows how to get around the security cameras and stuff," I suggested.

"Oh, you don't have to be a criminal to do that," Kristi said.

"What do you mean?" I asked.

"The security cameras inside the koala exhibit don't work. They threw up this building so fast—they wired them in, but they never connected them to the main system properly."

I sat up in surprise once again. "The cameras don't record at all? Then how did I get filmed last night?"

"Because the cameras *outside* the exhibit work. They were all installed when the park was built. But the ones *inside*, everything in the viewing area, Kazoo's pen, and even this one"—Kristi pointed at a camera mounted on the wall at the ceiling of her office—"they don't do a thing. I've been complaining about it for weeks, but no one's gotten around to fixing it. Marge told me not to worry because the cameras alone should have been a deterrent—as long as everyone *thought* they worked. But obviously, they weren't."

I shook my head sadly. "Did Charlie know the cameras didn't work?"

"I didn't tell him, but someone else might have. Or someone might have talked about it in front of him while he was wearing that ridiculous costume one day. Or maybe he just figured it out for himself."

"And Freddie Malloy could have figured it out too," I suggested.

"Absolutely," Kristi agreed.

My phone buzzed. It was a text from my father: *Done here. Where R U?*

"Is that important?" Kristi asked.

"Kind of," I said.

Kristi checked her watch and got to her feet. "I better get going. I didn't expect to talk so long. I have to get back to pretending a stuffed animal is real for the tourists." Kristi sighed. "Pete was wrong. Taking care of the fake *isn't* less work than caring for the real thing. It's more. Kazoo was easy to handle. But with the fake . . . I'm constantly worried someone's going to catch on. And when they do, it's going to be bad."

I got up too, and Kristi shepherded me toward the door.

"Can I tell my parents about Freddie and Charlie?" I asked.

"That's what I *want* you to do," Kristi said. "That's why I told you all this. I can't get the ear of anyone important here. I'm just a keeper. But your parents are more connected. Someone has to either get our security to focus on finding the real kidnapper—or the police need to be brought aboard. We need to locate Kazoo and get him back here as fast as possible. Every minute counts."

Her voice cracked, like she might be on the edge of crying. I froze, halfway through the door. "Why?"

"Most people don't realize it, but koalas don't eat just any eucalyptus," Kristi said. "The type Kazoo eats is very special. It doesn't grow in Texas, so we have to fly it in from Australia twice a week. Whoever stole Kazoo didn't take any of it—"

"He doesn't have any food?" I asked, concerned.

"No," Kristi said sadly. "So if we don't find Kazoo soon, he'll starve to death."

CARNIVORE CONTROL

I called Dad right after leaving KoalaVille.

"Where are you?" he asked.

"Near Carnivore Canyon," I replied. Technically that wasn't a lie. I thought my father might get upset if he knew I'd been to KoalaVille.

"Stay there," Dad told me. "I'll be there as fast as I can."

I hurried over to Carnivore Canyon, which was carved into a huge slab of rock close to the Land Down Under. During the summer it had been one of the most crowded exhibits at FunJungle, although today it was almost deserted. KoalaVille had siphoned off much of the attention. Plus, the really popular carnivores—the lions and tigers—had the good sense to stay indoors on cold days. Lots of smaller carnivores, like the otters and raccoons, stayed active during the winter, but for some reason, tourists didn't care about them much.

I liked the otters, though. So I posted myself in front of their exhibit and watched them cavorting until Dad arrived five minutes later. He was out of breath, having run across the entire park—and he was on edge, which was unusual for him. Dad was generally extremely unflappable. His work as a wildlife photographer had put him in plenty of dangerous situations. He'd faced everything from great white sharks to charging grizzly bears to third-world militias. But now he was a bundle of nervous energy.

"I thought we agreed you'd stay with the crowds," he said.

"There aren't many crowds to stay with today," I replied.

Dad frowned. "This isn't a game, Teddy. You need to be careful."

"Is something wrong?" I asked.

Dad hesitated a moment before answering, as though he was going to say one thing but decided to say something else instead. "I've just been worried about you. Come on." He put an arm around my shoulder and steered me off the main route through the exhibit.

I followed him down a thin dirt path through the land-scaping. "Where are we going?"

"To borrow a friend's office for a bit." Dad didn't have an

office at FunJungle. He could do almost anything he needed with a digital camera and a laptop computer, so he tended to work at home or borrow Mom's office—when he wasn't traveling the world on assignment.

"Is Mom coming too?" I asked.

Dad shook his head. "She really wants to, but she had another situation with Motupi."

I nodded understanding. Motupi was a five-year-old chimpanzee with severe anger-management issues. He had recently arrived at FunJungle, and while he behaved normally most of the time, every now and then he would have massive emotional eruptions. During these, he would tear up the landscaping, threaten the other chimps, and throw anything he could get his hands on—which was usually his own poop. FunJungle employees had started calling him Furious George.

"What'd he do this time?" I asked.

"Same as usual," Dad told me. "One second he was fine; the next he was screaming like a banshee and throwing stuff. Mom decided she can't leave him on display with the other chimps anymore, so she's shifting him to a holding cell until she can figure out what's triggering this behavior. If it weren't an emergency, she'd be here for you. You know that, right?"

"Yeah," I said. "I know."

Tucked behind the otter exhibit was a security door with the standard security keypad. Dad had written the day's code for this door on the palm of his hand. I figured whoever we were visiting must have given it to him. Dad typed it in, the door clicked open, and we entered the tunnels behind Carnivore Canyon.

Because the animal enclosures at the Canyon were built into the rock, the behind-the-scenes areas had needed to be carved out as well. The tunnel had the feel of a mine shaft and reeked of pee because all the big cats marked their territory several times a day. We passed behind the serval, bobcat, and mountain lion enclosures until we reached Carnivore Control. This was a surprisingly large room hollowed out in the rock. It was basically a man-made cave, albeit an incredibly high-tech one: There were computer monitors everywhere, providing live video feeds from the exhibits, although they could also be used to check everything from the feeding schedule to the animals' most recent health reports. It looked like the top secret underground lair of a James Bond villain.

A single keeper sat in the midst of the monitors, busily tracking all the carnivores at once. Most keepers tended to be darkly tanned from working hours outside each day. This keeper, however, was pasty from spending so much time underground, and the blue glow from all the monitors reflected off his white skin to give him a sort of ghostly pallor. He was so riveted to a video monitor that he barely glanced up when we entered.

"Teddy, this is Arthur Koenig," Dad said.

"Thanks for helping us," I said.

Arthur waved this off without taking his eyes off the monitor. "No big deal," he said. "Your father's helped me plenty of times. Grab any computer you need. I can't use them all."

Dad and I selected a computer right next to Arthur. Now that I could see his monitor, I realized what was so fascinating. He was watching video of FunJungle's four new Siberian tiger cubs, which were only a few days old. Siberian tigers are almost extinct, so any babies were a huge boon to the survival of the species. People around the world had been thrilled by the news of their birth. Pete Thwacker was chomping at the bit to get them on display—or at least to get photos of them in the papers—but for the time being the cubs needed rest and privacy. Most FunJungle employees hadn't even had the chance to see them yet. The cubs were all lodged at their mother's teats, nursing hungrily. They were so helpless; they couldn't even open their eyes yet.

"How're they doing?" Dad asked.

"Fantastic," Arthur replied. "In the wild, two would have been lucky to survive, but here, all four are probably going to come through. Even the little runt there." He tapped the screen, pointing to a cub significantly smaller than the others. His littermates kept shoving him away, but each time, he'd scramble back into the fray.

"Do they have names yet?" I asked.

Arthur shook his head. "Pete Thwacker wants to have a big contest to name them. He's gonna milk these cubs for as much PR as he can."

"Can't really blame him," Dad said. "This place needs all the good PR it can get."

"Maybe," Arthur grumbled, "but it'd be nice to call them something other than Cubs One, Two, Three, and Four."

Dad grabbed two chairs for us, then pulled a DVD out of his pocket. "My pal in security copied all the footage from the camera feeds outside KoalaVille last night," he told me. "Turns out, there's no footage from inside the exhibit. The morons never hooked it up properly."

I made a show of surprise, not wanting to tell Dad I knew this already. Because then I'd have to tell him *how* I knew, which was a conversation I didn't feel like having quite yet. There was too much else to focus on. "Have you watched all this already?"

"No. Only a few minutes of it. But I wanted to examine the rest more closely." Dad inserted the DVD into the hard drive, then brought up the file. It was quite large—a few hours of footage from multiple cameras—so it took a while to load. When it finally popped up, the computer screen displayed four different squares, each showing video from a different angle outside Kazoo's exhibit. The time was digitally stamped at the bottom of each. The video quality was surprisingly good; one of the many companies J.J. McCracken owned made high-quality surveillance cameras, so he'd given himself a deal on them.

The video began at four thirty p.m. There were no tourists lined up for the exhibit, as it was supposed to be closed for the night, although lots of people were jamming the bazaar, buying Kazoo merchandise.

Dad fast-forwarded a few minutes, then slowed down the video again. At 4:43 I ran past one of the cameras, then appeared on another, then showed up at the door to the keepers' office. My backpack dangled over one shoulder, obviously empty. I knocked, then entered Summer's code in the keypad and slipped into the office.

"Your knowing that code raised a lot of questions in security," Dad said. "Apparently, no one there knew J.J. McCracken had his own secret access code. Not even Marge."

"What Marge doesn't know could fill a library," I said.

"Marge—and most everyone else—assumes you must have stolen the code somehow," Dad went on. "Which indicates a lot of premeditation. Like you planned this theft well ahead of time."

I swallowed hard, concerned. "Why doesn't Marge just ask J.J. about the code?"

"I doubt he'd admit the truth about it," Dad said. "Then his secret code wouldn't be a secret anymore."

I sighed and nodded agreement.

Dad jumped two minutes ahead in the video. Four forty-five. The last of the tourists begrudgingly filed out of the koala viewing area. Then Kristi emerged and started toward her office, but Large Marge cut her off. There was no audio on the recording, but I knew Marge was demanding to be let into the viewing area and Kristi was telling her it was pointless because I wasn't inside. Marge grew angrier and angrier, so finally Kristi capitulated and let her in.

Dad jumped forward another few minutes. At 4:50 Marge and Kristi exited the viewing area, circled around to the keepers' office, and went inside. Two minutes after that, Marge stormed out, looking angry, and stomped off toward the bazaar. After another three minutes, Kristi exited, having tended to Kazoo, and headed home for the night.

Dad fast forwarded again. On the screen, it grew dark as the sun set and the video shifted from full-color to a night-vision green. Dad slowed the video a final time. At 5:31, I peeked out the door and looked around furtively. When I didn't see any security guards, I bolted for the back gate of the property.

Dad froze the video of me in mid-stride. "This is what grabbed everyone's attention," he said, pointing to the monitor.

My backpack was now on both shoulders. I knew it was still empty, but that wasn't obvious in the image.

"Looks like that backpack is full," Arthur said.

I turned, surprised to find him watching over my shoulder. "Well, it's not."

Arthur shrugged. "I just said it *looks* that way."

I was about to tell him to mind his own business when Dad cut me off. "It *does*," he said. "And that, combined with your suspicious behavior when you exited the exhibit, has raised a lot of concerns."

"I wasn't being suspicious," I said defensively. "I was looking around for the security guards."

"That's not suspicious?" Dad asked.

I suddenly realized why he was on edge. He'd already seen the footage and he knew it made me look bad. "I was looking for them because they'd been chasing me," I explained. "Not because I'd stolen Kazoo."

"*I* know that," Dad told me. "But we're talking about how it appears to other people."

"If Marge and all the other security guards were already chasing me, why would I pick that very moment to go steal Kazoo?" I asked. "That doesn't make any sense at all."

"Maybe not," Dad said. "And yet all the evidence is pointing directly at you. It's not just that they have this video of you. It's that there's no video of anyone else."

The gravity of my situation suddenly sank in. I felt terrible. It wasn't merely fear of being framed for a crime I didn't commit. I was also ashamed. I knew my father didn't believe I'd taken Kazoo, but one look in his eyes told me he was even more distressed by the situation than I was.

"There's no one else at all?" I asked.

"It doesn't look that way," Dad said sadly. "Security scanned through the rest of the footage and didn't see anyone else enter or leave the exhibit all night."

"They only scanned it?" I said. "No one ever watched it in real time?"

"No," Dad admitted. "Because that would take twelve hours, which probably seemed like a waste of time given that they already had video of you red-handed. That's why I asked for the footage, though. I figured I could go through it more carefully and see if anything interesting crops up."

"Now?" Arthur asked. "Sorry, but I can't let you guys stay for twelve hours. . . ."

"I wasn't planning on that," Dad told him. "I'll watch this myself at home tonight. I just wanted Teddy to see this much so he can understand what we're up against here." He turned to me solemnly. "You understand how bad this looks for you?"

"Yes," I said.

"Hopefully, I'll find something else on the footage," Dad

said. "Chances are, the security guys didn't pay very close attention to the rest of it—if they paid any attention at all. However, if I don't find anything else—"

"You have to," I interrupted. "Someone else took Kazoo. They have to be on the video. Security just didn't see it."

"I hope it's that easy," Dad said, though he sounded strangely pessimistic. He ejected the DVD and turned to Arthur. "Thanks for letting us use your office."

"Don't mention it," Arthur said. Something struck me as odd about how he said it, though. He didn't even look up. His eyes were riveted to his computer monitor again.

Dad sensed something was wrong too. "Arthur," he said worriedly. "What have you done?"

"My duty as a keeper," Arthur replied.

Dad grabbed me by the arm. "We have to get out of here, Teddy. Now!"

We ran for the exit, but we had only gone a few steps before Marge O'Malley and Bubba Stackhouse entered. The two of them filled the doorway, blocking any chance of escape. Marge dangled a pair of handcuffs from one meaty finger and gave me a big toothy grin. "Theodore Roosevelt Fitzroy," she said proudly, "you're under arrest."

CHAOS

Dad shot a look of betrayal at Arthur. "You tipped them off?"

Arthur couldn't even bring himself to meet my father's gaze. "Face the facts!" he mewled. "Teddy's guilty!"

"Mr. Fitzroy, please step away from your son," Bubba Stackhouse said. It was the first time I was seeing him up close. He was a big man in every way. He was at least six and a half feet tall, and his shoulders seemed four feet across. Muscles bulged under his shirt, but a large belly did too. He had a big nose, big ears, and a huge anvil jaw. Even his voice was big. It boomed and echoed inside the cave like a depth charge. "We'd like to make this as easy as possible for everyone."

Instead of doing what Bubba asked, Dad stepped in front of me, the way a buffalo would to protect its young from predators. "Teddy hasn't done anything wrong."

Bubba's muscles tensed in anger. "I don't want to hurt you, sir, but I will have to if that's what it takes."

"I'm not worried about me getting hurt," Dad replied. "I'm worried about Teddy. I don't think there's any need to put handcuffs on him. He's only twelve."

"*I'll* be the judge of what's necessary." Marge stepped forward as well, twirling the cuffs on her finger. "Now step away from the boy."

To my surprise, Dad complied. He suddenly shifted to the side, leaving me out in the open. Marge and Bubba loomed over me. I felt like a shrimp facing a pair of whales.

"Turn around, Theodore," Marge said. "And put your hands behind your back."

I looked to my father nervously, expecting him to stand up for me. Instead, to my surprise, he gave me a slight nod.

So I did exactly as Marge had asked. I turned around and put my wrists together at the base of my spine.

"Good boy," Marge said, like I was a dog. She took a step closer, still twirling the handcuffs.

Dad suddenly sprang into action. He snatched the cuffs off Marge's finger and, before Marge even knew what was happening, locked one around her left wrist.

"Hey!" Marge shouted.

Bubba spun toward Dad. He reflexively raised his fists . . .

And Dad snapped the other handcuff around his wrist.

Bubba grabbed for him, but as his right arm was now cuffed to Marge's left, his reach was suddenly cut short.

Dad easily leaped out of range, then yelled, "Teddy! Let's go!"

I didn't need to be told twice. I bolted for the exit. Arthur Koenig lunged for me, but I easily dodged the traitor. He slammed face-first into one of the computer monitors, gave a squeal of pain, and crumpled to the floor, clutching his bloodied nose.

Dad and I raced out of the control room. Marge and Bubba charged after us, though the two of them didn't coordinate their steps right. They crashed into each other and took out a desk full of computer equipment.

Dad led me back the way we'd come in. Behind us we could hear Marge screaming in rage and frustration. She was so angry she couldn't even form words. Instead she sounded like a wounded animal.

"Where are we going?" I asked Dad.

"I don't know," he admitted. "I'm making this up as I go."

We barged through the exit by the otter exhibit and startled a few tourists as we burst out of the landscaping— although Marge's angry howls echoing through the tunnel scared them even more.

"Sounds like something's escaped!" one tourist yelled,

and everyone fled in fear. A few more park guests near the lion exhibit overheard them and ran as well. (Given that a tiger had escaped at Carnivore Canyon's grand opening gala, their reactions actually made sense.)

Dad and I reached the entrance to Carnivore Canyon and found several security guards racing toward us from the center of the park. We turned toward the back gate, but guards were blocking that as well. There was only one way for us to go: For the second time in two days, I found myself running toward KoalaVille.

The number of guests fleeing Carnivore Canyon had snowballed, and the approaching phalanx of guards now confirmed everyone's fears that an animal had escaped. Panic set in. The tourists screamed and scattered across the park, not so much seeking safety as trying to outrun all the other visitors and thus let them get picked off first.

The guards made no attempt to calm the frightened guests. Instead they charged after me and Dad.

Marge and Bubba emerged from Carnivore Canyon and joined in the chase. Bubba was a surprisingly strong man. Marge would have been like an anchor to most people, but the policeman was dragging her right along with him.

Dad and I raced past the crowded Kazoo merchandise bazaar, but then stopped short on the other side, scanning the length of the back fence.

"What's wrong?" I asked.

"We shouldn't have come this way." Dad sounded upset with himself. "It's a dead end."

"So what do we do?"

"Create a diversion." Then, at the top of his lungs, Dad yelled, "The lion's out!"

Everyone in the bazaar started in fear, then noticed their fellow tourists panicking over at Carnivore Canyon. They dropped their koala merchandise and scattered. Within a second the entire shopping area became pandemonium. People were screaming and running everywhere. A shelf full of commemorative Kazoo snow globes toppled and shattered.

The security guards lost us in the chaos. Dad and I doubled back, using the racks of sweatshirts as cover, and circled around the koala exhibit. Despite everything, there was still a line of tourists at the door. Either they hadn't heard the warning about the escaped lion, or they were so determined to see Kazoo that they were willing to risk being mauled to do it.

Dad and I came around the back side, hoping to find a path to freedom. Instead we found trouble.

Bubba Stackhouse was smarter than we'd thought. He'd kept an eye on us and swung around to cut us off, bringing Marge with him. They ambushed us, blocking our escape.

Dad and I had no choice but to veer into the exhibit. We bulldozed in through the exit. The teenager posted there to make sure this didn't happen tried to chastise us, but Bubba and Marge flattened him before he could.

The exhibit was even more crowded than it had been earlier. Tourists were packed four deep at the glass, staring at the stuffed toy back in the trees. The newlyweds were still there, having spent an hour and a half patiently waiting for the fake koala to move. Kristi had resumed her post on the podium. Pete Thwacker was now with her. Apparently, the PR man had dropped by to see for himself how well his ruse was working. As always, Pete looked impeccable. His hair was perfectly combed, his teeth gleamed blindingly, and he wore a fancy suit that probably cost more than our trailer.

The crowds were too thick for Dad and me to wriggle through. We were trapped. Marge and Bubba cornered me against the glass.

"Everyone stand back!" Marge ordered. "This kid is dangerous!"

Her voice was surprisingly commanding. The crowd obediently cleared away from me, as though I were contagious.

Only Dad remained close. Once again, he placed himself between the authorities and me. "Leave my son alone," he warned.

"If you obstruct justice again, we'll arrest you, too," Bubba growled. "Your son is guilty of a serious crime."

"What crime?" Dad taunted. "It seems to me that Kazoo's right here." He pointed through the glass.

Bubba looked into the exhibit and gaped in surprise at the koala. Evidently, no one had informed him of Pete's amoral cover-up.

Dad took advantage of the diversion to try and slip by with me in tow, but Bubba instinctively grabbed for us with his free hand. Dad expertly deflected it, grabbing Bubba's wrist and twisting his arm down. Bubba, being a good old boy who'd probably had his share of fights, responded to the attack by trying to punch Dad in the face.

Unfortunately, Bubba forgot he was handcuffed to Marge. Marge had already started toward Dad, and now the force of Bubba's powerful swing yanked her off balance. Dad darted out of the way as Marge sailed toward him. She slammed into the glass wall.

Most animal exhibits are built with extremely strong shatterproof glass, but KoalaVille had been thrown up so quickly there hadn't been time to get it specially made. Marge hit the glass hard—and pulled Bubba along with her. The glass didn't stand a chance against the two of them.

The enormous pane shattered into a million pieces. Marge and Bubba stumbled into the exhibit and slammed into the eucalyptus tree where fake Kazoo sat.

The koala tumbled from its perch and landed on its head.

And then Marge and Bubba fell on it.

The tourists had watched the intrusion into the exhibit in stunned silence. But now, seeing what appeared to be Kazoo's lifeless limbs sticking out from beneath Marge and Bubba, the screaming began.

Tourists of all ages, men and women alike, completely freaked out.

"They killed Kazoo!" the bride wailed, and several dozen other people echoed her.

I stole a glance at Pete Thwacker. His normally tan skin had completely drained of color. He looked as though he'd swallowed a porcupine.

Beside him, Kristi Sullivan appeared to be laughing at his expense.

"People, please!" Pete yelled over the din. "I assure you, Kazoo is not dead!"

"He's not moving!" the groom yelled back. "They crushed him! Oh, this is horrible!"

A few adults rushed to Kazoo's aid and tried to pry Marge and Bubba off the prone koala. However, Marge and Bubba—neither being very spry to begin with—were tangled up together and having a great deal of trouble getting up.

Mothers and fathers tried to shield their children's eyes from the carnage. Most of the children, however, were equally determined to see it. Other guests wept. Still others had dialed 911 and were currently being told that emergency services only responded for human emergencies, not marsupial ones. However, a majority of the tourists were using their phones to record everything that was happening. I noticed at least twenty filming the "corpse" of Kazoo.

A few more security guards burst in through the exit, preventing Dad and me from running. I'm not sure that we would have, though. The disaster unfolding before our eyes was too riveting to ignore. Even the newly arrived guards forgot about us as they saw what had happened. Apparently, none of them were aware that Kazoo was fake either. Upon seeing the flattened koala, a few broke down and cried on the spot.

Finally, with a mighty yank, one of the tourists managed to extricate the koala from beneath Marge. Or at least he extricated most of it. The head popped off, leaving the koala's savior holding only the body of the doll. At the sight of this, more gasps and screams erupted from the crowd. The bride fainted.

The man holding the koala, however, grew enraged. He turned on Pete and Kristi, the most obvious representatives of FunJungle present. "This is a toy!" he yelled.

A new wave of gasps rippled through the room. Everyone stared at the headless, pancaked koala in shock, unsure whether or not to believe this.

For a moment Pete was at a rare loss for words, unsure

whether to admit the koala was fake or claim that it was actually dead. In a panic he went with his standard gut response: lying. "It's not a toy," he argued weakly.

The man holding the fake koala pointed dramatically to where the head had torn free from the body. Instead of blood and guts spilling out, there was only cottony white stuffing. "I'm pretty sure this isn't natural," the man said.

Every head now swiveled toward Pete, who grew even paler. Kristi Sullivan, fearing the wrath of the crowd, stepped away from him and pretended to have been conned herself. "Where's the real koala?" she demanded. "What have you done with Kazoo?"

Pete shot her a glare of betrayal, then tried to address the tourists. "Kazoo has temporarily been removed from public view . . . ," he began.

"Without telling us?" a mother cried. "That's reprehensible!"

"Was there ever even a real Kazoo?" the groom demanded, still trying to revive his unconscious bride. "Or was this all just a plot cooked up by FunJungle to take our money?"

Much of the crowd angrily seconded this thought.

"I assure you FunJungle has done no such thing!" Pete told them.

"Then tell us where Kazoo is!" one of the park's own security guards demanded.

Pete started to say something, but then caught himself. I knew Pete well enough to guess that he'd been about to tell another lie—perhaps that Kazoo had been sent to a nice, relaxing koala spa for a few days to deal with the stress of being on display—but had realized that sooner or later this would be uncovered as well and that he and FunJungle would end up looking even worse than they did now.

"Where's Kazoo?" more people demanded.

"If you have a real koala, then prove it!" the groom ordered.

"I, er, well, um . . . ," Pete stammered. He didn't have much practice telling people the truth. "The thing is, while Kazoo isn't dead, he's . . . uh . . . he's not exactly here . . . on these premises . . . at this exact time."

"Well, where is he?" asked the man clutching the remnants of the emergency backup koala.

"He's been kidnapped," said Large Marge.

The crowd gasped again and swung back to face her. She was now on her feet, pink from embarrassment and exertion, brushing glass shards off her uniform. "He was taken last night."

The crowd now reacted with a wide range of emotions. Some people were even more horrified than they had been before. Others were still angry at the deception. I saw astonishment, shock, confusion, and everything in between. The bride, who had just regained consciousness, fainted again.

Marge focused her beady eyes on me, but continued to speak to the crowd. "However, we are in the process of apprehending the number one suspect at this very moment. We have evidence that this boy is responsible and expect him to reveal the koala's whereabouts soon."

The gaze of everyone in the room shifted once again. To me.

Two security guards seized me from behind. When Dad tried to intervene, four more grabbed him.

The crowd exploded. No one seemed to know what to believe anymore. People were shouting at me, at Marge, at Pete, at the security guards.

"He couldn't have done it!" someone declared. "He's just a boy!"

But other people were glaring at me hatefully. "Where's Kazoo?" one demanded. "What have you done with him?"

"I never touched him," I replied. "I've been framed."

Marge and Bubba stormed toward Dad and me over the carpet of glass shards, which cracked and popped beneath their feet. At a nod from Marge, the guards quickly marched us out of the exhibit.

We reemerged into FunJungle to find the place completely desolate. While we'd been dealing with the chaos inside, everyone outside had evacuated, still fearing an escaped lion.

Pete Thwacker and Kristi Sullivan followed us. Pete was

walking backward so he could talk to the angry crowd. "I don't have the time to answer all your koala-related questions at this moment," he said. "But I assure you, full details will soon be available on our website."

The crowd roared in disapproval, wanting to know more.

Marge's radio suddenly crackled to life. "Marge, this is Tracey. Pick up now."

That was Tracey Boyd, FunJungle's manager of operations, second in command only to J.J. McCracken. She sounded angrier than a tiger that had been poked with a stick. The security guards all looked to Marge, concerned.

"I'll talk to her later," Marge said. "We deal with Teddy now." She made a move to turn the radio off.

"Don't you dare turn that off," Tracey said.

Marge froze, startled.

"I'm watching you on the security cameras," Tracey explained.

Marge gulped. She picked up her radio and responded. "Security Chief O'Malley."

"I want you to report to my office this instant," Tracey told her.

"Right now? We're in the process of apprehending a known felon."

"I can see what you're doing. It can wait. In fact, I want you to bring Teddy here as well. I want *all* of you here. The whole darn circus. *Now*. And tell that idiot Thwacker to come too."

"Me?" Pete asked, worried, but there was no answer. Tracey was off the radio.

Kristi turned to Pete with a devilish told-you-so grin. "So," she said. "Looks like that fake koala wasn't such a good idea after all."

THE THREAT

"Today was not just a disaster at FunJungle," Tracey Boyd said. "It was a catastrophe."

I was seated in her office, along with Dad, Large Marge, Bubba Stackhouse, Pete Thwacker, and half the security staff. It was a large office on the fourth floor of the administration building, with windows that looked out over the entire park.

Another wall of Tracey's office was filled with TV monitors. Some of these were connected to park security cameras, which was how Tracey had known about the latest Kazoo catastrophe almost as soon as it had happened. Other monitors were tuned to a variety of television channels, ranging from the local news to CNN to Animal Planet. All three local TV stations had interrupted their usual daytime programming to broadcast the latest news from FunJungle. The local anchors didn't know what to cover first: the escaped lion (which they had yet to determine wasn't real) or the revelation that Kazoo had been kidnapped. Out the windows, I could see three news copters circling Carnivore Canyon, searching for the lion—and then, on the TVs, I could see the live aerial footage they were shooting.

Tracey was tall, with long thin legs like a giraffe and a mane of dark hair. When she was excited about something, she could be extremely effusive. (Unlike Martin del Gato, the previous director of operations at FunJungle, Tracey really liked animals and often could be found interacting with them with great joy.) But when she was angry—as she was now—she could be terrifying. Even a giant like Bubba Stackhouse seemed afraid of her.

"It was a fiasco," Tracey went on. "A calamity. A complete and utter cataclysm. In the future, students learning about how to run a zoo will study this day as a shining example of incompetence, foolishness, and idiocy."

Everyone looked at their shoes, ashamed.

Tracey shifted her attention to Pete Thwacker. "I assume it was your numskull idea to put a toy koala on display?"

Pete did his best to meet her eyes. "You told me to keep the theft a secret," he said.

"No, I told you to keep a lid on the story," Tracey

snapped. "I thought you were going to say the exhibit was closed for maintenance—"

"The guests get upset when they come all the way to the zoo and find their favorite animals aren't on display . . . ," Pete explained.

"Ah, right," Tracey said. "Thank goodness we didn't upset any of the guests, then. Instead we completely horrified them. First they witnessed what they thought was the brutal death of Kazoo by blunt trauma—and then you went and revealed that Kazoo had been stolen anyhow."

Pete winced. "I thought it was better than everyone thinking the koala was dead."

"They *knew* the koala wasn't dead!" Tracey roared. "They figured that out when they noticed it had stuffing coming out of its neck! What they were upset at—and rightfully so—was the idea that they'd been conned! Duped! Bamboozled! Hoodwinked!" When Tracey got angry, she had a weakness for synonyms. Behind her back, many park employees called her Thesaurus Rex.

"I'm sorry," Pete said weakly. "It was a mistake."

"You're darn right it was!" Tracey cried. "It was a blunder. A beanball. A total boner. And because of it, every media outlet in this state is calling for our heads on a stick—and the rest of the country isn't far behind. So you need to get out there, face the music, and own up to this. Admit this was your lamebrain idea, not the park's—and that your actions in no way represented park policy."

Pete nodded obediently. "And what do you want me to say about the kidnapping?"

"First of all, don't call it a kidnapping. It's not a kidnapping until we get a ransom note, and we don't have one of those yet. This is a theft. But as for what to say about it . . . heck if I know. That's *your* job. Whatever it is, just make sure the park sounds good."

"Should I offer a reward for anyone who helps find the perpetrator?" Pete asked.

Tracey thought for a moment, then sighed. "I suppose we'd better. Let's say twenty thousand dollars. Maybe that will remind people that we're a business that cares about our animals, rather than a business that scams its customers. And while we're at it, we'd better offer free park passes to everyone who came to see Kazoo today."

"Consider it done." Pete sprang to his feet, happy to have permission to leave, even if it meant eating crow in front of the press.

"There's one more thing," Tracey said, freezing Pete in his tracks. "The only reason you still have a job right now is because I don't have anyone else to undo your mistakes. So you'd better take good care of this mess—or I'll can you, understand?"

"Yes, ma'am," Pete said meekly, then scurried out with his tail between his legs.

Large Marge instantly raised her hand and waved it in the air like an eager student with a question for the teacher.

Tracey turned to her. "What is it, Marge?"

"I don't understand the point of offering a reward to help catch the perpetrator," Marge said. "We've already caught the perpetrator. Right there." She pointed at me.

I started to defend myself, but before I could, Dad jumped in himself. "There is no proof that Teddy stole Kazoo."

"Yes there is!" Marge argued. "We've got him leaving the exhibit on tape!"

"Without a koala," Dad said.

"He has a backpack that was big enough to hide a koala in," Marge countered.

"That doesn't prove anything," Dad told her.

"It does when no one else entered the exhibit!" Marge shot back. "Teddy goes in, there's a koala. He comes out, there's no koala anymore. He took it. Case closed."

"Then where is it?" Dad demanded. "You searched our house this morning and didn't find so much as a hair."

"Then Teddy hid it somewhere else," Marge growled. "The woods, maybe. Wherever it is, I'll find it."

Before Dad could counter this, Tracey steeped into the fray. "Enough!" she shouted. "Silence! Clam it!"

Dad and Marge both fell silent.

"Face the facts," Tracey told Dad. "The evidence against Teddy here is awfully conclusive." Marge grinned at this, but then Tracey swung back to face her. "However, given the disastrous events of today—which you played no small part in—and the beating we're about to take in the media as a result of them, there is no way I'm going to let you arrest a young boy for this crime without ironclad proof that he did it. The last thing we need right now is to claim a kid took Kazoo and then find out he didn't."

Marge sagged like a popped balloon. "But he's our number one suspect," she whined. "If we let him go, he might skip town."

"No I won't," I said. "'Cause I didn't do it."

"You won't," Tracey told me, "because we're going to ensure you can't." She looked to Bubba. "What would it take to outfit Teddy here with an ankle bracelet?"

Bubba shrugged. "Not too much."

"What's an ankle bracelet?" I asked.

"A radio transmitter that we lock on your leg," Marge informed me. "So that we can tell where you are at all times."

"I've got some in the car right now," Bubba said. He started to get up.

"Hold on now," Dad said. "No one's fitting Teddy with one of those. They're for criminals."

"He *is* a criminal," Marge replied, glaring at me. "We just haven't proved it yet."

"And until you do, Teddy will be able to go about his normal life," Tracey ordered. She looked to Dad. "He can return to school, stay at home, or move about the park at will. The only difference will be that he has a tracking device on him. So if it turns out that he is indeed the thief, then we'll know where to find him."

Dad held her gaze for a moment. "I don't like it," he said. "Not at all."

"Well, tough," Tracey said. "Because that's what we're doing. And in the meantime, your family is going to fully cooperate with Marge's investigation."

Dad looked to me.

"I'm okay with it," I told him. "I don't have anything to hide."

"All right," Dad said with a sigh. "But I'd like to point out that every minute spent investigating Teddy is a minute no one's looking for the *real* thief."

"We're not focusing on Teddy to inconvenience you," Tracey told him. "We're doing it because, at the moment, he's our number one suspect. Either he's a criminal, or he's a foolish little boy who's only in this mess because he did a lot of things he shouldn't have in the first place."

Now everyone was staring at me, though the only one I

was ashamed to look back at was my father. Tracey Boyd was right. I'd gotten myself into this heap of trouble on my own.

Large Marge smirked at me, but Tracey then turned on her. "And as for you, let's have a few less catastrophes and a lot more careful investigating here. Teddy's father is right. If Teddy's innocent, then you've given the thief a big head start. So you had better either bring me proof Teddy did this—or find the real criminal, fast. The Australians are going ballistic about this. If we don't get that koala back, we're going to have an international incident on our hands. Every day that goes by, Kazoo's situation gets more and more desperate. So if he isn't recovered soon—or if we have any more disasters like today—heads will roll, do you understand?"

The smirk disappeared from Marge's face. "Yes, ma'am," she said.

"Good," Tracey said. "Then everyone here is dismissed—except Teddy." She met my father's surprised stare. "I'd like to talk to him solo for a bit."

"I'm not too comfortable with that . . . ," Dad began.

"You can wait right outside the door if it will make you feel better," Tracey told him. "I'll leave it unlocked. We'll only be ten minutes, if that. Any longer and you can feel free to come right back in here."

Dad glanced at me. I nodded that I was all right.

"Ten minutes," he told us. "And I'll be right outside."

He filed out behind all the security guards. Marge let him exit before her, then took one last long, hard look at me, wondering why I merited a one-on-one with Tracey and she didn't. Then she stormed out and slammed the door behind her.

Tracey let the silence hang there for a few seconds, allowing me to grow uneasy. Finally she asked, "Did you take that koala, Teddy?"

"No," I said. "But I have some ideas about who might have."

Tracey wasn't expecting that. She stiffened in surprise. "Really?"

"Well, they're not *my* ideas," I admitted. "They're Kristi Sullivan's. She says Freddie Malloy had a grudge against Kazoo."

"Freddie." Tracey rolled her eyes. "Let me guess. That idiot thinks the koala cost him his show somehow. Not the fact that he routinely traumatized the audience."

"Yes. Kristi said he'd threatened to throw Kazoo into the gator pit."

Tracey grimaced. "Who else?"

"Charlie Connor. He's been looking for a way to get some money out of FunJungle."

Tracey sighed, then dutifully wrote both names down on a legal pad. "Anyone else?"

"A rich animal collector named Flora Hancock. She might have hired Charlie to swipe Kazoo for her. Or maybe she had someone else do it."

Tracey wrote that down too. "Any more?"

I shook my head.

"Why didn't Kristi tell *me* any of this?" Tracey asked.

"She told *Marge*," I said. "But Marge didn't do anything."

Tracey sighed again, then tapped her fingers on her desk. "And how, exactly, did you come to learn this from Kristi?"

"She told me."

"Really? Of all the people Kristi could go to, she tracked down the twelve-year-old boy accused of the crime?"

"Well, she didn't track me down, exactly. I happened to be in KoalaVille."

"Why?"

"I was . . . well . . ." I squirmed in my seat, aware Tracey wouldn't like the answer. "I was sort of investigating."

Tracey stared at me for a long time. Then she said, "Teddy, there are a lot of people at this park who say you were a great help in finding out who killed Henry the Hippo—but there are also a lot who claim you were just a nuisance who stuck his nose where it didn't belong."

"They're wrong!" I protested. "No one would have even known Henry was murdered if it wasn't for me!"

"I highly doubt that," Tracey told me. "However, I do

know that Henry's funeral wouldn't have been such a disaster if it weren't for you."

"That wasn't entirely my fault," I argued. "The bad guys were after me. I was only trying to escape."

"In addition, you were also linked to the escape of a tiger from Carnivore Canyon—and the disappearance of a black mamba from World of Reptiles. A mamba that *still* hasn't been recovered. You have been accused of arming the chimpanzees with water balloons, spreading rumors that the meat in our hamburgers is kangaroo, and teaching the parrots to say bad words in Spanish. And now, in the past two days, you've planted a fake arm in the shark tank *and* been involved in the destruction of the koala exhibit." Tracey came out from behind her desk and approached me. "Now, I don't know if you took Kazoo or not, but I do know that wherever you go at this park, chaos and mayhem follow. I don't like chaos and mayhem. Not at all. So from this point forward, you are going to stop these shenanigans. I want you to lay off the cheap pranks—and I want you to stay far away from this investigation. If you can't—if there's one more PR disaster and I find you're even remotely connected—I'll ban you from this park forever."

"I can't stay out of the park," I said. "I *live* here. Both my parents work here."

"That can change," Tracey told me.

It took me a second to realize what she meant. And once I did, I couldn't believe what I was hearing. "You mean . . . you'd fire them?"

"Yes."

"Because of me?"

"I wouldn't *want* to," Tracey said. "Both your parents are extremely valuable assets to this park. However, at a certain point, the trouble you've caused outweighs their worth to us. FunJungle is already in a tenuous financial situation. We can't handle another event like *this*." Tracey pointed at the wall of TV monitors. The screens were all now filled with coverage of the chaos in KoalaVille. Tourists had already uploaded video to YouTube of Marge crashing through the koala exhibit, and every news station was running it. I caught a glimpse of myself ducking out of the way just before Marge sailed through the glass.

"My parents love it here," I pleaded. "Please don't fire them. I don't mean to cause all this trouble—"

"Whether you mean to or not, you cause it," Tracey said. "And that needs to stop. Cease. Desist. Come to an end. Right now. If it doesn't . . . I'll have no choice but to let your parents go."

10

THE GOOD CALL

I expected my parents to be angry when they heard Tracey had threatened their jobs. Enraged, even. But they weren't. Instead they just accepted the news sadly.

"You're not upset?" I asked at dinner that night. "It's not fair!"

"Maybe not, but I understand Tracey's reasons," Mom said. "This park has had more than its share of disasters . . . and you've been involved in every one."

"That's not true," I protested. "I didn't kill Henry. I didn't set the tiger or the mamba free—"

"I didn't say you *caused* all of them. I said you were involved." Mom gave me an unusually hard glare across the table.

"Are you upset at *me*?" I asked.

"We told you to stay away from this investigation," Mom chided. "And the first thing you did was run off to KoalaVille. And then you led Marge and Bubba right back there—"

"That wasn't his fault," Dad told her. "He was only trying to get away from them."

"Which he wouldn't have had to do if *you'd* been more careful." Mom shifted her glare to Dad. "You're just as much to blame for the madness today as he is."

"I was trying to protect our son," Dad argued.

"You shouted that a lion was loose in the middle of a crowd," Mom said coldly.

Dad looked down at his meat loaf. "I didn't have time to think. I was trying to help Teddy."

"I know you were," Mom said. "But it was a mistake. And we can't afford any more of them. So . . ." She turned back to me. "You need to listen to Tracey. Stay away from KoalaVille. Don't make any more waves—and try to keep out of trouble."

"All right," I said. "It ought to be easier now anyhow, seeing as Marge and Bubba aren't hunting me down." The electronic bracelet was clamped tight around my ankle. Bubba had locked it on right after I left Tracey's office. It was surprisingly large and bulky. The plastic strap was three inches wide, while the GPS transmitter was the size of a cell phone.

"We can track you anywhere you go with that," Bubba had warned me. "And right now, the only place you're approved to go besides FunJungle is school. If you try to make a run for it, we'll know. And then we'll come get you and toss you in a juvenile facility."

The bracelet wasn't very comfortable. The plastic strap was already rubbing my skin raw and making my ankle sweat (even though it was freezing outside). I itched right beneath the transmitter, where it was impossible to scratch. Now I tried to jab the blade of a butter knife under it to give myself some relief.

"Careful with that," Mom told me. "If it breaks and the signal drops, the police will probably come running."

I sighed and set the knife back on the table. "Marge and Bubba still think I'm the one who poached Kazoo. What if they don't try to look for any other thieves?"

"Don't worry," Dad said. "Somehow we'll find a way to prove you didn't take Kazoo."

"I'm not worried about *me*," I replied. "I'm worried about the koala. Kristi says he'll starve in another two days."

Mom and Dad shared a look, then turned back to me. Both looked pained by what they had to say next.

"Even so," Dad said. "That doesn't mean *you* have to save him. Tracey gave you specific orders to stay away from this investigation. I know you want to do the right thing, but . . . Kazoo isn't worth losing our jobs over."

"But he could *die* . . . ," I began.

"It's not your job to save him," Dad said sadly. "It's not any of our jobs. If Kazoo dies—and I truly hope that doesn't happen—it won't be because *we* failed him. It will be because Marge and the rest of FunJungle security did."

I stared back at him, feeling angry and helpless. I was upset that my own father was putting his career—and my mother's—before the welfare of Kazoo. But I also knew he was right. Just because I'd solved one crime at FunJungle didn't mean I could solve another. And my involvement so far had been pretty disastrous—although I certainly wasn't the only one responsible for that.

"Can I be excused from dinner?" I asked. "I don't feel very hungry anymore."

Mom and Dad exchanged another look, this one a bit sad.

"Of course," Mom said. "Teddy, I know all this isn't easy to hear. We just want you to know, we don't blame *you* for anything that's happened. Sometimes there are events we simply can't control."

I nodded understanding. I think Mom was hoping that I'd say something, maybe stick around and let them explain their reasons to me a bit more, but I didn't feel like it. I simply cleared my plate and then headed to my room.

The moment I shut the door, my phone buzzed in my

pocket. I almost tossed it aside. I didn't feel like talking to anyone . . .

With one exception. So I checked the caller ID.

To my surprise, it was her.

I quickly accepted the offer to video chat, and Summer McCracken popped onto the screen on my phone. She was in her school dormitory, wearing pink pajamas, her blond hair done up in a ponytail with a pink scrunchie cinched around it.

"Hey," I said.

"You have an amazing gift for causing mayhem," Summer told me. "This time was almost as crazy as Henry's funeral—"

"It wasn't my fault," I said quickly.

"I know that," she replied. "It's the adults who screwed up here, as usual. You just have a talent for ending up in the middle of things."

"I wish I didn't."

"I wish I'd been there today. I would have loved to see Marge flatten that fake koala in front of everyone. It must've been hilarious. Especially Pete trying to explain it all. I don't know what he was thinking, putting that toy in the exhibit. Serves him right how all this went down."

I thought back to the events in the koala exhibit, imagining them from someone else's perspective. "It actually was pretty funny," I admitted.

Summer laughed. "I hear Tracey Boyd chewed out Pete and Marge pretty hard afterward."

Any bit of joy I'd felt quickly dissipated. "Tracey got on my case too. In fact, she told me that if anything like this ever happens again, she'll fire my parents."

Summer stopped laughing. "Listen, Teddy . . ."

"Could you tell your dad about this?" I asked. "Maybe he can convince Tracey to go easier on them if I screw up again."

"I'm sorry. I can't . . ."

"Sure you can! You're his daughter. You're practically the only person he listens to—"

"That wasn't Tracey's decision to threaten your parents. It was Dad's."

I stared at Summer a moment, feeling stunned and betrayed. "I thought your father liked my parents," I said finally.

"He *does*." Summer bit her lip, obviously uncomfortable about what she had to say. "It's just that . . . he's a business-man, and what happened today was very bad for business."

"Do you agree with him?"

"Well, I see his point. FunJungle's not doing so well, Teddy. And every time something like this happens, it scares more tourists away."

"I thought you said it was hilarious—"

"It was. To *me*. But not to everyone else in America. Fun-Jungle's doing poorly enough as it is. Remember how my dad was thinking about building roller coasters through the animal exhibits?"

I did. My parents and I had found the plans. It would have been disastrous for the animals if J.J. had gone through with them. "I thought he promised you he'd never do that."

"Well, he's getting desperate enough to break that promise. The park's in trouble, and today's disaster didn't exactly help things."

"So you want me to back off trying to find who took Kazoo too?" I asked.

"No!" Summer said quickly. "I only said I understand why my father did what he did. And that's why I can't get him to undo Tracey's order. But as for finding out about Kazoo . . . you *have* to keep investigating."

I scowled, frustrated by the mixed messages I was getting. "Your father will fire my parents if I keep investigating."

"No, he'll fire them if you cause another disaster."

"I can't control that. I'm not *trying* to cause all this trouble. My parents say I need to just back off and let Marge handle the case."

"I don't think that'd be in your best interests," Summer said.

"Why not?"

"Because Marge is stepping up her attempts to prove you're the thief. She just e-mailed my father a whole report detailing why she's positive you did it."

"How'd you get it?" I asked.

"I know Daddy's e-mail password. Sometimes, on a day like today, I like to check in to see what's going on. Lucky for you, I did. She's really out to get you."

"But Tracey just told her she'd better find the thief ASAP or heads would roll."

"Yes, and Marge is convinced the thief is *you*. To her, following any other leads is a waste of time. Instead she's doubling down on trying to prove you're guilty."

I rubbed my temples. Trying to understand Marge's thinking was giving me a headache. "So Tracey tells Marge to find the thief . . . and Marge's response is to come after me even harder . . . which is allowing the thief to get away."

"Yes, although Marge wouldn't see it that way."

"Any idea what she has on me?"

"Nothing new. You're caught on video coming out of the koala exhibit the night Kazoo got kidnapped—and no one else is. But you have to admit, that's pretty strong stuff. If someone else stole the koala, how'd they do it without being recorded?"

"That's what Marge is supposed to be finding out," I said sullenly.

"Well, she's not," Summer said. "She's only building a case against you. Which means the real bad guy is still out there with Kazoo somewhere—and no one's looking for him. That's why you *have* to try to figure out who did it."

"I can't," I told her.

"If Kazoo isn't found soon, he's going to die! If I were there, you know I'd be helping find him . . ."

"That's easy for you to say. If you get caught investigating, your father isn't going to lose his job."

Summer sighed. She seemed disappointed in me. "Look, Teddy, I know this is asking a lot—"

"It's asking a *ton*."

"But Kazoo needs you. No one else is helping him. You were willing to look for Henry's killer when no one else was—and Henry's life wasn't even in the balance. He was already dead."

I frowned. I was feeling disappointed in myself, too. "Things are different this time," I argued. "Can't you get your father to replace Marge with someone who actually knows what they're doing?"

"My father doesn't know Marge like you and I do. He trusts her."

"Why?"

"Because he didn't promote Marge to be a detective. No one expected there to be another case like this. Marge is only supposed to be the head of security, which isn't exactly brain surgery. The biggest crime at theme parks is usually shoplifting—and Marge is great at busting shoplifters. She's really made a dent in crime at FunJungle since she took over."

"Maybe, but she has no idea how to catch a *real* criminal. Doesn't your dad understand that?"

"Know what would make him understand?" Summer asked. "You finding the real kidnapper. Then he'd realize it wasn't a fluke when you and I found Henry's killer."

"He thinks we just got lucky?"

"I don't know. Maybe. But think, if Marge is spending all this time trying to prove you're the criminal, and then *you* figure out who the criminal actually is, then you reveal Marge to be a complete bozo. Dad won't be able to ignore that. He'll give her the ax—and he'll never even *think* about firing your parents again. He'll see you as an asset, rather than a liability."

"He should *already* see me as an asset," I groused. "I've already solved one crime around here, haven't I?"

"Which means you can solve this one too. And I'll be available to help you in any way that I can. So what do you say?" Summer batted her eyelashes at me, although she did it in an exaggerated way, playing up the damsel-in-distress thing. "Please? Will you do it for me?"

I took my time before answering. Although I'd been given a lot of reasons to steer clear of the investigation, Summer had given me a decent number to investigate as well. To my surprise, despite all the threats, I realized I *wanted* to help find Kazoo. In part this was because I was worried about the koala and it seemed like the right thing to do. In part it was wanting to prove my innocence—and Marge's idiocy. And in part it was because I was excited to have another adventure with Summer. Talking to her now, I realized how much I'd missed her over the past few months. Investigating would give us the excuse to have lots more conversations.

However, I still had plenty of concerns. "How am I even supposed to do this?" I asked. "I can't just wander over to KoalaVille and start poking around for clues."

Summer broke into a big, brilliant smile. "Does this mean you're in?" she asked. "You'll help find Kazoo?"

"I'm thinking about it," I said. "It won't be easy. I don't even know where to start."

"*I* do," Summer said.

"Where?"

"How did the thief get in and out of the koala exhibit without being seen?"

I shrugged. "I have no idea."

"Exactly," Summer told me. "And neither does anyone else—except the thief. No one's even tried to figure it out yet.

But it's important, right? I mean, it couldn't have been easy to get into the exhibit."

"Right," I agreed. "There was only one door, with a key-pad entry, and there were four security cameras outside."

"So there's no way anyone could get through all that without leaving some evidence behind."

"I'm not so sure. After all, the thief didn't show up on any of the cameras."

"That's just not possible," Summer told me. "A ghost didn't steal Kazoo."

"I don't know how they avoided being filmed," I said. "But they did."

"Are you sure there's *nothing* on any of the cameras?"

I thought back to the conversation I'd had with my father at Carnivore Canyon that afternoon. "No," I admitted. "My dad said he was going to watch all the footage tonight, though."

"So when's that happening?"

I realized I hadn't heard my parents in a while. I crept to my door and peered out. Sure enough, Dad had his computer on the kitchen table. He and Mom were both watching the security tapes.

"It's happening right now," I reported to Summer. "But it's gonna take a while. There's almost twelve hours of footage."

"Well, let's hope they find something," Summer said. "In

the meantime, there's still the security door to consider."

"How so?"

"It has a keypad entry, Teddy. Only the keepers know the entry code for it."

I thought about that a moment. "No one else does? Not maintenance or security?"

"Not that I know of. It's designed to protect the animals. If maintenance or security needs to get in anywhere, a keeper has to let them in."

"Does anyone else have an entry code for all the doors like you do?"

"No. And I don't even have one anymore, thanks to you. Daddy wasn't happy to find out I knew his and had passed it on to you. So he changed it."

"Oh. Sorry."

"Don't sweat it," Summer told me. "You've got enough to worry about. Now, do you know all the koala keepers at FunJungle?"

I shook my head. "The only one I know well is Kristi Sullivan. She's the head keeper, so she's there most days. But there are some others who fill in for her on weekends and such. I'm not even sure of their names."

"Hold on. I'll get them." Summer propped up her phone and got on her computer.

"What are you looking at?" I asked.

"The administrative database for FunJungle."

"Are you supposed to have access to that?"

"Of course not." Summer gave a triumphant cry. "Here we go: assistant koala keepers are Elizabeth Ames, Jennifer Weeks, and Ashley Thomas."

"That sounds right."

"Think any of them could have pinched Kazoo?"

"Definitely not Kristi," I said quickly.

"Why not?" Summer shot back.

"She just wouldn't have," I said. "She cared about Kazoo too much."

"Maybe she cared so much that she wanted him as a pet."

"No. She's not like that. In fact, she was helping me come up with other suspects today."

"Maybe she was only doing that to divert attention from herself."

"She didn't do it, all right?" I was surprised by how defensive I was where Kristi was concerned. "She wouldn't have."

Summer raised her hands. "Okay. Take it easy. I'm only trying to make sure we don't rule anyone out too quickly. But if you say we can trust her, we can trust her."

"Good," I said, although as I did, a thought niggled at the back of my mind. Could we *really* trust Kristi? Did I know her as well as I thought?

"What about the others?" Summer asked.

"I don't really know any of them at all," I said. "I suppose they could have done it."

"I guess you'll have to investigate them a bit closer then," Summer told me. "And while you're at it, you should have a look around the exhibit. Make sure there's no way to get in besides the security door. If there's not, that narrows down our suspects quite a bit."

"And if there is?"

"Then maybe it offers another clue as to who the thief is."

I nodded agreement. "There's one big problem, though. How am I supposed to do any of this? Tracey gave me a direct order—thanks to your dad—to lay off the investigation."

"You'll just have to do it without being seen, then."

"How am I supposed to do that?"

"It's easy." Summer flashed a wide, knowing grin. "As usual, I have a plan."

THE TOILET OF DOOM

Once Summer had told me her plan for how I could investigate unnoticed, I had to admit it was pretty clever. However, I had to wait before I could put it into action.

I had to go back to school.

I returned the next day, the monitoring bracelet strapped to my ankle. Worried that it looked dorky and branded me as a potential criminal, I did my best to hide it under the cuff of my jeans, but it was still noticeable if anyone looked at my feet. No one said anything—except Xavier, of course—but I got the sense that everyone was staring at me. When I tried to catch them at it, they'd all pretend to be doing something else, but the moment I turned away again, I could feel all their eyes return to me.

I made it halfway through the day before Vance Jessup caught up with me.

I was on my way to lunch with Xavier. We were a little late, as Xavier's locker had jammed, and the halls had cleared out. We were about to enter the cafeteria when Vance and TimJim blocked our path.

"Hey, Teddy," Vance said, completely ignoring Xavier. "We missed you yesterday. Where were you?"

"Sick," I said, trying to duck past him.

He stuck out an arm, blocking my path. "Sick, my butt. You've been up to no good, haven't you?"

"No."

"That's a nice piece of jewelry you've got there." Vance pointed at the ankle bracelet, and TimJim snickered. "Where'd you get it?"

"It's a long story," I said. "I'm late for lunch . . ."

I tried to squirm past Vance again, but this time he seized my shoulder. "It's not because of our little prank the other day, is it?" he asked.

"No," I told him.

Vance clapped his other hand under my jaw, then forced my chin up so I was looking him in the eye. "You're sure? 'Cause if the police are involved, you'd better not rat me out. That'd be a very bad idea." To drive the point home, he gave my shoulder a menacing squeeze. He barely flexed his fingers, and yet it felt as though he were leaving divots in my shoulder blade.

"Teddy's not lying to you!" Xavier said quickly, trying to help me. "The bracelet's not for the shark prank. It's because the cops think Teddy stole the koala from FunJungle."

Vance swiveled his giant head toward Xavier, surprised. Then he looked to TimJim. Then back to me.

"Is that true?" he asked.

"Yes," I admitted.

Vance let go of me in surprise. And then he broke into his weird, strangled laugh. TimJim laughed even harder.

"You?" Vance asked me, incredulous. "*You're* a suspect in that?"

"I didn't do it," I said sullenly. "I was framed."

"Sure you were." Vance turned to TimJim. "Wow, we get this kid to pull one prank and the next thing you know, he's off stealing koalas."

"He's telling the truth," Xavier said.

Vance stopped laughing and glared at Xavier. "Bug off," he snarled.

"Okay." Xavier scurried into the cafeteria.

Vance returned his attention to me. "Well, Teddy, now that you've got a taste for this, my posse and I were just talking about how we ought to pull another prank at Fun-Jungle."

I winced. There was no way I could do anything like that again. Not when my parents' jobs were on the line. But saying no to Vance was always a dangerous proposition. I decided to try using logic instead. "We can't," I told him. "We almost got busted last time."

"That's what made it so classic!" Vance crowed. "When that cow from security slipped in the puke, I laughed so hard I almost busted a gut. Now, we've been thinking about what to do next, and we've come up with a good one. What if we do the same sort of thing like we did with the shark tank, only with the lions? But this time, instead of just an arm, we could put a whole mannequin in the cage and cover it with ketchup so it looks like there's a dead, bloody person in there? Maybe we could even get some calf's brains to really sell it. . . ."

I shook my head, desperately trying to get out of this. "It wouldn't work. The lion exhibit is completely fenced off. There's no way for us to get the body inside."

"Oh," Vance said, disappointed. "Well, what about doing that with the tigers?"

"All the carnivore exhibits are the same," I said. It was a lie, but I figured Vance didn't know FunJungle as well as I did. "The shark tank's the only one you can get things into, and after our prank the other day, they've really stepped up security there. There's two guards posted full-time now."

Vance frowned, buying my story. "Okay," he said. "Then how about this: You know about cow tipping, right?"

I nodded, worried where this was going. Cow tipping was the act of sneaking onto a ranch, finding a sleeping cow—cows sleep standing up—and shoving it over. It was the sort of thing incredibly bored teenagers in the sticks were rumored to do.

"Well, we're pretty good at it," Vance said. "In fact, we're so good, it's not very exciting anymore. The cows all just lie there after you shove them over."

I wondered what Vance ever *thought* a sleeping cow would do after being shoved over that would qualify as exciting. Explode, perhaps?

"But," Vance went on, "we know there's all kinds of crazy animals at FunJungle that would be a lot more interesting than cows. Rhinos and hippos and all those weird, freaky antelope. I mean, how cool would it be to shove over a sleeping rhino, right?" He laughed at the thought of this, and TimJim echoed it.

I couldn't believe what I was hearing. "It wouldn't be cool," I said. "It'd be idiotic. Rhinos are incredibly dangerous. They'd trample you to death the moment you came near them."

Vance stopped laughing. His eyes narrowed angrily. "Did you just call me an idiot?"

I gulped. I'd been so astonished by the insanity of Vance's idea, I'd forgotten to be properly submissive to him. "Uh, no. I wasn't talking about *you*. I was talking about your plan."

"Yeah," Vance snarled. "You said it was idiotic. Which means you think *I'm* an idiot."

"No," I said. "I just think you don't understand how dangerous rhinos are. A lot of people make that mistake." I tried to back away.

Vance didn't let me go. Instead he clamped one hand on my shoulder again, then shook a fist in front of my nose. "Nobody calls me an idiot," he growled.

Vance had been in a fight recently. His knuckles were wrapped in bloodied bandages. I stared at them, terrified that in the next few seconds some of my blood was going to be adorning them as well. "I didn't mean to insult you," I said. "I was only trying to explain—"

"I ought to punch your lights out," Vance told me. "But we need you. So I'll give you a choice: Either help us prank FunJungle again . . . or feel the pain."

I should have just agreed to the prank. It would have been a lie, of course, but it might have convinced Vance to not hurt me for a little while. But instead I made the mistake of trying to reason with a bully. "We'll never get away with another prank," I protested. "We were lucky to get away with the last one. Forget about it."

"That sounds like you're saying no to me," Vance growled. "So I'm gonna give you one last chance to change your mind . . ."

"I'm trying to protect you!" I told him. "You guys try anything else at FunJungle and they'll be ready for you. We'll all get busted."

"Don't give me that," Vance said. "You're just chicken." He turned to TimJim. "Looks like Teddy here has chosen to feel the pain. Give him a swirlie."

Before I knew what was happening, Vance shoved me toward TimJim, who grabbed my arms and hoisted me off the ground.

Xavier had told me about swirlies. They were by far the worst of a long list of abuses Vance and his pals were known to dole out. The victim was dragged to the most disgusting toilet in the school and inserted headfirst into it, after which Vance would flush. There was a great deal of competition for the most disgusting toilet at our school. Many of them tended to be clogged and were thus full of more poop than FunJungle's hippo pools. Although I really didn't want to cause any more trouble at the park, I wanted to get a swirlie even less.

"Wait!" I said. "Let's talk about this!"

"You already had your chance to talk." Vance led the way to the bathroom, grinning devilishly.

"Help!" I yelled, desperately looking around for anyone else. To my dismay, all the other students were either at lunch or wisely staying out of Vance's sight.

I thrashed about, trying to break free from TimJim's grip—or to at least boot one of them in the shins—but they held my arms tightly and kept their legs away from mine with the skill of boys who'd performed swirlies many times before.

Vance kicked open the door to the boys' room closest to the cafeteria. This bathroom was renowned as one of the least sanitary places at school, if not on planet Earth. Someone— probably Vance—had wrecked the pipes with cherry bombs. The toilets still worked, in theory, but they tended to back up and overflow. Thus this bathroom was generally avoided like the plague. I think even the janitors stayed clear. It looked as though it had been several weeks since the last cleaning. Toilet paper was strung everywhere, and water was puddled on the floor. The place smelled worse than anywhere I'd ever been, which was saying something, given that I lived at a zoo.

"Please, Vance," I pleaded. "Don't do this. I'll do whatever prank you want." I wasn't proud of myself, but desperate times called for desperate measures. "You want to tip rhinos, fine. We can go tip rhinos." Maybe I'd made a mistake in talking them out of that before. I should have let them try it and all get trampled.

Vance acted like he didn't even hear me. He now seemed more excited about the swirlie than about any prank at Fun-Jungle. "Let's do stall five," he said. "That one's been really foul lately."

TimJim laughed, although rather than the usual sniggering, this sounded almost diabolical. The boys upended me and carried me to stall five.

I knew about stall five. It was the worst of the worst. The kids at school called it the Toilet of Doom.

I stopped pleading. It wasn't doing any good. Plus, given that I was about to end up headfirst in foul water, I thought it was best if I kept my mouth closed.

Vance opened stall five and faked a gasp of disgust for my benefit. "Ooh. This is even worse than usual. Looks like someone with a disease used it today. And forgot to flush."

TimJim laughed again and carried me forward. I caught my first glimpse of the Toilet of Doom. It was worse than I'd ever imagined.

I shut my eyes, held my breath, and prepared for the worst.

Before TimJim could plunge me in, however, the bathroom door banged open.

"Put him down," someone said.

I couldn't see who was speaking, since I was facing the wrong way and unable to turn around, but the voice was obviously that of a fellow student rather than a teacher.

I *could* see Vance, although it was a little hard to make out his expression, as I was upside down, looking up his nose. At first he seemed to be a little unsettled by whoever had entered, but he quickly played the tough guy again. "You gonna make me?"

"No," said a second person, entering the room. "*We're* gonna make you."

Now that he was facing *two* people, whoever they were, Vance's tough act faltered, though he struggled to seem imposing. "There's three of us," he said. "Try anything and we'll crush you."

"I don't think so," the first voice said calmly. "Now put the kid down."

Tim and Jim turned around, taking me with them, so I could now see who'd come to my rescue.

It was Ethan Sokol and Dashiell Alexander. They were eighth graders and, better yet, stars of the school football team. In the Texas middle school system, this meant they might as well have been gods. Ethan was a wide receiver and Dash was the quarterback. Though neither was quite as big as TimJim, they were in much better shape. I had no idea what they were doing standing up for me. Neither of them had ever said a word to me before. Up to that point, I'd have guessed they didn't know I existed.

"This isn't any of your business," Vance told them. "Just walk away." I noticed that Vance was saying this from safely behind TimJim rather than in front of them.

Ethan and Dashiell came toward us, unfazed. "Put the kid down . . . or we'll make you," Ethan warned.

TimJim flipped me upright and set me on my feet, although this wasn't out of any kindness. They were simply getting ready to attack.

Before I could make a move, Vance locked his arms around me, holding me tight. "Get them!" he yelled.

TimJim lunged forward, as obedient as a hunting dog.

Ethan and Dash were ready, though. Ethan quickly side-stepped Tim, then used the thug's momentum against him, grabbing his arm and whirling him headfirst into the wall. Tim's skull bounced off the tile and he went down. Dash took the more direct approach. He simply punched Jim in the stomach. Jim folded like a pocketknife and collapsed to the floor.

Just like that, Tim and Jim were out of commission.

Without his muscle, Vance suddenly wasn't so tough anymore. "Stay back!" he yelled, his voice cracking, and then turned me toward stall five, using me as a hostage. "Let me go or I'll dunk Teddy!"

Vance wasn't as big and strong as TimJim, however, and he was distracted. I had a chance against him—and I definitely didn't want to end up in that toilet. Before I knew what was happening, my instincts had kicked in. I lifted both legs and kicked off the door frame of stall five, forcing Vance and me backward. Vance, caught by surprise, slipped on the wet floor and tumbled. He landed flat on his back and I landed on top of him, my skull cracking him in the face. That hurt me—but it hurt Vance a lot more. The back of my head caught him right in the lips.

Vance howled in pain, relaxing his grip on me. I quickly wriggled free and scrambled to my feet.

However, Vance got up just as quickly and snagged my arm, spinning me to face him. His mouth was now full of blood—I'd smashed his lips into his own teeth—making him look even more devilish than usual.

I tried to pull free of him. I may have been a lot smaller than Vance, but I was having a major adrenaline rush. Vance tried to keep his grip on me, but his feet slipped on the wet floor and he pitched forward. I leaped out of the way—and as I did, I saw the look on Vance's bloodied face shift from anger to terror.

He pitched past me, straight into stall five—and landed face-first in the Toilet of Doom.

I didn't actually see him do it. Even though Vance had made my life miserable every chance he got, I couldn't bring myself to watch and averted my eyes. The sound was disgusting enough. There was a sickening wet slap as his face plunged in, then a brief moment of silence—and then the sound of Vance pulling himself back out and screaming in horror.

He lurched out of the stall, wild-eyed, wet toilet paper and things I didn't even want to think about dangling from his hair. He'd immediately forgotten all about me. Now he only wanted to be clean. He raced to the sink, only to find that, as usual, the taps weren't working. "No!" he moaned, and then bolted from the bathroom, racing right past Ethan, Dashiell, and TimJim in search of clean water. It almost sounded as though he was crying as he ran down the hall.

Ethan and Dashiell turned to me—and then burst into laughter.

"That was awesome!" Ethan cried.

"Classic," Dashiell agreed. "Students here are gonna be talking about this for *years.*"

"Thanks for saving me," I told them.

"You should thank your pal Xavier," Ethan said. "He's the one who came and got us."

"Are you all right?" Dashiell asked me.

I realized my heart was still hammering in my chest, the result of the adrenaline. My whole body felt numb. I had to check the mirror to make sure I wasn't hurt. "I'm fine," I said.

"C'mon," Ethan told me. "Let's get some lunch."

After witnessing—and smelling—everything that had just transpired, I wasn't the slightest bit hungry. But I'd learned some rules of middle school, and one of the major ones was, when the varsity football players invite you to lunch, you eat with them.

"Sure," I said, and we headed for the cafeteria, leaving TimJim sprawled on the bathroom floor behind us.

THE ROYALS

For the first time in either of our lives, Xavier and I ate lunch with the popular kids. Dash and Ethan invited us to sit with the Royals in the center of the cafeteria.

It wasn't as amazing as I'd expected. Everyone had regarded the Royals so highly; I had figured they'd all be fascinating. Instead they were surprisingly normal. They were just like everyone else—except maybe a bit more attractive and better at sports. They hadn't ignored me—and most everyone else—out of spite. They were simply sticking to their own clique of friends, the way pretty much everyone else did.

Now that they had a reason to be introduced to Xavier and me, however, the Royals were all welcoming and friendly. No one seemed upset that we were suddenly at their table—although they weren't really paying that much attention to us. Instead they were riveted to Dash and Ethan, who were recounting the story of Vance and TimJim's defeat in sickening detail.

If the Royals weren't focused on us, however, everyone else in the cafeteria seemed to be. As I ate my lunch, I could feel the eyes of the entire school on me, hundreds of fellow students watching my every move with curiosity and jealousy, already spreading rumors about what I had done to gain access to the exalted center table.

Meanwhile, Xavier was beside himself. "How cool is this?" he whispered to me as he dug into his food. "We're eating with the cheerleaders!"

I faked an enthusiastic smile, then glanced toward a gaggle of the Royal girls. They were all laughing at Dash and Ethan, who were recounting Vance's face-plant into the Toilet of Doom—except one.

Violet Grace, the head cheerleader, was looking at me. But the moment I caught her at it, she turned away and pretended as though she hadn't been. The same way I'd noticed plenty of other kids doing that day.

I began to get the feeling that something was going on at school. Something everyone else knew about that somehow I didn't.

Ethan and Dash wrapped up their story, and the Royals cheered with approval.

Violet looked back toward me. This time, however, she didn't turn away again. Instead she asked, "So you're really the kid in the koala video?"

I was thrown for a moment. If our school had royalty, Violet was the queen. She was the quintessential Texas cheerleader: beautiful, brunette, and green-eyed, and a fountain of energy and enthusiasm. While the other cheerleaders were cute, Violet was so attractive it was intimidating. My immediate thought was that she had to be talking to someone else besides me.

"Er . . . what video?" I asked.

Now Violet seemed thrown. "On YouTube," she clarified. "The one with a million hits."

"I don't know what video that is," I said.

"You don't?" Violet turned to her fellow cheerleaders and said, "He doesn't even know!"

The cheerleaders all giggled in response.

I felt my ears and neck get hot. I must have been turning red in embarrassment.

Violet noticed. "Oh!" she cried. "Don't be upset. It's cool. I just figured you knew. *Everybody's* seen it."

So that was why everyone had been stealing glances at me all day. "*I* haven't seen it," I said.

"Hold on." Violet quickly dug her phone out of her purse and brought up YouTube on it. She slid next to me so we could both watch, and several of the Royals crowded around us to see it again. I was now so close to Violet I could smell her. She smelled surprisingly good—like the rain forest in bloom—and I suddenly worried what I smelled like. Hopefully not the zoo—or worse, the Toilet of Doom.

I caught Xavier staring at Violet nestled against my side. He didn't seem excited to be with the Royals anymore. Instead he looked jealous of me.

I quickly turned my attention to the video on Violet's phone. It was one of the many that had been posted showing Marge and Bubba smashing into the koala exhibit the day before. However, this one was from a better angle than the others I'd seen in Tracey's office. And unlike many of those, it was shot from close by, in focus.

It started on the stuffed koala. Whoever was filming was right at the glass trying to get a decent shot of it, thinking it was really Kazoo. "He's just sleeping," someone off camera said disappointedly. "C'mon. Let's go see something interesting."

There was a sudden commotion by the exit door. The camera swung that way in time to see Dad and me push through and then get cornered by Bubba and Marge against the glass. The guy filming was right next to us, though I hadn't even noticed him in the heat of the moment.

"That's you, right?" Violet asked.

"Yeah, it's me," I admitted.

A murmur of excitement went through the Royals.

"Everyone stand back!" Marge ordered on the video. "This kid is dangerous!"

"Are you?" Violet asked.

I looked up from the video to find she and everyone else were now watching *me*. "Am I what?"

"Dangerous," Violet said.

"Vance Jessup certainly thinks so," Dash said, and everyone laughed.

"No," I told them all. "I'm not dangerous."

"Then why did that security lady say you were?" Violet asked. Her green eyes were fixed tightly on me.

"She thinks I stole Kazoo," I said.

A lot of the Royals went "oooh" in response.

"Hey!" Ethan called. "This is the best part!"

Everyone returned their attention to the video in time to see Marge and Bubba crash through the glass. Only whoever had filmed it had slowed it down. Instead of happening in a few seconds, the chaos now played out leisurely. Even on the tiny phone screen I could see the panic on Marge's face as she tumbled into the exhibit, then Bubba's surprise as he sailed in after her, followed by the looks of horror on the spectators as they watched the koala get crushed flat.

The Royals were laughing hysterically, even though

they'd seen it many times over. "That must have been wild, being there," Dash said, and everyone echoed agreement.

The video resumed normal speed, zooming in on the pancaked body of what everyone thought was Kazoo. "Oh my," the person recording it said. "That doesn't look good."

"I didn't steal him," I said.

Everyone looked up from the video again and back at me.

"In case you were wondering," I explained. "Marge—the guard who just squashed Kazoo—is wrong about me."

Violet stared into my eyes for a moment, then nodded. "Cool," she said. "I believe you."

The Royals around us nodded in agreement. I wasn't sure if I'd sounded convincing or if they were all merely following Violet's lead, but it was reassuring to see.

"Is that why you've got the ankle bracelet?" Ethan asked.

Most of the Royals, including Violet, looked at him curiously, not knowing what he meant. Ethan kept his gaze locked on me, though.

"I saw it in the bathroom," he told me. "Go ahead and show everyone. It's pretty sweet."

I pushed my chair back from the table and hiked my jeans up, revealing the monitor cinched around my leg.

I'd expected that my fellow students would be put off by the hardware, lumping me in with future criminals like Vance Jessup. Instead everyone seemed impressed.

"What's that for?" Violet asked.

"It tracks me," I said. "So the cops know where I am."

"Can I touch it?" Violet asked.

"Uh, sure. I guess." I propped my leg up on a chair.

Violet tentatively touched the monitor, like it might explode. "Excellent," she said.

The other Royals crowded in to examine the bracelet as well. I had to lean back to give them all room.

As I did, I caught a glimpse of the video, still playing on Violet's phone. The camera was now panning back and forth between Pete Thwacker and the people trying to extricate the stuffed koala from beneath Bubba and Marge. As it did, it repeatedly caught a man in the background. He was dressed like all the other tourists, but something seemed strange about him.

"Can you pause that?" I asked Violet.

She did. "Do you not want to watch it anymore?"

"Actually, I want to take a closer look," I said. "Can I borrow your phone?"

"Sure." Violet handed the phone to me, intrigued.

I rewound to the man. He was thickset and muscular, like a wrestler, wearing jeans, a winter jacket, and an orange Houston Astros baseball cap. While everyone around him seemed to be either disgusted or saddened, he was watching the whole scene stoically, his mouth a flat, emotionless line.

That was understandable, however. Not everyone reacted to tragedy the same way. There was something else about him that had caught my attention.

"Do you know that guy?" Xavier asked.

"No," I said. "I've never seen him before."

"Then why are you so interested in him?" Dashiell asked.

"He's wearing sunglasses," I said.

"So?" Xavier asked. "Lots of people wear sunglasses."

"He's inside," I said. "Plus, it's pretty dark inside the koala exhibit. And it was cloudy yesterday. Not the kind of day anyone would be wearing sunglasses *outside*."

Now everyone's attention had shifted from the bracelet back to me again.

"Suspicious," Ethan said. "You think he stole Kazoo?"

"I don't know," I admitted. "Maybe." In truth I knew the sunglasses weren't *that* suspicious. Wearing them inside on a cloudy day wasn't much evidence against someone. But something still struck me about the man in the Astros cap. I suddenly had the feeling that maybe I *had* seen him before, only I couldn't recall where. It was hard to get a good idea of what he looked like on the tiny screen.

I handed the phone back to Violet. "Thanks."

"No problem," she said. "Can I ask you something?"

"Sure."

"Word is, you live at FunJungle, right?"

I swallowed, surprised Violet knew that about me—or anything about me, for that matter. "Yes. Both my parents work there."

"That's pretty cool," Dashiell put in, and a lot of the Royals echoed agreement. "So you get to hang out there after the park closes?"

"Sometimes," I said.

This was met with murmurs of excitement from the group.

I couldn't help but smile. I'd always figured that living at a zoo would be considered weird by the Royals. Instead they were all intrigued.

"Do you ever get to play with any of the animals?" Ethan asked.

"Well, that's not really good for the animals," I said. "But I've been in with the gorillas a few times."

This produced even more excitement.

"Ooh! I *love* gorillas!" one of the cheerleaders squealed. "Could you ever get me in there?"

"Maybe," I said. In truth the answer was *no*, but I wasn't about to shoot down a cheerleader right then and there.

"That's not what I wanted to ask about . . . ," Violet began.

Before she could finish her thought, however, a football player called out, "How about the tigers? Have you ever been in with the tigers?"

"No," I said. "But I was right there when the tiger escaped at that big party last year."

That *really* got everyone's attention. Now I was being peppered with too many questions to answer. Some kids wanted to know about the tiger escape. Others wanted to know what other animals I'd been able to interact with. Most wanted to know if I could get them free tickets.

Violet kept trying to get a word in edgewise, but the others drowned her out. Finally she snapped. "Hey! Let me speak!"

Everyone fell silent deferentially. They seemed almost embarrassed that the queen had been forced to raise her voice.

Violet returned her attention to me. "There's a rumor going around about you," she began. "I just want to know if it's true."

"Shoot," I said, wondering what it could be. The fact that I'd grown up in the Congo? Or that I'd helped solve the mystery of Henry's death last summer? Or that I'd been responsible for the debacle at Henry's funeral?

"Are you friends with Summer McCracken?" Violet asked.

I hadn't expected that, although I realized I should have. Sometimes I forgot Summer was just as famous as FunJungle. As the daughter of one of the richest men in America, she routinely ended up on the Internet or the covers of tabloid magazines.

"He is," Xavier said proudly. "In fact, he talked to her last night!"

This provoked the most excitement so far. The Royals immediately forgot about everything else.

"What's she like?" Violet asked, and everyone else quickly seconded the question.

I took my time answering. I didn't mind milking my life at FunJungle to get in with the Royals, but it seemed wrong to use my friendship with Summer the same way. I'd always thought the major reason Summer liked me at all was because I had never taken advantage of our relationship. Now, I was afraid that the moment I said anything revealing about her, it would spread like wildfire through the school.

So I went with the blandest thing I could think of. "She's nice."

"I knew it!" Violet said triumphantly. "She always seems nice on TV."

The others jumped in, bombarding me with questions.

"Have you ever been to her house?"

"How often do you talk to her?"

"Does she dye her hair?"

Violet, however, was front and center, commanding the most attention. She put her hand on my knee and got face-to-face with me. "Next time she's in town, could you introduce us?"

"I don't think she's going to be in town for a while," I said, trying to duck the question.

Before Violet could follow up, the bell rang, signaling the end of lunch. All around the cafeteria, students snapped to their feet and hurried off for their next class—although the Royals took their time, less concerned about getting tardies. However, the bell gave me an excuse to break away from them. As much as I'd enjoyed getting to spend time with the popular kids, I didn't want to have to share any more about Summer. "It was really nice meeting all of you," I said, then turned to Ethan and Dashiell. "Thanks again for saving me."

"Get Summer McCracken to go to the school dance with me and we're even," Ethan said, and everyone laughed.

"Don't listen to this moron," Dashiell told me with a grin. "It was no big deal."

I smiled back and turned for the door.

Xavier was right on my heels. "That was crazy," he said. "In my whole life, I never thought I'd get to sit with the Royals. . . ."

"They're just kids," I told him. "They're no different from us."

"They're *way* different from us," Xavier corrected. "They're popular. And now *you* could be popular too. Did you see their faces when they heard you knew Summer? The cheerleaders flipped. *You* ought to ask Summer to the school dance. If she came with you, you'd be the coolest kid in the history of this school. Maybe the history of Texas."

I started to tell Xavier I would never use Summer like that, but before I could, someone tapped my shoulder.

I spun around to find Violet there. For once she wasn't surrounded by her fellow cheerleaders. They were all heading out the door. Violet checked to see if they were watching her, then handed me a scrap of paper. "This is my cell number," she said. "Call me."

I was so surprised, all I could think to say was "okay."

"Great!" Violet flashed a quick, surprisingly shy smile, then ducked away before anyone noticed she'd been talking to me.

Xavier's jaw dropped in astonishment. "Whoa," he gasped. "Violet Grace gave you her digits! That's incredible!"

"She just wants to meet Summer," I said.

"Maybe not," Xavier replied, though he didn't look like he fully believed that either.

"I'm a seventh grader who nearly got swirlied at the beginning of lunch and she's the head cheerleader," I argued. "You really think she wants to go out with me?"

"*I* think you're cool," Xavier said.

"That makes one of us." I slipped Violet's number into my pocket.

And then, out the window behind Xavier, I saw Vance Jessup.

He'd cleaned himself off and changed his shirt, probably in the school gym. Now he was staring at me. Vance had always been scary, but at that moment the look of hatred in his eyes was downright terrifying. I wondered how long he'd been watching me.

He pointed through the window at me. It was a subtle gesture, but it was loaded with meaning. Things weren't over between us. Not by a long shot.

Then, before anyone else noticed him, Vance ducked away and vanished from sight.

UNDERCOVER WORK

I managed to avoid Vance for the rest of the day.
He'd apparently ditched school after I saw him by the cafeteria. Even bullies could be embarrassed, and Vance's plunge
into the Toilet of Doom was the primary topic of conversation at school that afternoon.

Still, I doubted Vance had gone far. Several times I had
the eerie feeling he was watching me. Once, as I was boarding the bus after school, I even thought I caught a glimpse
of him inside a store across the street, glaring balefully at me
through the window. But when I looked again, he was gone,
leaving me to wonder if it had really been Vance, or if my
skittish mind was playing tricks on me.

On the ride home, however, I received two texts that
made me forget all about the bully.

The first was from Summer:

Heads up. Large Marge is meeting with Daddy tomorrow at FJ to make her case against you. Don't think LM has any new evidence, but still, I thought you'd want to know.

Have you learned anything new?

The next was from my father:

Bad news. I've gone through all the security footage from the night of Kazoo's disappearance. I didn't find anything on it. No one went in or out of the koala exhibit except you.

I have to photograph a surgery for Doc this afternoon but should be done by 5. Mom is at her office. Check in with us when you get home from school.

I pocketed my phone, feeling frustrated. How could anyone have possibly swiped Kazoo without showing up on the security tapes? It didn't seem possible. Meanwhile, Large Marge was briefing J.J. McCracken the next morning, and all the evidence still pointed directly at me. If I didn't figure out who Kazoo's kidnapper was before then, J.J. might not have any choice but to order my arrest.

It was time to put Summer's plan into action.

Once the bus dropped me off at FunJungle, I returned home just long enough to ditch my backpack, then headed right into the park. Darlene, the guard, paid far more attention to me than usual. She actually stopped watching her movie for once when I walked in.

"Where you headed today, Teddy?" she asked suspiciously.

"Mom's office," I said.

Darlene wrote that down.

As I passed through the metal detector, my ankle bracelet set the alarm off.

"Hold it," Darlene said. "I need to pat you down."

"It's only my monitor," I said, hiking my pants leg.

"I gotta make sure," Darlene told me. "Marge's orders."

So I spread my arms and legs and let her wave the security wand over me. It crackled like crazy around my ankle, but nowhere else.

"You're clean," Darlene said. "Stay out of trouble, now."

I called Mom as I passed into the park.

"Are you home?" she asked.

"Just got back."

"How was school today? Anything interesting happen?"

"Not really," I lied. I planned to tell her and Dad the whole story about Vance, but it made more sense to wait until dinner. The moment Mom heard, she'd want every detail, and I didn't have the time for all that. "How about you?"

Mom sighed. "I'm still having trouble with Motupi."

"Furious George? Did he go nuts again?"

"No. He didn't do *anything* wrong," Mom said. "That's

the problem. I can't figure out what's triggering these epi-sodes. If anything, he behaved beautifully all day. Gentle as a teddy bear. It's killing me to keep him in solitary. Chimps are such social creatures; it's obvious he's unhappy away from the others."

"Can you move him back, then?" I asked.

"Unfortunately, no," Mom told me. "I can't risk putting him with the others until I find out what's going on. I need to spend a bit more time with him today. Were you planning on coming to the office to do your homework?"

"Shouldn't I?"

"Maybe not right now. I'd prefer to have as few distrac-tions here as possible. Are you all right with that?"

"I guess so," I said. "I'll see you later."

I hung up, relieved. If Mom had demanded I come to her office, I'd have been hard-pressed to get out of it. But now both Mom and Dad had their hands full, leaving me the opportunity to investigate Kazoo's disappearance.

I made a beeline for the character changing room.

This was located near the front entrance, in the employees-only area of the park. It was the place where the motley crew who'd been hired to dress as FunJungle's animal characters put on their costumes. The actors—as they were known—were, for the most part, an unimpressive lot. After all, their job essentially involved standing still and letting people take pictures with them. The most demanding thing they ever had to do was wave their hand on occasion. However, the costumes could be quite uncomfortable—especially on summer days when it hit over a hundred degrees at FunJungle—and thus, even though the job was ridiculously easy, it wasn't very desirable. Only three types of people tended to apply: slackers who were incredibly unmotivated, screwups who weren't skilled at anything else—and aspiring actors who mistakenly believed that dressing as a giant animal was a good way to break into show business.

Charlie Connor fell into the last category. Apparently, he was quite a good clown, and had even gone to a prestigious clown school. He'd expected that as a character he'd be allowed to put some of his skills into effect to amuse the crowds: juggling, perhaps, or riding a unicycle. To his dismay, he'd learned he wasn't supposed to do anything at all. (In the first few days FunJungle had been open, the actor playing Zelda Zebra had tried juggling some bowling pins and had accidentally brained a tourist with one. The tourist had threatened to sue, FunJungle had settled quickly, and the lawyers had nixed any further character performances.) Charlie suspected that he'd merely been hired because of his size. Sadly, this was probably true. As a dwarf, Charlie was the only person who could fit in some of the smaller, "cuter" costumes. Unfortunately for him, as much as he hated his job, he couldn't find another. Being an ex-con severely cut down on the number of people willing to hire him.

Summer's plan relied on the fact that Charlie was no longer playing Kazoo. No one was. Now that the public knew the koala was missing, Tracey Boyd had decided that keeping the character around was a bad idea. So the Kazoo costume had been shelved and Larry the Lizard, Charlie Connor's old character, had been revived from the dead for him to play once again.

However, Summer suspected that while FunJungle's administration had informed the *actors* that no one was supposed to play Kazoo anymore, they most likely hadn't informed *everyone* at the park about this. Therefore, most employees wouldn't think twice about seeing a giant koala wandering about—if they even thought once about it. As we knew, it was amazing how quickly people forgot the characters were actual people.

There was moderate security to get into the employee area at the park—which I passed through easily, as the guards all knew me—but there was no security at the changing room at all. I found it empty. During the first months the park had been open, the room had often been filled with actors slacking off rather than doing their jobs, but one of Marge's major initiatives had been to crack down on this. ("Lollygagging while you're on the clock is the same as stealing," she'd explained.) The actors hadn't taken her seriously at first, but then she'd managed to get their pay docked for any time they didn't work. After that, the changing room was almost always deserted.

Without anyone in it, the room was kind of spooky. The costumes hung on hooks on the wall, while the disembodied heads were all lined up on a shelf above them. It looked somewhat like a zoo full of gaily colored animals had been skinned and decapitated.

There were two Kazoo costumes, wedged between Eleanor Elephant and Alexander Aardvark. (There were two of every costume, just in case one got dirty, which happened quite a lot. Children rubbed everything from snot to melted ice cream on them, while the actors didn't treat them so well either. A few days before, an actress who'd caught the flu had vomited inside Rhonda Rhino's head.) I grabbed a Kazoo, pulled it on over my clothes, and walked right out the door.

Since Charlie Connor wasn't much shorter than me, the costume fit pretty well, but it was still a pain to wear. It was made of thick material that trapped my body heat, so even though it was a cold day, after going only a short distance I felt like I was in a steam room. Plus, the giant head was incredibly difficult to see out of. I could only look out through some mesh in the mouth, but the mouth was angled downward. This was designed to make sure whoever was inside didn't bowl over any toddlers, but it made it almost impossible to tell where I was going. Every time I wanted to look straight ahead, I had to tilt backward, but then the head was so heavy I'd nearly fall over. No wonder Charlie was always so grumpy, I thought. He spent eight hours a day in a koala-shaped torture chamber.

Between my inability to see and the bulkiness of the costume, I couldn't move very fast. I was a bit worried that with my slow, shambling gait, everyone would think I was drunk. However, no one seemed concerned by it. Perhaps, since koalas are known for being slow and shambling, everyone figured I was method acting. I walked right through the employee area without anyone saying a thing, then entered the main park and headed for KoalaVille.

Getting there took a lot longer than I expected. Not only because I couldn't move quickly, but because half the tourists I passed wanted pictures with me. No one seemed to think it was weird to have a giant Kazoo around when the real one had been stolen. Instead it appeared that many tourists were even *more* excited to see me because Kazoo was gone: Robbed of the chance to see the real koala, they could at least take photos of the fake one. In fact several families, perhaps worried their young children would melt down if they didn't see a koala, tried to pass me off as the *real* Kazoo.

Despite all this, the costume worked perfectly, allowing

me to hide in plain sight. I walked right past several security guards, who barely even noticed me.

I was passing Carnivore Canyon when I spotted Arthur Koenig lurking behind some bushes, talking on his phone. Something about him struck me as odd. He kept glancing around furtively, the way a kid who's cheating on a test keeps an eye out for the teacher. Plus, it was unusual to see Arthur outside. Why was he making a phone call out there, in the cold, when he had a nice warm office—unless he didn't want anyone at Carnivore Canyon to overhear him?

For once, no tourists were tailing me. So I slowed down as I approached Arthur, trying to test the idea that even employees forgot there were humans inside the costumes. It actually seemed to work. Arthur glanced at me, but then continued his call, as though maybe I were a real giant koala who happened to be wandering by.

"That's not enough money," he said. "What I'm offering is easily worth twice that." He listened a bit, then grew annoyed. "Do you have any idea what I went through to get this? Do you understand the risk I've taken? If anyone finds out, I could go to jail! At the very least, I'd lose my job. . . ."

Unfortunately, the wind kicked up then, drowning out the rest of Arthur's words. I tried to sidle a little closer, but it wasn't easy to sidle in a koala costume. I got a bit too close, and Arthur froze in midsentence, eyeing me suspiciously.

I had no choice but to continue onward, acting as though I were merely strolling past rather than eavesdropping. Arthur seemed to relax, but I couldn't keep watching him and walk at the same time. I headed on toward Koala-Ville. By the time I felt comfortable enough to look back at Arthur again, he was gone.

Could that have been about Kazoo? I wondered. Was it possible that Arthur had taken the koala and was now trying to sell it? He'd obviously been up to something illegal. He didn't work in KoalaVille, but he worked awfully close—and he knew a great deal about the park's technology. Maybe he'd come up with a way to circumvent the alarm system. He'd also been very quick to turn me over to the cops and declare my guilt; maybe he'd been doing that to distract everyone from him.

There was no way for me to follow him now, however. I didn't know where he'd gone. Most likely it was back into Carnivore Control, but I couldn't get in there. Then again, maybe he was hiding somewhere, keeping an eye on me to see if I'd overheard him. Either way, I needed to stick with my original plan.

I turned back toward KoalaVille—and found Large Marge blocking my path.

"What do you think you're doing?" she demanded.

I gulped, wondering how she'd figured out it was me, but

before I could say anything, she told me, "You've got your costume on all wrong."

I heaved a sigh of relief. Marge hadn't recognized me at all. Instead she thought I was an actor. Although now my silence had started to make her suspicious. "Hey," she said, knocking on the koala head to get my attention. "You listening in there? What's your name?"

"No hablo inglés," I said.

Marge sighed, annoyed. "Figures," she muttered. Then she began to speak very loudly and slowly to me, as if this would magically make someone who didn't speak English understand it. "Your costume is on wrong! The head is cockeyed! You look like Kazoo has been in a car accident! Stand still!" Marge seized the head in both hands and heaved. The head twisted a bit and locked into place.

"There!" Marge stepped back to admire her work. "Much better."

I nodded as well as I could with the giant head. *"Muchas gracias."*

"That costume is your uniform," Marge informed me, apparently having already forgotten she was talking to someone who didn't speak English. "You represent this park when you wear it, just like me. So you wear it right, and you wear it with pride. Got it?"

I nodded again. *"¡Sí, señora! ¡Sí!"*

"Okay, then," Marge said. "Don't let me catch you improperly dressed again. Now get to your post." She pointed off toward KoalaVille.

I hurried off that way. I was slightly worried Marge might follow me to see if I committed any more infractions, but then I heard her in the distance behind me, berating some tourists for putting recyclable bottles in the regular trash.

I headed into KoalaVille. The place was deserted. Even the bazaar had been closed down. After all, with Kazoo gone, FunJungle had made the wise—if rare—decision to stop selling any merchandise with the koala on it, feeling this was in bad taste. Kazoo's exhibit was shuttered, the doors locked. According to my parents, the koala keepers had already been transferred to other locations. (Kristi Sullivan was now working at the small mammal house.) I was all alone, able to wander the area freely without any tourists clamoring to take my picture.

As Summer had instructed, I went right to the exhibit to see if there was any way in or out that wouldn't be seen by the cameras.

My first thought was that perhaps there was an entrance I didn't know about, but this quickly proved to be wrong. The building wasn't big, so it didn't take much time to thoroughly examine the exterior. There were no hidden doors.

I also determined that there was no route to the exhibit

that avoided the security cameras. I knew where the four closest ones were, having figured out their positions from the footage I'd been unlucky enough to appear in. They covered every angle of the exhibit—and in addition, I spotted two more cameras close by.

So the question remained: How had the thief gotten in and out without being seen? I could come up with only two answers:

1) There was a secret underground entrance.

This was doubtful. There was almost nothing underground at FunJungle, as the park was built on solid rock, which was very expensive to dig through. (J.J. McCracken had declared that building Carnivore Canyon into the rock had been a colossal, money-sucking mistake he was determined to never repeat.) The koala exhibit was far from the rest of the park and thus would have required an extremely long tunnel. Plus, the building had been erected so quickly there probably hadn't been time to dig one anyhow.

2) Whoever had stolen Kazoo was a master of camouflage.

This seemed far more likely. Now that I considered it, camouflaging oneself was a surprisingly common skill in southern Texas. Lots of hunters lived in the area, and sporting-goods stores were chock-full of camouflage clothing and greasepaint (which the hunters used to cover their faces). There were also several military bases close by, which meant there were lots of current and retired soldiers. The schools all had big ROTC programs, where the art of camouflage was taught. And on top of all that, there were tons of paintball enthusiasts. In fact a twenty-five acre paintball range sat only a few miles from FunJungle, where hundreds of men, women, and children showed up in full camouflage every weekend to play pretend war. Until FunJungle had come along, Killer Paintball had been the biggest tourist attraction in the region.

Even my own parents knew a decent amount about camouflage: Dad used it all the time to photograph animals, while Mom had employed it to get close to gorillas in the wild. There were plenty of other field biologists employed by FunJungle; many of them had probably used camouflage as well.

I wondered if someone could have concealed themselves so well that they would have been invisible to the cameras. After all, the theft had happened during the night, when it would have been easier to blend into the shadows. Whoever had stolen Kazoo would have still needed to open the exhibit door, but maybe if they'd done it quickly enough, that would have been hard to spot in the twelve hours of recorded footage. Yes, Dad had gone through all of it, but staring at video of nothing happening for that long must have been mind-numbing. He'd probably only been looking for something dramatic, like the thief blatantly approaching the door, rather than someone more stealthy.

That might account for how Kazoo had been stolen, although the question of who'd done it was still wide open.

I poked around the exhibit a bit longer, but didn't find any more clues. In truth I didn't even know what I was looking for, short of a handy note saying *I took the koala* and signed by the thief.

It was already starting to get dark, which made it even harder to see inside the koala costume. I figured I ought to get back and return it soon. It was nearing closing time anyhow, and both my parents would soon be wondering where I was. I couldn't help feeling frustrated. Despite Summer's brilliant plan for me to remain incognito, I hadn't learned enough, meaning I would still be suspect number one when Large Marge presented her case to J.J. McCracken the next morning. I decided to make one last sweep of KoalaVille, just in case I'd missed something, though I didn't have high hopes.

And then I saw the man in the Astros cap.

It was the same man from the YouTube video Violet Grace had shown me at lunch, the man who'd been oddly stoic during the revelation that the koala had been poached. Even in the dimming light, it wasn't that hard to recognize him. His orange cap stood out, and he was still wearing sunglasses, despite the darkening skies. He was standing near one of the closed-up koala merchandise tents, talking to someone I couldn't see.

I crept closer. Unfortunately, now the koala costume was working against me. It was hard to be inconspicuous while dressed as a giant marsupial. There were no tourists around I could pretend to be entertaining. In fact, it occurred to me that Astros Cap was probably here for that exact reason: no tourists. Therefore no one to see or overhear him. I simply had to hope that because I was in KoalaVille, I'd look like part of an advertisement for Kazoo merchandise that someone had forgotten to clear away.

I finally reached a point where I could see around the corner of the merchandise tent. The person Astros Cap was talking to came into view.

It was Freddie Malloy.

It was tough to make him out at first, as he had a safari hat pulled down tightly over his head, but when he gestured, I could see there were only three fingers on one of his hands.

Freddie and Astros Cap definitely seemed to be familiar with each other. They were standing close together, like friends or business associates rather than two people who had just met. Freddie was pointing up the hill, away from KoalaVille, toward the rest of FunJungle.

Astros Cap listened intently, nodding every once in a while. At one point he reached forward, as though Freddie had handed him something small, and tucked it into the pocket of his jacket.

Unfortunately, I was too far away to hear what they were saying, and there was no way I could get closer in the koala costume. I'd have to ditch it and hope no one from security noticed me.

Just as I started to wriggle out of it, however, Astros Cap and Freddie started to walk away. They disappeared around the corner of the tent, heading back toward the park.

I kept the costume on and followed.

By the time I had made it to the tent, they had already split up. Apparently, the two of them didn't want to be seen together. Freddie was moving quickly toward Carnivore Canyon, while Astros Cap was angling toward the park exit.

I couldn't follow both of them, so I quickly opted to go after Astros Cap. I could always track down Freddie, while I might never see the other man again.

Astros Cap moved cautiously, pretending to be a regular tourist but keeping a close eye on his surroundings. I kept my distance until we made it back to Adventure Road, where there were a few tourists and it made at least some sense for a giant koala to be wandering about. Then I stepped up my pace to try to catch up to him.

Astros Cap suddenly stopped in front of Shark Odyssey.

I stopped as well and pretended to wave at some tourists.

Astros Cap looked around to see if anyone was watching him. His eyes fell right on me, but he didn't seem to think anything of it. Eventually he decided the coast was clear, then ducked around the side of the building into the employees-only area.

That certainly seemed suspicious. Now that Astros Cap couldn't see me anymore, I hurried toward Shark Odyssey as quickly as I could. It was hard to run in the costume, though, and despite the cold weather I began to sweat. A tourist family yelled at me to stop so they could take a picture, but there was no time. I pantomimed pointing at my watch and kept on going, as though perhaps Kazoo had a big appointment he was late for.

I reached the point where Astros Cap had slipped off Adventure Road. A small walkway wound through the landscaping along the side of Shark Odyssey. I followed it, although it was difficult to fit my giant koala head through the dense brush. My huge ears got hung up in the branches several times.

The path led to a door marked MAINTENANCE. EMPLOYEES ONLY. As with almost every other door at FunJungle, there was a keypad entry for it. I looked around. Astros Cap couldn't have gone anywhere except through the door. The landscaping was too thick for him to have left the path without breaking some branches or leaving a footprint in the mud, but there was no sign of that.

I pulled off my koala glove and tried entering J.J. McCracken's secret code.

As Summer had warned, it no longer worked.

Whoever Astros Cap was, he must have had the proper code for Shark Odyssey. Was he an employee there? Or was that what Freddie had given him? If so, how had Freddie gotten it? He didn't work at Shark Odyssey himself.

Whatever the case, I'd hit a dead end. I schlepped back down the path, figuring I'd just have to wait until Astros Cap emerged from Shark Odyssey again.

The moment I stepped out of the landscaping, someone broadsided me.

For a moment I thought I'd been ambushed. But then I realized my attacker was only three feet high.

The tourist family had caught up to me. The three-year-old daughter was now clamped tightly to my left leg, hugging Kazoo for all she was worth. "Kazoo! I love you!" she crowed.

I did my best to give her a friendly rub on the head, the way I'd seen Kazoo do to other kids, although I ended up bonking her pretty hard. She didn't seem to care at all. In fact she giggled happily.

"Isn't that cute?" her mother cooed. "Kazoo loves you, too!"

While the parents snapped pictures, a line started to form. It was now past closing time. All the exhibits had shut down for the night, so I was the only thing left for people to see. The last batch of tourists filed out of Shark Odyssey, and every kid among them clamored to have their photo taken with me. Before long there were more than twenty families waiting to see me.

I didn't want to make any waves, so I dutifully stood for photos with everyone. But more and more people kept showing up. Some people didn't even know what they were lining up for; they simply saw a line and got in it, figuring it must be for something important. (This happened quite a lot at FunJungle.) I posed with one German family that seemed to think I was Yogi Bear. After a while, I lost track of how long I'd been standing there.

I was having my photo taken with a busload of Japanese tourists when Astros Cap finally emerged from Shark Odyssey again. He slipped out of the landscaping and headed for the park exit. There were still lots of people in line to meet me, but I had to go after him. Even though it was a direct violation of FunJungle character protocol, I spoke for Kazoo, using what I assumed was a cute, koala-like voice, "Sorry folks! The park's closed and I have to get home for dinner!"

Unfortunately, the tourists weren't so easily put off. As I tried to leave, several blocked my way. "Come on," one father implored. "My kid's been waiting fifteen minutes to see you."

"Sorry!" I chirped again. "I'm real hungry! I haven't had any eucalyptus since lunch!"

A child latched on to my leg. "Don't go, Kazoo! Please!"

Astros Cap was gaining ground. I didn't have any more time to be polite. I dropped the koala voice and used the gruffest one I could. "Let me go, kid! I've really got to pee."

The kid released me, startled.

Several adults weren't quite as obliging. They all grabbed for me, but I shoved through them like a running back gunning for a touchdown. I knocked over at least two people with my giant ears, but I couldn't even stop to see if they were all right. Instead I ran after Astros Cap as fast as I could.

He was trying to fit in with the other tourists, so he was only walking and I was able to close the gap on him. I wasn't too far behind him when he suddenly ducked off the main path again.

He'd gone behind the Polar Pavilion. I rounded the corner after him.

This time, however, he wasn't heading inside the building.

Instead, he was waiting for me.

LARRY THE LIZARD RETURNS

Astros Cap completely caught me by surprise.
Between the darkness and the Kazoo head, I could barely
see as it was. He ambushed me easily, grabbing me by the
fur and slamming me against the wall of the Polar Pavilion.

"Why are you following me?" he demanded. Because
he was much taller then me, I couldn't see his face through
the downward-angled mask. He had a strong Texan accent,
though.

"I'm not!" I said quickly, though I still had the presence
of mind to use the gruff voice, hoping he wouldn't realize I
was a kid. "I'm just working!"

"Don't give me that bull," Astros Cap growled. "I know
a tail when I see one. Now tell me the truth . . . or I will hurt
you."

He held one of his hands where I could see it. It was clenched into a fist.

I gulped. I'd made it most of my life without anyone shaking a fist in my face, and now it had happened twice in one day. I didn't think telling Astros Cap the truth would make him any happier with me, though, so I tried lying again. "I swear, I wasn't following you! I'm only an actor!"

"I warned you," Astros Cap said. The fist withdrew from sight, then slammed into the koala nose hard enough to dent it.

Luckily for me, Astros Cap wasn't that bright. Apparently, he hadn't realized that punching the koala in the face wouldn't actually hurt *me*. The blow still knocked me off balance, however. I stumbled and, already top-heavy in the costume, tumbled backward into the landscaping.

Astros Cap loomed over me. Now that I was on the ground, he looked prepared to kick me—and my body didn't have nearly the protection in the costume that my head did.

"Wait!" I said. "Please . . ."

"You had your chance to talk," Astros Cap snarled, then cocked back his leg.

"Hey!" someone yelled. "Leave Kazoo alone!"

Since I was on my back, the mouth in my mask was angled up toward Astros Cap. Behind him I could see one of the families I'd just posed for. The father was the one who'd shouted. His wife was shielding the eyes of their two children from the sight of a grown man beating up their favorite koala.

Astros Cap turned to face the father, unfazed. "This doesn't concern you, amigo. Mind your own business and move along."

The father didn't back down. Instead he turned and yelled to some other tourists. "Help! Some psycho's beating up Kazoo!"

Within seconds a dozen other people rushed to his side. Most were parents, though a few park employees were in the mix. They all gasped upon seeing Astros Cap looming over me, and then grew angry.

"I'm only going to say this one more time," the father told Astros Cap. "Leave the koala alone."

"What's wrong with you?" a mother demanded. "This is a family park!"

"Don't hurt Yogi!" yelled the German father, who still didn't know who I was supposed to be.

Now that he was outnumbered, Astros Cap wasn't so tough anymore. He raised his hands, signaling the others to back down. "Hold on," he said meekly. "This is all just a big misunderstanding. There's no need to get nasty."

"Yes there is!" I yelled. "He stole my wallet!"

The mob grew even angrier.

"You mugged an innocent koala?" a grandmother shouted at Astros Cap.

"Get him!" one of the park employees yelled.

Astros Cap ran. Several of the adults went after him. Astros Cap crashed through the landscaping and made it to Adventure Road just ahead of the mob, which pursued him toward the front gates like hounds going after a rabbit.

The other adults came to my side. "All you all right?" a mother asked.

"No," I said. "Can you help me out of this costume?"

I knew it might cause trouble to reveal my identity, but there was no time for caution. I needed to learn who Astros Cap was and I couldn't do it dressed like a koala.

Someone popped the head off my costume. Everyone reacted with surprise.

"You're just a kid!" a father gasped.

"After-school job," I lied, then wriggled out of the rest of the costume and bolted after Astros Cap.

He—and his pursuers—were well ahead of me, but I poured on the speed. Without the bulky, heavy costume, I suddenly felt a hundred times lighter. Plus, after so much time in the stuffy suit, the fresh night air was invigorating.

Astros Cap was most likely heading for the park's main exit. There was really no other place for him to go. Everyone came to FunJungle by car, and the only place for guests to park was the giant lot out in front. The crowd grew thicker as we went, as everyone was funneling the same way. Astros Cap ducked and jibed through the other people, trying to shake his pursuers. I lost sight of him in the crowd.

Luckily, I knew a shortcut. I veered between the carnival midway and the nocturnal-animals building. There was an access to the employee area between them. I shot through it and cut behind a few exhibits to the employee exit. I emerged outside the front gates just in time to see Astros Cap barge through.

The thug was in such a hurry he was shoving people aside, even young kids and old ladies. He'd managed to lose the mob pursuing him, however. They all must have been stuck back in the crowd.

Astros Cap darted into the parking lot. I paralleled him through the lines of cars, trying to keep a safe distance. He hadn't seen me without the koala costume on, so he wouldn't recognize me—but then, I'd already been caught following him once that day and it hadn't been pleasant.

It was so dark now that Astros Cap finally had to remove his sunglasses, but in the dimly lit parking lot I still couldn't get a good look at him. We zigzagged through the cars until we reached the Giselle Giraffe section, where Astros Cap quickly ducked into a white sedan. I hurried over as he started the engine, arriving right before he slammed the pedal down and peeled away.

I had just enough time to memorize the license plate. TEXAS, SDP 5967.

Then I turned around and headed right back for the park. It was now well after five, which meant my parents would soon be looking for me. As I crossed the parking lot, I dialed Summer McCracken. I wasn't expecting to get her, thinking I'd just leave a message—but to my surprise, she answered on the second ring.

"Hey!" she said. "I've been waiting to hear from you."

"You have?" I asked.

"Of course. How'd the investigation go today? Did my plan for you to go undercover work? You didn't chicken out, did you?"

"No," I said, a bit too defensively. "I did exactly what we talked about. And it worked just fine."

"Ha!" Summer crowed. "I told you it would! So? Did you find out who stole Kazoo?"

"Maybe. I need a little help from you, though. Can you write something down?"

"Give me a second." I heard Summer scrambling for a pencil. "Okay. Shoot."

"I need to find the owner of the car with this license plate: Texas, SDP 5967."

There was a pause while Summer copied that down. "Got it. I'll send it to my dad right away. I'm sure he knows someone who can handle it. But he'll need to know why I'm asking for it. Is it the koala thief's?"

"Could be." I told Summer all about Freddie Malloy and Astros Cap as I reentered FunJungle. It took longer than I'd expected, as Summer could never let me go more than three sentences without asking a question. By the time I'd explained everything, I was back by the Polar Pavilion again.

"So you really think this Astros Cap guy is our man?" Summer asked me.

"I don't know," I admitted. "But he's certainly up to something around here. Someone ought to look into it— and I know Marge won't. If I gave her this info, all she'd do would be to try and arrest me for impersonating a koala."

"You're probably right," Summer laughed. "But Daddy will get to the bottom of this. I'll make sure of it. You did good work, Teddy. I wish I could have been more help."

"You helped plenty," I assured her. "I never would have found Astros Cap if you hadn't thought for me to dress up as Kazoo."

"That was pretty brilliant, wasn't it?" Summer teased.

"There's just one thing," I said. "When you tell your dad about the license plate, you probably shouldn't tell him I'm the one who gave it to you."

"But I'd have to," Summer countered. "How else would he believe I got the info?"

"He's already threatened to fire my parents if I did any more investigating. You think he'll be pleased that I stole a

Kazoo costume and wandered around the park in it?"

"That was my idea. I'll own up to it."

"But I *did* it. Can't you just make something up?"

"I can try—but knowing Daddy, he'll figure out the truth anyhow. Hold on." It sounded like someone had entered Summer's room. I heard them say something, after which Summer groaned. "Sorry, Teddy. I've got to go. It's supposed to be study time here, which means no phone calls."

"Since when do you care about rules?" I asked.

"Since I got put on probation," Summer answered, now keeping her voice low. "I got busted for sneaking out after curfew last week. If anything else happens, they'll boot me out of here—and Daddy will have a cow. Thanks for calling with the update. I'll let you know the moment we hear anything."

Summer hung up before I could even say good-bye. I tucked my phone back in my pocket and trudged into the landscaping beside the Polar Pavilion.

The Kazoo costume lay crumpled right where I'd abandoned it. There was no one around. Everyone who'd witnessed the attack had apparently gone home. I figured I should return the costume to its rightful place; if someone noticed it was missing, Marge might comb through the security footage and find me entering the changing room. It was easier to wear it than to carry it, though, so I quickly pulled it on and hurried across the park.

There were no longer any tourists to stop me, so I made good time and was soon back at the changing room. No one was there, which wasn't surprising; the actors tended to take off the moment their shifts ended, and it was now well after closing time. I pulled off my koala pelt and hung it on the wall.

Before I could make it out the door, however, Charlie Connor entered.

He was wearing his old Larry the Lizard costume, although since it was after park hours, he had the head tucked under his arm and a cigar in his mouth. Charlie was normally in a bad mood, but it got considerably worse upon seeing me. He stopped in his tracks and pointed accusingly. "You! What are you doing here?"

I stuttered for a moment, scrambling to come up with something, then realized I actually had a legitimate reason to be there. "I —well—I . . . was looking for *you*."

"Me?" Charlie's eyes suddenly lit up with understanding. "Oh no. This is about that missing koala, isn't it?"

"Yes," I said.

"Of course." Charlie stormed past me, threw his lizard head up onto the shelf, and unzipped his costume. "There's been a crime, so naturally, you're playing detective again. Well, just like last time, I didn't do anything. I had no beef with that koala."

"Kristi Sullivan said you did."

Charlie froze in shock, halfway out of his costume. He looked like a mutant lizard shedding its skin. "She ratted me out? That girl's a piece of work. First she refuses to go out with me on the grounds that I'm a little person—"

"She refused because you tried to scam FunJungle."

"That was a legitimate injury claim, and this lousy park rejected it!" Charlie angrily kicked off the rest of his costume. "And even if it wasn't on the up-and-up, that doesn't make me a koala-napper. If you want to know who did that, maybe you ought to look at Kristi herself."

"What?" I asked. "Kristi wouldn't steal Kazoo. She loved him."

"Exactly," Charlie told me. "She was always going on about how adorable he was and how she'd be so upset when the time came for him to go back to Australia. More than once she told me she might swipe him so she could keep him forever."

"I'm sure she was only joking."

"Was she? 'Cause the koala's gone, and she had better access to his exhibit than anyone."

I started to counter that, then bit my lip, realizing Charlie had a point. The real reason I'd discounted Kristi as a potential thief was that I liked her, but just because someone was nice—or at least pretending to be nice—didn't mean they couldn't do something wrong. "But she was so worried about him . . . ," I began.

"Smoke and mirrors, kid. Totally threw you off her scent, didn't she?"

"I guess, but . . ."

"Let me ask you something else: Why'd she say I took Kazoo? To ransom him? Shake the park down for a few million?"

"Yes."

"Then where's the ransom note?" Charlie asked. "That's the number one rule of kidnapping, isn't it? Ask for a ransom. If you don't do it, you don't get the money. But there isn't a note. Therefore, either the kidnapper is an idiot, which I'm not—or Kazoo wasn't kidnapped at all."

I nodded understanding, but added, "You could still make money off a stolen koala."

"How?"

"By selling it."

Charlie laughed. "Right. Exactly how easy do you think it is to fence a koala?"

I shrugged.

"It's impossible," Charlie said. "It's not like there's a couple hundred koalas for sale on eBay every day and I could just slip Kazoo in there without being noticed. Right now there's exactly *one* koala at large in this country, and the very moment whoever took it tries to sell it, every cop, Fed, and animal-rights activist is gonna come down on them."

"Not if Flora Hancock had already hired you to steal it for her."

Charlie seemed legitimately confused by this statement. "I don't know any Floral Peacock."

"Flora Hancock," I repeated. "The rich lady from Waco who collects exotic animals."

"Never heard of her." Either Charlie was being honest or he was one heck of an actor.

"You're sure?" I asked. "Because she spent a lot of time in KoalaVille."

"So did plenty of people. I didn't meet any of them. I just stood around in that stinking koala suit and let people take my picture." I tried to say something else, but Charlie cut me off. "And besides, if this fancy-pants collector really did want Kazoo, why would she come to me? I don't know squat about stealing koalas. Long ago, I was a two-bit mugger who took cash and jewelry. Nothing more intricate than that. And I've been clean for over five years now. I'm trying to live a normal, law-abiding life—which isn't easy when every time there's a crime you start pointing fingers at me because I'm the only criminal you know."

"Kristi said you had a new plan to bilk FunJungle."

Charlie backed down a bit, busted. "All I was gonna do

was inflate my hours a bit. That's not exactly the crime of the century. And for your information, I never actually did it. I only bragged about having a plan to impress Kristi. Being a schmo who dresses like a marsupial for a living wasn't exactly knocking her socks off."

For a moment I almost felt sorry for Charlie. But then I caught myself. After all, Charlie had tried to con FunJungle with a bogus medical claim, which meant he wasn't exactly law-abiding—and he'd mentioned Kazoo as a potential moneymaking target to Kristi. Or had he? If Kristi *had* taken Kazoo, then she'd certainly picked the right person to divert my attention from her.

In fact she'd picked *two* people. And right now, of those two, Freddie Malloy was the one who really looked like he was up to no good. He was the one who'd been talking to Astros Cap, not Charlie Connor. The idea of Charlie stealing Kazoo on behalf of Flora Hancock now seemed quite farfetched—although not completely impossible.

"You're not the only criminal I know," I said. "There's also Freddie Malloy."

Charlie stared at me for a moment, a little off guard. Then he shook his head again. "Freddie's a moron, not a criminal."

"Are you sure?" I asked. "I hear he was really angry at Kazoo."

"Who'd you hear that from? Kristi?"

"No," I lied, although I apparently wasn't convincing; Charlie saw right through it.

"Sounds like you did," he said. "More smoke and mirrors. I don't blame you, though. She's a cute one, that Kristi. And the cute ones can be very convincing, because you *want* to believe them. A guy who looks like me, though, has a hard enough time trying to get anyone to ever believe the *truth*."

"I don't think Freddie's completely clean," I said. "I saw him talking to a known criminal today."

Charlie laughed again. "Oh, you did? And who, exactly, was this criminal?"

"I don't know his name," I admitted. "But he's a big, mean guy who always wears sunglasses and a orange Astros baseball cap."

I was looking right into Charlie's eyes as I said this. He didn't betray an ounce of recognition. "That's all you've got?" he asked. "Not even a name?"

"No."

"I thought you said this guy was a known criminal."

"He tried to beat someone up here today."

"Who?"

"I don't know," I lied. "But I saw it happen."

I was more convincing this time. Charlie bought it. "That doesn't make the guy a criminal," he said. "It makes him a jerk. And besides, I have no idea who he is or what Freddie Malloy was doing with him. Here's my two cents: If you really want to find this koala, take a good, hard look at Kristi Sullivan." With that, he stormed out of the changing room.

I followed him. "Where are you going?"

"Home. My shift's over. I'm done—and so is this interrogation. Now leave me alone."

I stopped. Charlie kept on going without a look back.

Was he right about Kristi? I wondered. I had a hard time imagining she could have ever taken Kazoo, but then, as Charlie had suggested, maybe I was letting her off easy because she seemed nice.

My phone buzzed in my pocket. I checked it and found I'd missed a call from Dad a few minutes before. The costume room had lousy reception. I was about to call back when I got the feeling someone was watching me.

I spun around to find Marge O'Malley leaning against a lamppost. She grinned in a taunting way. "What were you talking to Charlie about, Teddy?"

I wondered how long Marge had been there, and if she'd seen me enter the room with the costume earlier. "I'm doing your job," I told her. "Trying to find out who stole Kazoo."

"I *know* who stole Kazoo," Marge said. "*You* did. And I've got all the proof I need to put you away. In fact, I even picked up a little bonus tidbit of information today that ought to be the final nail in your coffin."

I doubted Marge could have recognized a piece of evidence to save her life, but her confidence made me uneasy. "What is it?" I asked.

"You'll find out tomorrow," Marge said, "after I present my case to J.J. McCracken. You'll be heading straight to juvenile hall—though the cops might go easier on you if you cough up the koala first." Marge stomped over and fixed me with her hardest stare. "So where is it?"

I tried to muster my own hard stare in return. "I don't know, Marge. I didn't take him."

Marge laughed. It sounded evil, like the deep-throated rumble that hippos make. "You want to play it like this, that's fine with me. You'll only end up doing more time." She grinned and strode away with an actual bounce in her step. "It's gonna be a great day tomorrow: the day I finally get rid of Teddy Fitzroy once and for all."

15

FURIOUS GEORGE

According to Dad's message, he was done with his photography session. He grabbed some sandwiches at the Gorilla Grill and we met up at Mom's office for dinner.

Normally, Mom hated eating dinner in her office. She said she spent enough time there during the day. However, it was cold that night, which meant that our trailer would be freezing, and besides, she wanted to keep an eye on Furious George.

George was now in chimpanzee solitary, a cell situated right next to Mom's office. There was a large window between them, allowing us to observe George (and allowing him to observe us, too). The cell was really two rooms, divided by a wall of bars down the middle, so that someone could be in there with a quarantined animal but not be in danger of getting hurt. George's side of the cell was actually quite nice; it wasn't supposed to be a punishment so much as a safe place to take an animal off display. There were plenty of ropes to climb and toys to play with. George was swinging about, looking happy and perfectly mentally balanced.

Therefore Mom wasn't paying much attention to him. Instead she was completely focused on me.

I told her and Dad everything that had happened that day, with one exception. I didn't own up to swiping the Kazoo costume, figuring that would get me in trouble. Instead I said I'd merely "happened" to stumble across Freddie and Astros Cap colluding. (I still told them Astros Cap had threatened me, but claimed he was run off for picking on a kid.) Normally, Mom might have seized on the gaps in my story, but that night she and Dad had too much else to deal with. They listened silently as I recounted facing the bullies, my run-in with Astros Cap, and my conversation with Charlie Connor. But when it was all over, Mom was so worked up she didn't know what to discuss first. She kept starting to say one thing, then changing her mind and trying to say something else, before finally deciding to focus on Vance.

"I can't believe—why didn't you—? I specifically told you not to—this bullying has gone far enough! I'm calling your principal again!" She reached for her office phone, but I blocked her.

"Mom, don't," I pleaded. "That will only make Vance Jessup angrier at me."

"Don't be ridiculous," Mom told me. "The school needs to handle this. Those boys need to be punished!"

"Vance and TimJim don't care about being punished," I said. "But I *know* they don't want to face the football players again. I think they'll leave me alone after what happened today."

"Maybe not," Dad cautioned. "And the football team won't always be there to protect you."

"That's right," Mom echoed.

"So the next time one of these guys comes at you," Dad said, "you just haul off and punch him square in the nose."

"Jack!" Mom gasped. "Don't tell Teddy that! It'll only get him in more trouble!"

"He's in enough trouble as it is," Dad countered, then turned back to me. "Your average bully is really a coward. He only survives by intimidation. If you fight back, it'll completely catch him off guard. One good sock, right here." Dad pointed to his nose. "You'll bloody him up nice and good and he'll never bother you again."

"Or he'll get angry and pound our son to a pulp," Mom said tartly.

"He won't, Charlene," Dad said. "Trust me. This works."

"How would you know?" Mom asked suspiciously. "Have you done this?"

Dad shrugged. "I've dealt with a few bullies in my time."

Mom's mouth dropped open. This was obviously news to her. "When?"

"Middle school," Dad said. "High school too. And a couple years ago in South Africa, this meathead in a bar tried to shake me down—"

"Enough," Mom said, before he could go on. "Teddy, don't listen to your father. Violence is never the answer. Promise me that you won't try to fight anyone."

I glanced at my father. Behind Mom's back, he signaled me to say yes, though when Mom looked at him, he pretended to be scratching his head.

"Okay," I said. "But right now I'm more worried about Astros Cap than Vance Jessup."

Mom put a reassuring hand on my shoulder. "Oh, I doubt he'll threaten you again. He was probably just trying to scare you off."

"I'm not worried about him hurting me," I said. "I'm worried about what he's up to."

"What do you mean?" Mom asked.

"Well, Freddie was already angry at FunJungle," I explained. "So maybe he hired this guy to get rid of Kazoo. But the guy's still hanging around. That doesn't make any sense unless they're planning to do something else nasty. Something to Shark Odyssey, maybe."

Mom and Dad shared a look, mulling this over. Neither seemed to completely buy it.

"We don't really have any evidence that this Astros Cap guy had anything to do with Kazoo," Dad told me. "All we know is that he was at the scene of the crime *after* it happened—like a lot of other people. And that he knows Freddie."

"He *looked* suspicious," I said. "And he got really upset when he thought I was following him."

"That doesn't make him a criminal," Mom said. "And no matter how angry Freddie Malloy was, I can't imagine him hiring anyone to get rid of Kazoo. He loves animals. No one would even attempt a show like his if they didn't."

I sighed, frustrated by my parents' arguments. And then I thought of something else. "Arthur Koenig also might have taken Kazoo." In all the excitement with Astros Cap, I'd forgotten about Arthur.

Mom and Dad stared at me, surprised. "Why do you say that?" Dad inquired.

"I overheard him trying to sell something to someone today. He was being really suspicious and asking for a lot of money."

"Did he mention Kazoo specifically?" Mom asked.

"No," I said. "But he said he'd taken a big risk to get whatever he was selling, and that if people found out, he could go to jail."

Dad and Mom shared an intrigued look. "Sounds like he was definitely up to something," Dad agreed.

Mom frowned. "It does, but Arthur's a good, caring keeper. I can't see him taking Kazoo either. . . ."

"Well, someone had to!" I exclaimed. "And if we can't figure out who, I'm going to jail for this!"

"What about Charlie Connor?" Mom suggested. "We *know* he has a criminal background."

"Charlie actually had some good reasons to explain why he *hadn't* done it," I said. "He said he didn't have the slightest idea how to steal or fence a koala."

"Well, you wouldn't expect him to admit that he did, would you?" Dad asked.

"No, but I still believe him." I hesitated before adding, "Charlie said we ought to consider Kristi."

Mom recoiled slightly. "Kristi? Why would *she* steal Kazoo?"

"To get a koala," I answered. "Charlie said she knew the koala exhibit better than anyone."

Mom shook her head. "No one who knew anything about koalas would steal one. They're virtually impossible to care for."

I thought back to Kristi and how concerned she'd been about Kazoo. It was hard to imagine her faking that to throw me off her trail. She was the one who had told me that Kazoo had such a specialized diet—and that he'd starve to death if he wasn't rescued soon. If she knew that, why would she take him?

"I'm just telling you what Charlie told me," I said.

"Well, Charlie's wrong," Mom told me. "I think we can rule Kristi out."

"What about the other koala keepers?" Dad suggested. "There were three of them, right? Elizabeth Ames, Jen Weeks and . . . shoot, I can't remember the third."

"Ashley Thomas," Mom said. "They worked with Kazoo less than Kristi did, but they all had to learn just as much about koalas. All of them would have known the extreme difficulties involved in taking care of Kazoo."

"Maybe they didn't do it to get a pet for themselves," I said. "Maybe some rich collector like Flora Hancock paid them to steal a koala for her. She has enough money to buy all the eucalyptus in the world."

"None of those keepers would have stolen Kazoo," Mom stated flatly.

"Maybe Arthur Koenig stole him for Flora Hancock," I said.

"I don't think *any* keeper would steal a zoo animal," Mom told me.

"Well whoever did it had to know how to get in and out without being seen," I argued. "Which means the thief had to know the koala exhibit really well. If it wasn't a keeper, then who was it?"

"What about one of the contractors who built the exhibit?" Dad suggested. "Suppose some carpenter had his eye on Kazoo all along. Maybe he knows Flora Hancock is willing to pay big bucks for a koala. So he builds a secret entrance into the exhibit, bides his time for a few weeks, then sneaks into the zoo one night and swipes Kazoo."

Mom frowned at him. "You really think so?"

Dad shrugged. "It's possible. And it explains how the thief got Kazoo without showing up on tape. Even if Kristi or Arthur or this Astros Cap guy took the koala, we still haven't figured out how they did it without going through the door."

"Maybe Astros Cap *was* one of the carpenters!" I exclaimed. "Maybe Freddie approached him at some point during the construction of the exhibit and they came up with a plan to steal Kazoo."

"Or maybe he works for the company that installed the security system here!" Dad was getting excited now. "Maybe he built in his own secret access code—which would explain how he could get into the koala exhibit *and* Shark Odyssey. And he might know how to override the security cameras as well so he could get in and out without being recorded."

He and I both looked to Mom expectantly. The frown

hadn't left her face. "It seems awfully far-fetched," she said.

"Maybe, but it's still possible," Dad countered. "In fact, I'd say it's the best we've come up with so far." He turned to me. "What'd you do with his license plate number?"

"I called Summer," I told him. "And she's going to pass it on to her father. She says he knows people who can trace it."

"We ought to pass it on to Marge, too," Mom recommended.

"She won't do anything with it," I said. "All she cares about is framing me for this."

Mom sighed. "Marge might have a chip on her shoulder where you're concerned, but she's still in charge of security here. She should know about this. Maybe if it comes from one of us rather than you, she'll take it more seriously."

"I guess it can't hurt." I dutifully wrote down the license plate number for my mother, who began texting it to Marge. "And while we're at it, we should let her know about Arthur Koenig, too."

Mom paused in midtext. "Teddy, for the last time, I don't see Arthur doing this—"

"Well he was selling *something* he wasn't supposed to have," I argued. "Even if it wasn't Kazoo, Marge should know about it."

"Good point." Mom went back to composing her message. "Did you say there was footage of this Astros Cap online?" Dad asked. "Maybe we could forward that to Marge and the McCrackens as well."

"Sure," I said. "I'll see if I can find it."

I got on my mother's computer, feeling more upbeat than I had in a while. Astros Cap being a construction worker was certainly the best explanation we'd come up with to explain how Kazoo had been taken. And there was no shortage of people he could have been working for—Freddie, Arthur, Flora—if not a combination of any of them. There was only one thing that still nagged at me: What had Astros Cap been doing at Shark Odyssey?

It took me a few tries to find the right YouTube video; a dozen more recordings of the disaster at KoalaVille had been uploaded since lunch. But I eventually located it.

We watched it play on the computer. Mom, who'd only heard about the events from Dad and me, just shook her head in dismay as they unfolded before her. Dad, who'd lived through it, stood behind her, struggling to keep from laughing. Finally the camera settled on Astros Cap, and I paused the video. "There!" I said. "That's him!"

Dad zoomed in so that Astros Cap's face filled the screen, then squinted at the pixelated image. "It's not easy to make him out with the glasses and the hat," he said. "I might have seen him before, but I can't be sure. How about you, hon?" He looked to Mom.

"He seems familiar to me, too," Mom said. "Though I can't figure out why."

"Maybe we saw him around one of the construction sites—" Dad began, though he didn't get to finish the thought, because Furious George suddenly went nuts.

He'd been so quiet up until then; even Mom had forgotten about him. Now he let out a nerve-jangling scream that made all of us leap out of our seats.

We spun around to find him racing about his cell like a maniac. He bounded off the walls, flinging everything he could get his hands on, screeching the entire time. Every few seconds he would return to the viewing window and pound on it so hard I thought he might break through. Most people don't realize that chimps have extremely sharp teeth. The sight of George gnashing them with rage in his eyes was terrifying. I'd never seen him like this. In fact I'd never seen him be anything other than sweet and kind.

Mom sensed I was frightened and put a hand on my shoulder to calm me. "It's all right," she said. "He's not trying to get to us. Something else triggered this reaction."

"Like what?" Dad asked. "He's in solitary. He can't see anything but *us*."

"Something must have changed," Mom said. "We weren't doing anything. We were only looking at . . ." She trailed off and turned toward the computer.

I looked that way too. On the screen, in full view of Furious George, was the blown-up photo of Astros Cap. "It's *him*," I said.

Mom wiped the photo from the computer.

George calmed down almost as quickly as he'd flipped out. He stopped banging on the glass and baring his teeth. The rage in his eyes was replaced by a pained, almost ashamed expression, as though he was embarrassed about his behavior.

"Could that man have done something to him?" Dad asked.

"Perhaps." Mom had a faraway look in her eyes, which she got when she was trying to solve a problem. "But, like you said, it was hard to make him out—and George was a lot farther from the computer than we were. He wouldn't have been able to recognize a specific person. I wonder if he was responding to something else instead."

"Like what?" I asked.

"What he was wearing." Mom returned her attention to the computer and did a Google image search for "orange baseball caps." "Get ready," she told me. "This might get scary again."

The monitor screen filled with photos of people wearing orange caps. Mom clicked on one and then stepped aside so that Furious George could see it.

He went nuts again.

One second he was calm. The next he was screeching and banging the glass.

Mom wiped the screen once more.

George went back to his normal self.

Mom came to the viewing window and placed her palm against it. "You poor thing," she said sadly. "You poor, poor thing."

George put his hand on the other side of the glass, so his palm was facing hers.

"It's all right," Mom told him. "You're going to be okay."

"What's going on?" I asked.

"George's behavior is consistent with an ape that has been abused," Mom said. "I can't say for sure whether or not the man in the video did it, but it seems quite evident that whoever did was wearing an orange baseball cap."

I sat down, feeling like the wind had been knocked out of me. Even though I'd seen plenty of examples of humanity's cruelty, they still always caught me off guard.

"Do you think it was someone here?" Dad asked.

Mom shook her head. "It wouldn't have been any of my people. And the exhibits here are designed to prevent any visitors from harming an animal on display. I'd suspect that this was done to George *before* he arrived. He's only been here for a few months."

"Where was he before that?" I asked.

"A research facility in Houston," Mom replied.

"Home of the Astros," Dad said. "Probably a lot of orange baseball caps there."

Mom nodded, then swiveled her computer monitor so that George could no longer see it and opened a folder filled with movie files.

"What are those?" I asked.

"Video from the security camera that faces the crowd in the chimp exhibit," Mom told me. "FunJungle records everything that the cameras see and keeps it for two weeks."

"Why just two weeks?" I inquired.

"There are over ten thousand cameras at this park," Dad explained. "All that video takes up a huge amount of memory. The servers aren't big enough to keep everything forever. So security only holds on to what's important."

"Like this." Mom pointed at the video clips. "I asked security to send me the feeds from the exact times that George had his episodes. I've gone over them a few times already, figuring something in the crowd might be triggering him, but until now I didn't know what to look for."

She clicked on the file from the previous morning. The camera footage filled her screen. It was grainy and shot from an angle near the ceiling, so it was almost impossible to make out anyone's face. A time stamp at the bottom of the screen showed that the film was starting at 10:55 a.m.

There were sixteen people in the crowd. One of them was wearing an orange baseball cap. It wasn't Astros Cap, just a random visitor.

"There," Dad said.

"Got him," Mom said, then brought up the next video, which was from three days before, at 1:37 in the afternoon.

The crowd was much bigger this time. There was a group of elementary school children on a field trip. It took us a bit longer to find the kid in the orange baseball cap.

"There," I said.

"Looks like we have our trigger." Mom sighed. "I can't believe I didn't notice this before."

"Don't blame yourself," Dad said. "It's almost impossible to see until you know what to search for."

Mom nodded, but still looked upset with herself. She brought up a third video to confirm her theory. It was from a week before, just after three in the afternoon.

There were only five people this time, so it wasn't hard to find the man in the orange baseball cap.

"Hey," I said. "That's Astros Cap!"

Mom paused the video and enlarged it. It wasn't a great picture, given the angle of the security camera, but it definitely looked like the guy I'd seen around. He had the same thick build and was wearing sunglasses, even though he was inside.

"Looks like he's been spending a lot of time around here," Dad said suspiciously.

Before I could respond, the phone rang. Mom snapped up the receiver. "Charlene Fitzroy."

The person on the other line said something. I couldn't hear it, but it made Mom look toward me, surprised. "Yes, he's here," she said. "But I'm his mother. Whatever you need to say to him, you can say to me."

She then listened, nodding a few times. "All right," she said finally. "I'll give him the message." She hung up and rolled her eyes.

"Who was that?" I asked.

"The personal assistant to J.J. McCracken," Mom replied. "The boss wants to see you first thing tomorrow."

16

ENEMIES

J.J. McCracken's office was on the top floor of the administration building. It was the nicest office in the entire park, which didn't make that much sense, given that J.J. only used it one day a month, if that. Most of the time he was traveling around the world, overseeing the dozens of companies he owned—or cutting deals to buy yet another one.

The room was twenty times the size of my mother's office, with huge windows that normally offered a panoramic view of all of FunJungle. Today, however, it was sleeting so badly that I couldn't see a thing. When the secretary showed my parents and me in at nine a.m., J.J. was already seated at his enormous desk. The size of the office and the desk were probably supposed to signify J.J.'s power, but to me they had the opposite effect. J.J. was a short man, and surrounding himself with big things only made him seem smaller. He looked kind of like a kid who'd snuck into his father's office.

J.J.'s personality wasn't small at all, however. He was effusive and opinionated, and spoke in a voice that seemed to come from somebody three times bigger. J.J. had grown up close to where FunJungle was built and still acted like a local good old boy rather than a Wall Street billionaire. His standard outfit was a denim shirt, a bolo tie, and cowboy boots. When I entered his office, I was worried he might be angry with me. Instead he seemed thrilled to see my whole family.

"Well, if it isn't the Fitzroys!" he crowed. "Three of my favorite members of the FunJungle family!" He came out from behind the desk to greet us, shaking Dad's hand and mine and giving Mom a peck on the cheek (which he had to stand on tiptoe to do). "I really appreciate y'all coming down here this morning. I know you've got things to do and places to be."

"Like school," Mom said pointedly, nodding toward me.

J.J.'s smile faltered, but only for a second. He wasn't used to people talking to him the way Mom did, but he always seemed to appreciate her cutting to the chase. "You're right," he admitted, then spoke directly to me. "It was probably bad form, demanding to meet you right now, when you're supposed to be studying. But the fact is, I wanted to talk to you face-to-face, ASAP. This was the first opportunity I had. I just flew in from Berlin this morning." He gave me a grin.

"Don't you worry, though, Teddy. If that school gives you any trouble about truancy, just tell Principal Dillnut to call my office. I'll set him straight."

I grinned back. J.J. McCracken was the most revered person in all of Central Texas. It was kind of like having the president of the United States offer to write me a note excusing me from class. "You really mean that?"

"I never say anything I don't mean," J.J. told me. "How is old Lyndon B. Johnson Middle School anyhow?"

"Honestly?" I asked. "Lousy."

J.J. chuckled. "I hear you. It wasn't too much fun for me, either. I had this one teacher, Mrs. Orton, who made my life downright miserable."

"I have Mrs. Orton now," I said.

J.J. took a step back in surprise. "She's still alive? Jumping jackalopes! She was ancient when she taught *me*—and I'm no spring chicken. The old bat must be two hundred years old by now! She giving you any trouble?"

"Yes," I said.

"Mrs. Orton doesn't always seem that fair when it comes to grading Teddy's papers," Dad offered.

"I wouldn't put too much stock in what Mrs. Orton thinks," J.J. said. "She always told me I wouldn't amount to much." He waved to his office. "I think we can agree she missed the mark on that one."

J.J. might have happily rambled on about his old teachers all day, but Mom cut him off. "I'm sure you didn't call us in just to talk about old times, J.J.?"

"Right as usual, Charlene." J.J. waved us to a couch, then sat in a large, overstuffed armchair. "I wanted to talk to you about something far more terrible than middle school—which is saying something. Teddy, I know you've been nosing around in this whole Kazoo business."

I looked toward my shoes. Either Summer had spilled the beans about me, or she'd been right and J.J. had seen through her story. "I'm sorry. I didn't mean to cause any trouble. . . ."

J.J. laughed. "Hold on there, kiddo. I'm not planning to tan your hide for this. In fact, I want to thank you."

I lifted my head, surprised. On either side of me, Mom and Dad seemed equally caught off guard.

"You do?" Mom asked, before I could.

"Sure," J.J. said. "Now, I know there's been some trouble, but I doubt that Teddy's entirely to blame for that. Your son shows gumption, Charlene, and I respect that. In fact, sometimes I wish my security staff here behaved a bit more like him."

I glanced at my parents, unsure what to make of this. I'd heard J.J. was upset with my snooping—but now he seemed pleased with it. "So . . . you don't think I stole Kazoo?" I asked the billionaire.

J.J. hesitated for a little too long before answering, like

he was choosing his words very carefully. "I'll admit, there was a moment or two when I had my suspicions. Not that I thought you were up to anything criminal, Teddy . . . but you do have a reputation for pranks around here, and I thought perhaps this might have been one that had gone a little too far."

"Now hold on there . . . ," Dad began, but J.J. held up his hands to signal he wasn't finished.

"All I'm saying is that I considered the possibility," he explained. "And you have to admit, the evidence was stacked pretty high against your son."

Dad backed down. "I suppose."

"Well, that's probably all moot now anyhow," J.J. said. "In light of what Teddy turned up with his snooping last night."

Mom and Dad looked to me curiously, then back to J.J. "Is this about Astros Cap?" Mom asked.

"In part," J.J. replied. "Though the big piece of evidence Teddy got was that license plate number. Once Summer sent it to me, I passed it on to my security division."

"You mean Marge?" I asked.

J.J. laughed again. "No, I mean the security division for my entire corporation. I often have to deal with issues quite a bit more serious than what normally takes place here: things like embezzlement, fraud, and corporate espionage. That division is staffed mostly by former FBI agents and the like who still have plenty of connections in law enforcement, so it wasn't too hard to trace the plate. Seems the car was rented by an employee of the Heisenbok Company."

"I've never heard of that," Mom said.

"No," J.J. told her. "You wouldn't have. Because the company's just a front. It doesn't make a thing. Its only purpose is to hide the identity of its owner, but once again, my people know how to get through to the bottom of corporate shenanigans like this. The point being, Heisenbok is actually owned by the Nautilus Corporation, which is owned by none other than Walter Ogilvy."

Mom and Dad both reacted with surprise. Obviously, they knew who Walter Ogilvy was. I'd never heard the name, though. "Who's that?" I asked.

"Another billionaire capitalist," Dad said. "Sort of like J.J. here."

"Walter Ogilvy is nothing like me!" J.J. spoke so sharply he even seemed to take himself by surprise. He hopped to his feet and paced around his office. "The man is an unethical, greedy bottom-feeder whose only talent is leeching off other companies. He's no better than a common thief. In fact, he's worse. When a thief gets caught stealing, he goes to jail. When Ogilvy gets caught, he just bribes his way out of trouble and gets away with a wrist slap."

Mom leaned over and whispered in my ear. "As you can see, there's some bad blood between J.J. and Walter."

"That weasel has stolen dozens of ideas from me over the years," J.J. was saying. "And then he had the unmitigated gall to accuse *me* of stealing the idea for FunJungle from him! That man's less trustworthy than a raccoon in a henhouse—"

Dad interrupted. "J.J., I think Teddy needs a little more background to understand what's going on here."

J.J. paused in mid-rant and swung back toward us, as though he'd forgotten we were there. "Good point," he said, and then focused on me. "Even though it is extremely well documented that the idea for this park was generated by none other than my own daughter several years ago, Walter Ogilvy has repeatedly claimed that it was actually *his* idea. In reality, he was just jealous of the concept and tried to steal it for himself. He made multiple attempts to block the construction of FunJungle while racing to build his own animal-based theme park in New Mexico. ZooTopia, he called it. He filed injunctions, dragged me to court, and cost me an arm and a leg in legal fees—and when that didn't work, he played dirty, making several attempts at sabotage—"

"I heard that was never proven," Mom said.

"Of course it wasn't," J.J. groused. "Ogilvy's more slippery than a moray eel. The man's never had an original thought in his life, but he knows how to cover his tracks. I assure you, though, there was definite sabotage of this park during construction—and I know Ogilvy was behind it."

"Like what?" I asked.

"World of Reptiles mysteriously caught fire," J.J. told me. "There was an explosion at Hippo River. Someone ripped out all the wiring of two dozen bulldozers. Penny-ante stuff, really. But it all cost time and energy—and it put the lives of innocent workers in jeopardy. And the worst thing is, there wasn't a point to any of it. Ogilvy knew I was going to finish FunJungle no matter what. He knew his own park wouldn't ever be finished before mine. He was just being a sore loser, like the kid who sticks tacks in your bike tires because you're dating the girl he has a crush on."

"Is ZooTopia still being built?" I asked.

For the first time since the subject of Ogilvy had come up, J.J. smiled. "No, Teddy. It's not. Ogilvy bought a lot of land and started clearing it, but once FunJungle opened and grabbed all the press, Ogilvy's backers realized they'd never be able to rival us. So the project got canned, leaving the Nautilus Corporation on the hook for all the cash they'd laid out. The whole incident left Ogilvy looking like a fool, and yet he still hasn't backed down. He's continued to file suits against me, looking for a cut of FunJungle's profits. And I've suspected all along that he's not done with his dirty tricks. Teddy, do you recall that in the midst of the whole Henry the Hippo investigation, I'd suggested there might be some corporate interests behind Henry's death?"

"Yes," I said. I remembered the conversation quite well. It was the first time I'd ever met J.J. McCracken.

"Well, Walter Ogilvy was one of the folks I had in mind," J.J. told me. "In fact, he was my primary suspect—until the truth came out. Now, Ogilvy might not have murdered Henry, but it seems he's still determined to cause trouble here."

"You think *he* swiped Kazoo?" Mom asked.

"I think it's darned likely." J.J. circled back behind his desk. "The only way Ogilvy will ever get ZooTopia off the ground is to drive FunJungle out of business. Now, I won't kid you: We're having a tough go of things right now. We're far below where our numbers ought to be in terms of ticket sales. That Henry business didn't help this summer—and the nasty weather this winter has been a real kick in the knees. Kazoo was proving to be our salvation—not just in tickets, but in merchandising as well—and suddenly he goes missing. Look at what that accomplishes: It takes away a major revenue stream *and* it makes FunJungle look bad. Coming on the heels of Henry's death, we look like a bunch of knuckleheads over here. And it's not like we can get a replacement koala. The Australian government is pitching a fit over this and threatening to sue me for gross negligence. Ogilvy couldn't have picked a better way to hurt us."

A frightening thought occurred to me. "Does this mean you're going to build those roller coasters through the animal exhibits after all?"

J.J. looked offended that I'd even posed the question. "I promised Summer I wouldn't. She convinced me that was a mistake. I'm not about to go back on a deal with my daughter."

I glanced at my mother, unsure if I should believe this. She nodded, signaling she thought J.J. was telling the truth. "Okay," I said.

J.J. unlocked a desk drawer, pulled out some eight-by-ten photographs, and slid them across the desk. "Teddy, is this the fellow you saw snooping around yesterday?"

I stood up and grabbed the photos. They were all somewhat grainy, as if they had been taken by a surveillance camera from a long distance away. Astros Cap was in each one of them. He was always wearing sunglasses and a baseball cap. "That's him," I said.

J.J. nodded knowingly. "And can you tell me exactly where you saw him?"

"First, he was talking to Freddie Malloy in KoalaVille," I reported. "And then he went into Shark Odyssey. Not the main entrance, but the employee area. He knew the code to get through the door."

"Malloy must've given him the entry code," J.J. muttered. "That nut job's still friendly with the shark keepers. He could've convinced one of them to give him the day's code and then passed it on."

Mom tapped one of the grainy photos of Astros Cap. "Who is he?"

"His name's Hank Duntz," J.J. replied. "Though in certain circles he's known as Hank the Tank. He's an employee of the Nautilus Corporation. Officially, he's the vice president of internal development. In truth he's in charge of doing Ogilvy's dirty work."

"You've had your eye on this guy for a while," Dad said.

J.J. looked at him curiously. "Why do you say that?"

Dad fanned out the photos. "These have been taken over at least a year. Probably more. The seasons change. Duntz goes from wearing winter clothes to summer ones. His hair changes length. He even seems to have gained about thirty pounds over the course of them."

J.J. was impressed. "I should have known a professional photographer would pick up on that. Yes, I've had people keeping tabs on Duntz for a while. We've found him in the vicinity of trouble several times—he was lurking around here just before the fire at World of Reptiles—but we've never been able to link him to anything. And now here he is again."

"Do you know where to find him?" I asked.

"Unfortunately, no," J.J. replied. "Most likely he's staying in a hotel under an assumed name."

"What about Freddie Malloy?" Mom asked. "He must know something."

"I'm sure he does," J.J. said. "Only, as of this morning, we don't know where Freddie is either. He called in sick today, but when I sent some of my people out to his house, he wasn't there. He flew the coop."

"Do you think he knows you're onto him?" Dad asked.

"It's the only thing that makes sense," J.J. replied. "I'm not sure how that happened. Maybe he and Duntz spotted Teddy here while he was snooping on them. . . ."

"Sorry," I said. "I tried my best."

"No need to apologize," J.J. told me. "There's a ton of other reasons Freddie might have gotten wind we were onto him—and the fact is, we *wouldn't* have gotten wind if it wasn't for you. If anything, Freddie's disappearance now confirms that he and Duntz both had a hand in this Kazoo business. Rest assured, we'll find them, though. I've got some of my top men on the case."

There was a knock at the door. J.J.'s secretary poked his head into the office. "I hate to bother you, Mr. McCracken, but your call with London starts in two minutes."

J.J. frowned, like he was annoyed he had to do this. "All right," he sighed, then handed the photos of Hank Duntz to his secretary. "Call Mark Middleman at corporate security right now. Tell him Teddy here confirmed it was Hank the Tank on the property yesterday—and that he was poking around Shark Odyssey."

"Do you think we should close that exhibit?" the secretary asked.

J.J. considered that. "Run it past Middleman. And get Pete Thwacker in on it too." He turned back to my family. "I'm sorry I have to bring this to a close, folks. But duty calls."

We were already on our feet, knowing our time with J.J. was up.

"We understand," Dad said. "Thanks for taking the time to listen to Teddy."

"My pleasure." J.J. bent to look me in the eye. "Although this doesn't give you a free pass to keep snooping—*comprende*? Hank the Tank is a dangerous man. My people have got this now. So leave it to us and get to school."

"All right," I said.

"You've got a good kid here," J.J. told my folks, and then ushered us out the door.

I glanced back at J.J. as we passed through his secretary's office. The smile was already gone from his face. Instead his eyes were narrowed in my direction. J.J. quickly forced the smile back on, then closed his door.

J.J.'s secretary saw us to the elevator, and before I knew it, we were out of the administration building again.

It was cold and raw outside. The sleet was falling even harder. My parents and I paused under the eaves of the building, in no hurry to head out into it.

The nasty weather echoed my mood. I probably should have been happy, given that J.J. McCracken himself had just complimented me, but I wasn't.

"What's wrong?" Mom asked. I could never hide my feelings from her.

"I kind of get the feeling that, well . . . that J.J. was only pretending to be nice to us so he could get the information he wanted."

Dad and Mom shared a look, then nodded. "I kind of got that feeling myself," Dad said.

Mom pulled my winter jacket tight around me and zipped it up. "And now you're upset because, after all you've done, he's only giving you a pat on the back and sending you off to school?"

"Sort of," I said. "But more than that, I feel like he wasn't being completely honest with us. Like the deal with him and Walter Ogilvy isn't exactly what he says it is."

Dad grinned. "J.J. was right: You *are* a smart kid. I can guarantee you J.J.'s version was whitewash. J.J. McCracken's no saint when it comes to business. Ogilvy isn't the only one with dirty hands here."

"Now, now," Mom chided. "You're talking about the man who cuts our checks. The man who has given both of us very nice jobs."

"Jobs that he threatened so he could keep Teddy in line," Dad countered. "And now he's acting like that never even happened, like he's been Teddy's biggest fan all along. I'm thankful for J.J. McCracken's jobs, but I don't trust him. And I know you don't either."

Mom frowned, but she didn't deny this.

And then Large Marge emerged from the sleet. Bubba Stackhouse was with her. And there were four other police officers with him. They all wore heavy parkas over their uniforms to protect them against the lousy weather, which made Marge and Bubba even thicker than usual.

"Well, well, well," Marge said with a grin. "Isn't this a surprise? I was just on my way to make my case to J.J. to arrest you—and here you are."

Bubba Stackhouse nodded to his officers, who surrounded us.

"You're wasting your time," Mom said. "We're coming from J.J.'s office right now. He knows who's behind Kazoo's kidnapping."

"No, he only *thinks* he does," Marge shot back. "I'm sure you folks fed him all sorts of lies to keep Teddy looking innocent. But J.J. hasn't seen the evidence I've got. And when he does, I can guarantee he'll change his tune."

"What evidence?" Mom asked. Though she was trying to hide it, I could hear she was worried.

So was I. Marge seemed way too sure of herself. I felt like a young deer that was surrounded by wolves.

"We just visited your trailer again," Marge said. "While you were snowing J.J., we were inspecting Teddy's room. And look what we found." Marge held up two evidence bags. One of them had a clump of gray fur that definitely looked like it came from a koala. The other held several small, oblong black pellets.

"Is that . . . ?" Dad began.

"Koala fur and koala poop," Marge said. "Meaning your precious son here has been in possession of a koala recently."

"I've never seen any of that before!" I protested. "Someone must have planted it!"

Marge ignored me completely and turned to the police. "Arrest him," she said.

HANK THE TANK

Two policemen grabbed me. One forced my hands behind my back while the other whipped out a pair of handcuffs.

"Get your hands off my son!" Dad shouted. He started toward me, but the other two policemen blocked him.

"You're making a mistake!" Mom told them. "Just call J.J. McCracken. He'll set everything straight."

"There's no mistake here," Marge sneered. "Your son was the only one at the crime scene—and now we've found ironclad evidence he had the koala in his room. Case closed. Now back off or we'll arrest both of you, too, for interfering with police business."

Dad didn't listen to her. Even though he was outnumbered, I could tell he was only thinking of me. Dad had been in plenty of dangerous places before, and he knew how to handle himself. He made a feint around the police and charged toward me. One of the policemen caught his arm and tried to twist it back behind him.

Dad swung around and slugged the cop in the chin.

The cop staggered backward, shaken.

His partner tackled Dad, knocking him down. "Bad idea," he snarled.

Dad did his best to fight back, but the second cop was now on him as well. They overwhelmed him, pressing him into the icy ground.

The other policemen cinched the cuffs around my wrists and started to lead me away.

"No!" Mom cried.

"Teddy didn't do anything, Marge!" Dad yelled. "He was framed!"

"Face the facts," Marge taunted. "Your kid's a bad egg. He should've been shipped off to juvenile hall long ago."

Mom came toward Marge, looking ready to claw her eyes out, but Dad's voice stopped her in her tracks. "No, Charlene! Get back to J.J.'s office. Tell him what these idiots are doing!"

Mom obviously didn't want to abandon Dad and me, but realized she wouldn't be any help if she got herself arrested too. "Don't worry, Teddy," she told me. "We'll get this all sorted out. You're going to be okay." Then she raced back toward the administration building.

Bubba Stackhouse looked to Marge, unsure what to do.

Marge stopped the policemen who were leading me away. "I can handle the boy," she said, then handed them the bag full of koala poop. "Run this up to J.J.'s office. When he sees the evidence, he'll back us over Mrs. Fitzroy."

The police seemed happy to get an assignment that took them out of the sleet. They quickly left me with Marge and hurried into the administration building.

Bubba turned to the two cops pinning Dad to the ground. Neither looked pleased that Dad had called them idiots. "You two take Mr. Fitzroy here to headquarters and book him for assault. Marge and I will run the kid to juvenile hall."

Dad stopped struggling, aware it would only get him into more trouble. The cops pulled his arms behind his back and cuffed him as well.

Then Marge and Bubba marched me around a corner and I couldn't see Dad anymore. We passed out of the employee area and into the park. Marge and Bubba each held one of my arms, keeping me squeezed in between them. Since my hands were behind my back, none of the tourists approaching us could see the cuffs on my wrists. Instead I probably looked like a kid on vacation with two very overprotective parents. Not that there were many tourists. The nasty weather had kept everyone but the diehards home.

I started to feel scared. Really scared. Although I'd been worried about Marge for the past few days, I hadn't expected it would come to this. I figured that I'd have found the real thief—or someone else would have. Or at least Marge would have come to her senses and realized I hadn't done it. Instead the stakes had been upped against me—and my parents hadn't been able to protect me.

Even more disconcerting, however, was the fact that whoever had stolen Kazoo had planted evidence against me. Originally, my being at the crime scene had seemed like mere dumb luck: I was in the wrong place at the wrong time. But now I had to wonder if that was true—just as my father had first warned the morning after. The real thief obviously knew I'd been suspected of the crime and had taken further steps to implicate me. Had I been set up all along, then? How much did the thief know about me?

As I thought about this, something occurred to me. "Why'd you decide to search our trailer again?" I asked.

"Because we did, that's why," Marge said, although she couldn't keep eye contact with me, which I figured meant she was lying.

I turned to Bubba. "What really happened?"

"We got a tip," the cop replied. Marge spun on him, annoyed that he'd spilled the beans, but he shrugged it off. "It's not a secret, Marge. He has the right to know."

"What kind of tip?" I asked.

"A phone call," Bubba told me. "Yesterday afternoon."

I thought back to Marge confronting me outside the costume room the day before. She'd been so confident; she must have just gotten the call.

"From who?" I asked.

Bubba shrugged again. "It was anonymous. The caller claimed they'd seen the koala at your place."

"That's a lie!" I said. "I never had the koala there!"

"The evidence says otherwise," Bubba countered.

"It was planted!" I told him. "Probably by whoever called you! They set me up! You should be arresting them, not me!"

"Oh, so it's a conspiracy against you?" Marge asked.

I said, "If I took Kazoo, where is he now?"

"You tell me," Marge growled.

I was about to argue further, but something caught my eye. A glimpse of orange in the distance. I peered through the sleet. A thickset man with an orange baseball cap was passing the Polar Pavilion. He was moving away from us, so I couldn't see his face, but I thought I recognized the lumbering gait. Hank the Tank. And he was heading toward Shark Odyssey.

"There!" I shouted. "That's the guy you should be arresting, not me!" I reflexively tried to point, but couldn't with my arms cuffed behind my back.

"Who?" Bubba asked.

"The guy in the orange Astros Cap by the Polar Pavilion! His name's Hank Duntz and he works for Walter Ogilvy! J.J. was just telling me about him. That's the guy who took Kazoo!"

"Can the lies," Marge told me. "What do I look like to you, an idiot?"

Almost any other time I would have answered yes. But right then I was at Marge's mercy.

"I don't see anyone," Bubba said.

I looked off toward the Polar Pavilion again. Sure enough, Hank had disappeared. There was simply too much sleet to see him. "He was there," I insisted. "He's probably heading for Shark Odyssey. I saw him poking around there yesterday. J.J. says he does the dirty work for Ogilvy, who wants to bankrupt FunJungle. Hank stole Kazoo. And now he's planning to do something in the shark tank."

"The only person who's messed with the shark tank lately is *you*," Marge sneered.

"Just call J.J. and tell him Hank the Tank is here," I pleaded. "It'll only take a few seconds."

Marge didn't even respond to me. Instead she turned to Bubba. "Don't pay him any attention. You can't trust a thing that comes out of this kid's mouth."

"I'm telling you the truth!" I shouted. "If you don't listen to me, something very bad is going to happen to this park—and it's going to happen on your watch."

"And if you don't shut your trap, I'm gonna tape it shut," Marge snapped.

I turned my attention to Bubba, who seemed at least a little more reasonable. "Please, Mr. Stackhouse. I'm not as bad as Marge says I am. She only has it in for me because I once swapped her black jelly beans with rabbit poo."

Bubba wavered. For a moment I thought I'd gotten through to him. But then he shook his head.

We were almost to the front gates. A tourist family was coming through the turnstile, braving the lousy weather. Two parents and three kids, all around my age.

I wasn't thrilled about what I had to do, but Marge and Bubba weren't leaving me any choice.

"Help!" I yelled to the tourists. "I'm being kidnapped! Help!"

The tourists looked at Marge and Bubba, alarmed. They backed away, not wanting to get involved.

"Help me!" I screamed, like my life depended on it. "Please! You're my only hope!"

The father reluctantly stepped forward, blocking Marge and Bubba's path. "What's going on here?" he asked.

"Don't listen to this kid," Marge told him. "I'm with park security—"

No she isn't!" I yelled. "She's only pretending to be! ...ey grabbed me in World of Reptiles when my parents weren't looking!" Normally, my ruse probably wouldn't have worked, but today Bubba's and Marge's parkas were concealing their official uniforms.

The mother pulled out her cell phone. "I'm calling the police," she said.

"Wait!" Bubba held up a giant hand. "I'm a cop and I can prove it. Let me show you my ID." He let go of me to unzip his parka.

I spun away from Marge, wrenching my arm free from her grasp. Bubba realized his mistake and tried to grab me, but Marge lunged for me at the same time and they slammed into each other. Marge slipped on a patch of sleet, stumbled, and pulled Bubba down with her.

The tourists watched it all, unsure what to do. The mother still had her phone in her hand.

"Tell the cops to come to Shark Odyssey at FunJungle!" I told her, and then took off.

It isn't easy to run with your arms cuffed behind your back, but I did my best, charging toward the shark exhibit as fast as I could.

Marge and Bubba scrambled to their feet and came after me. Both were seething with anger, which seemed to make them faster than usual. Between that and my slower-than-average pace, they closed the gap on me as we raced through the park. Marge kept yelling at people to stop me, but I kept yelling at people to stop her and Bubba instead. No one seemed sure what to make of the situation. If I'd been much older, I probably wouldn't have gotten away with it, but the few tourists around seemed to doubt Marge's claim that a twelve-year-old boy could be a wanted criminal. So no one intervened. They all simply stood back and hoped someone else would handle things.

Marge and Bubba both got on their radios. Bubba called the two cops he'd left in charge of Dad, while Marge put out a general APB to all FunJungle security. "I am in hot pursuit of Teddy Fitzroy in connection with the kidnapping of Kazoo the Koala and need backup. All available security personnel please respond. We are proceeding along Arctic Way—"

"Tell them we're heading to Shark Odyssey!" I yelled back. "They can ambush me there!"

I knew the park well enough that if I'd wanted to, I probably could have given Bubba and Marge the slip, but that would only have bought me a little more time. However, if I could get a few dozen security agents to converge on Hank the Tank, they could catch him—and maybe get him to confess that *he'd* stolen Kazoo, not me.

As I neared Shark Odyssey, there was still no sign of Hank. I wondered if he'd already gone inside—or if he was even there. It occurred to me that I'd merely assumed Hank was heading to the sharks—if he wasn't, then I'd just made a huge mistake. I could see several other security guards closing in on the exhibit from various directions.

Even though I'd seen Hank enter through the security door before, I couldn't do it. I didn't know the code—and if I had, I couldn't have entered it with my hands locked behind my back. I still wanted to draw security inside, though.

Some tourists were coming out the exit as I arrived, holding the door open. I barreled through them.

"Circle around to the entrance!" Marge ordered the security guards. "We'll trap him inside!" Then she and Bubba came through the exit as well.

I charged into the shark tube. For once it was devoid of tourists, a sign of what a slow day it was at the park. However, Bubba was bearing down on me. Halfway through the tube, he snagged my arm.

"Gotcha!" he wheezed, exhausted from his run.

Marge staggered into the tube, even more worn out than Bubba. She was so winded I thought she was going to throw up. "Nice work," she gasped.

A few sharks swam past us outside the tube.

I was suddenly overcome by a very bad feeling. If Hank Duntz was plotting something at Shark Encounter, the tube at the bottom of the tank now seemed like the worst place to be. "We have to get out of here!" I said.

Bubba and Marge didn't move. They were both too wiped out from their run. Bubba glared at me, as though he was angry I'd made him exert so much energy. "We'll go when *I* say it's time to go."

"You don't understand!" I said. "Something bad is about to happen here!" I tried to pull free of Bubba's grasp, but he wasn't going to let me get away with that again.

Instead he clenched my arm tighter. "Marge was right," he told me. "You can't be trusted. So do us all a favor and shut your trap."

"We're in danger!" I yelled.

"You never learn, do you, Teddy?" Marge asked.

At both ends of the shark tube, metal doors slammed shut, sealing us inside.

"I *do* learn," I said. "You just never listen."

Now, Marge and Bubba finally grew concerned.

"What are those doors for?" Bubba asked, his eyes wide with fear.

"Safety," Marge told him. "They seal off the rest of the exhibit in case something goes wrong with the shark tube."

"But we're *in* the shark tube!" Bubba wailed. In the space of a few seconds he'd gone from imposing to terrified. Rather than a big, tough policeman, he now seemed like a little kid. "I don't like sharks. I don't like them at all."

"I'm sure it's nothing," Marge said, although she didn't

seem to believe this herself. "Just a glitch in the security system."

"It's not a glitch!" I told her. "It's Hank the Tank! I told you he was up to something bad!"

Bubba let go of me. He stared at all the sharks circling above us and trembled in fear.

I ran to the closest metal wall and kicked it. It didn't do a bit of good. The steel door was sturdy as a sequoia tree. "Help!" I yelled. "Is anyone outside? Help!"

There was no response from the other side of the door. I looked up through the glass ceiling, wondering if any of Marge's security guys were in the viewing area above. If so, there was a chance they could see us down in the tube. I couldn't make out anyone, although it was tough to see through all the water.

Above us, Taurus the bull shark slid past ominously.

"I *really* don't like sharks," Bubba whimpered. "And I'm not so good in enclosed spaces, either."

Now that I was looking up, I noticed something else in the tube. The ceiling wasn't entirely glass. It was supported every twenty feet by steel ribs, which arced around the tube. Along the central rib was a thick wad of what looked like gray Play-Doh. Normally, I might have thought it was some kind of sealant for cracks in the glass, but there were wires snaking out of it. They connected to a small receiver that was taped to the steel rib.

"What is that?" I asked.

Bubba glanced up at it. I wouldn't have thought it possible, but he grew even more frightened. "Get away from it!" he yelled. "It's an explosive!"

We all scrambled to the far end of the tube and flattened up against the steel door.

The receiver beeped.

"Don't look at it!" Bubba ordered.

I turned away and tucked into a ball.

The putty exploded.

It wasn't a huge blast. If it had been outside, it probably wouldn't have even been that loud. In the enclosed tube, however, it echoed like crazy. A concussion of air hit me and the scent of acrid smoke filled the air. And then I heard the cracking.

I spun around.

Smoke drifted all along the top of the tube. Above us, the blast had spooked the sharks, which all darted about wildly.

A web of cracks was spreading quickly through the glass in the center of the tube. Water began dripping through, raining onto the floor. The cracks grew bigger as the water pressed down from above. The glass wasn't going to last more than another few seconds.

And when it went, the shark tube was going to flood with us inside it.

SHARK ODYSSEY

The cracks in the glass ceiling widened. Water began to gush through.

My hands were still cuffed behind my back. "You need to unlock these!" I yelled. "I can't swim like this!"

Marge ignored me, staring at the glass. Thankfully, Bubba came to my aid, though his hands were shaking with fear so badly he could barely hold his keys.

Marge whipped out her radio and called to her security men. "We are trapped inside the shark tube and it's about to blow. Get down here and open the doors. Now!"

I watched the web of cracks spreading through the tube all around us. "I don't think we have time for that," I said.

Bubba had given up any pretense of being tough. "I

don't want to die," he whined. "Not like this. I don't want to be eaten by sharks!"

"We don't have to worry about the sharks," I told him. I wasn't completely sure if this was true—Taurus might be trouble—but I needed Bubba to calm down and unlock my cuffs. "None of them are man-eaters."

"Except for that bull shark," Marge said. "That guy's a cold-blooded killer."

Bubba burst into tears. It wasn't dignified in any way. For a big man, he cried like a little girl. "Why?" he bawled. "Why is this happening to us?"

Someone responded on Marge's radio, but between the steel doors and the water above us, the transmission came through garbled. "I do not copy," Marge said desperately. "If you can hear me, get off the radio and open the doors!" Then something else occurred to her, and she added, "And if you see a man in a orange Astros cap up there somewhere, arrest him!"

Bubba was so upset he couldn't control his hands. He fumbled the keys onto the floor.

"Officer Stackhouse, please," I pleaded. "If you don't unlock my cuffs, I'm going to die."

"We're all going to die," Bubba moaned. "We're gonna be ripped to shreds by sharks!"

"We won't," I said. "If we don't panic, we'll be fine. In fact, I think we'll be able to swim right out of here."

Marge turned to me, surprised. "How?"

"The water's going to come through pretty strong at first," I said. "But once the tube fills up, that will stop. And then we ought to be able to swim. It's not that far to the surface."

"But if the tube is filled, we'll be underwater," Bubba mewled.

"I know," I said. "We'll have to time it just right."

Bubba nodded. His cheeks were still wet with tears, but my plan made sense. "And you're sure the sharks won't come after us?"

"Absolutely. Even the bull won't. He's too well fed to come after something as big as a human." I did my best to lie as confidently as possible, although it was difficult. Taurus was circling the tube slowly, like he knew what was going on. It was extremely unnerving.

My words still worked, though. Bubba calmed down enough to grab the keys off the floor. He made another attempt at the lock.

There was a loud pop as a huge crack shot across the ceiling. A web of smaller fractures blossomed around it.

To my surprise, Marge was staying calm. She was definitely scared, but unlike Bubba, she was holding it together. "I think this is it," she said. "Get ready."

At the last second Bubba finally managed to fit the key into the lock. There was a click as he turned it, one of the cuffs sprang open, and suddenly my arms were free.

There was no time to thank Bubba, though. Instead I sucked in as much air as I could and clamped my jaw tight.

The middle of the glass tube collapsed. A wave of water exploded toward us. I tucked down and braced for it, but it still bowled me off my feet. I tumbled backward and bounced off something hard, maybe the steel door, maybe the floor . . . I had no sense of where I was, or even of up and down. The water surrounded me, chilling me through. As I struggled to figure out which way was up, a few dark shapes shot past me. Sharks. They were only small ones who'd been dragged along in the surge of water, but they still triggered a primal fear in me.

The salt water stung my eyes, but I kept them open, trying to figure out where I was. I'd been pushed back down the tube, close to the steel door. Marge and Bubba were close by. If the sharks had scared me, they'd completely terrified Bubba. His eyes were so wide they looked like headlights.

I had no idea how long I'd been underwater. It was probably only a few seconds, but it seemed like much longer. The miniature tsunami had hit me so hard it had knocked the wind out of me. I was desperate to breathe, but I didn't have time to swim all the way to the surface.

Then I noticed that directly above me was a large bubble of air. Some of the glass had still held, and there was a gap at the top, though the water was rushing to fill it. I kicked upward and broke through. There were only a few inches left, but there was oxygen. I tilted my head back and sucked in air.

Marge and Bubba surfaced close to me, having followed my lead. They both gasped for breath as well, but the water was rising quickly.

"We have to swim now," I told them, then took in as much air as my lungs could hold.

The water swallowed us up again.

The tube was now full, but as I'd figured, the rush of water had abated. There was no more current pushing against us. It was still a long way to the surface, though. And there were sharks everywhere.

I willed myself to be calm. I found myself thinking back to the first time my father had ever taken me snorkeling, off the coast of Kenya. "If you ever get pulled under," he'd told me, "don't panic. Panic uses oxygen. You have a lot more air in your lungs than you realize. Just stay calm, ride out the undertow, then swim up."

I swam toward the middle of the tube. Almost all the glass had been blown out, save for a jagged fringe along the edge of the steel ribs. I steered clear of that. The last thing I needed was to cut myself, get blood in the water and spark a feeding frenzy. I rose through the gap in the tube and kicked for the surface. Below me, Marge and Bubba followed.

The shark tank was thirty feet deep: three stories, though it seemed more like a hundred as I swam up through it. The water was deathly cold—and my heavy winter jacket was of no use against it. In fact the jacket was now an additional threat to my life. There hadn't been time to peel it off after Bubba had finally undone my cuffs. Now it was saturated with water and weighing me down like an anchor. I tried to wriggle out of it, but couldn't get free and only ended up wasting precious seconds. As much as I tried to be calm, my muscles were still screaming for air. I kicked desperately, struggling toward the surface.

I was only about ten feet short when Taurus slammed into me.

I don't know if the bull was attacking. He might have merely been trying to chase me out of his territory. After the blast, he was no doubt on edge—and then I came swimming through his turf. Whatever the case, getting rammed by a seven-foot-long man-eater is absolutely terrifying. The shark knocked me sideways, blocking me from going any higher— and in my fright I coughed out the rest of my air.

Taurus circled around and came at me from the front this time. The bull moved with staggering speed, carving through the water like a torpedo. His mouth gaped open, displaying several rows of razor-sharp teeth.

Somewhere in the back of my brain, I remembered Dad telling me about swimming with sharks and what to do if one ever got too aggressive. Oddly, it was the exact same advice he'd given me for dealing with Vance Jessup.

I made a fist, and as Taurus closed in, I punched the shark in the nose.

The sensation was surprisingly soft, like hitting a sponge. The bull veered away, disappearing into the distance with only a few flicks of his tail.

I had no idea if I'd scared him off, or if he was merely circling to hit me from behind again. I didn't plan to stick around and find out. I aimed for the surface.

Unfortunately, the remaining ten feet might as well have been a mile. The cold water had sucked the energy from my body, and my saturated jacket was so heavy I could barely move my arms. Swimming was now a herculean task. I tried as hard as I could, but I didn't seem to make any progress at all. My brain grew fuzzy from the lack of oxygen. My vision tunneled. My body felt like it was shutting down.

Suddenly someone plunged into the water beside me. The sharks around me darted away in fear. In my addled state, I couldn't even make out who the person was through the cloud of bubbles surrounding them.

Whoever it was reached out, grabbed my jacket, and yanked me upward.

I burst through the surface, gasping for air. The moment fresh oxygen hit my lungs, I felt like I was back from the dead. My strength instantly came back. My mind sharpened and my vision cleared. I started treading water and found out who'd jumped in to save me.

My mother.

Her eyes were wide with fear. At the time I thought she was worried about the sharks, though I later realized she was really worried about *me*. She'd just witnessed my near death by drowning and shark attack. "Are you all right?" she asked.

"Yes," I gasped.

"Hang on to me," she ordered. "I'll get you out of here."

Now that Mom had proved it was safe, two security guards leaped in beside us, splashing into the shark pool like depth charges. Seconds later they surfaced with Bubba and Marge, who both gulped air as I had.

Mom looped an arm around me and sidestroked to the shallowest area of the shark tank. There was a low glass wall here that normally rose to only a few inches short of the surface. This allowed the smaller sharks to access the shallows while keeping the bigger sharks out. Since the water level had dropped in the shark pool due to the flooding of the tube, the glass wall now poked out above the surface. Mom helped me clamber up onto it. Water cascaded out of my clothes.

"I thought you were with J.J.," I said to her.

"I never made it," she said. "Building security kept me waiting in the lobby. And then word came over the radio about you and Marge being trapped in the tube. So I ran over. I didn't realize that . . ." Mom's voice hitched, as though she were having trouble finishing the thought. "I had no idea that it'd collapse." After that, she threw her arms around me and hugged me as tightly as she could.

I hugged her back, thinking about what she'd done. I wasn't quite sure how long it had been from when the tube had locked until Mom had rescued me. Fear screws up your sense of time. It had only been a few minutes at most, though. And Mom had run halfway across the park in that time. That would have been a practically Olympian pace. I could hear her heart thumping wildly in her chest, still spiking from the exertion.

Beside us Marge, Bubba, and the two guards who'd saved them clambered up onto the glass wall as well. Marge looked exhausted. Bubba was still gibbering with fear. "Sharks," he whimpered. "Sharks everywhere."

I broke the hug with my mother. "The tube *didn't* collapse," I informed her. "Hank the Tank blew it up."

Mom reacted with astonishment. "How?"

"He put some kind of explosive on it. There was a remote detonator."

Mom's eyes narrowed angrily, but then I started shivering and she grew concerned about me again. "We need to dry you off," she said.

From the top of the glass wall, we could get to the edge of the exhibit. There were now lots of people crowding the viewing deck. Most of them were park security, but there were also the Shark Odyssey staff and some random Fun-Jungle employees who'd raced over from other exhibits. (It appeared someone had thought to prevent tourists from coming in.) Several people reached out to help Mom and me climb over the wall onto the viewing deck. Others helped us pry off our wet jackets and put their dry ones around us.

Bubba and Marge came over the wall behind us, though they needed the help of a lot more people to do it.

The park's emergency medical staff burst through the doors. I caught a glimpse of a crowd of tourists gathered around the building, being held at bay by a few guards. The medics surrounded Bubba, Marge, and me, wrapping us in warm blankets and checking our vital signs. Mom and the guards who'd gone into the tank for Bubba and Marge grabbed blankets too.

Next, the policemen who'd been assigned to take Dad into custody arrived with Dad in tow. Apparently, they'd realized this was more important, although Dad was still handcuffed. The cops brought him directly to me.

"Are you all right?" he asked.

"Thanks to Mom," I said. "She dove into the shark tank to get me."

Dad looked to Mom, who shrugged as though this were no big deal. "Of course she did," Dad said. Then he gave her a kiss so big I had to avert my eyes.

The other police were checking on Bubba right next to us. He was wrapped in several blankets, but a great deal of his pale white flesh still peeked out from under them. He didn't seem to care, though. Now that he was safe, his fear had turned to anger. "Did anyone catch the guy who did this?" he demanded. "The guy in the Astros cap?"

"We got him," a security guard reported. According to the patch on her uniform, her last name was Patmore. "He was caught trying to slip out of the employee entrance to the park."

"Where is he?" Marge asked.

"The park-security holding cell," Officer Patmore replied.

Bubba glanced toward my father. "Unlock his cuffs," he ordered his policemen.

"But he interfered with an arrest—" one began.

"An unlawful arrest," Bubba corrected. "He was only trying to protect his kid. The guy in the holding cell is our man. Has he said anything?"

Everyone looked to Officer Patmore expectantly.

"No," she admitted. "He took the fifth and demanded a lawyer."

Bubba sighed with annoyance. "Of course he did. The guy's a pro. We won't get squat out of him."

An idea suddenly came to me. Despite everything that had happened, I broke into a smile. "I know how to make him talk," I said.

THE INTERROGATION

Dad ran home to get Mom and me some new clothes, and once we were dressed and warm, we headed to Mom's office at Monkey Mountain. Marge and Bubba met us there. While Marge had some spare uniforms at FunJungle, Bubba didn't, so he'd been forced to dress in clothes from FunJungle Emporium: neon-blue sweatpants, an Eleanor Elephant T-shirt, and a lime-green XXXL "FunJungle Fanatic" sweatshirt. Rather than a policeman, he now looked like a color-blind tourist.

None of the other police or security staff were with us, although a few guards were posted outside the office door. The office wasn't big enough for a crowd—and Bubba wanted privacy anyhow. Dad and I were only there because Mom had insisted on it in return for the police using the Monkey Mountain facilities.

The GPS tracker on my ankle bracelet had shorted out in the shark tank, so Bubba removed it. He didn't bother putting a new one on, as he now had another suspect in the crimes at FunJungle:

Hank the Tank sat in a chair with his hands cuffed in his lap. He still wore his orange Astros cap, but for once he didn't have his sunglasses, as Bubba had confiscated them. This was the first time I'd ever seen his eyes: They were surprisingly small and dark, like a pig's. Although he'd been caught fleeing the scene of a crime, Hank didn't look the slightest bit concerned. In fact he wore a cocky grin, as though facing off against us was going to be fun.

Bubba, however, was back to his normal, tough-guy self. Any weakness he'd shown in the shark exhibit was long gone. "I'm only giving you one chance to come clean," he warned Hank. "And if you don't, we'll do this the hard way."

"What's that?" Hank asked, nodding toward Bubba's protruding belly. "You gonna sit on me?"

Bubba furrowed his brow. "Why'd you rig the tunnel to blow?"

"I don't know what you're talking about," Hank replied.

"Like heck you don't," Marge snarled. "We've got security video of you entering the shark exhibit shortly before the tube went and taking off right after."

"There's a lot of guys who look like me," Hank said, knowing full well that wasn't true.

There was a sudden commotion outside the door. Then J.J. McCracken stormed in, seething with anger. Everyone snapped to attention, but J.J. didn't pay us any mind. He went right up to Hank and demanded, "Where's my koala?"

"I don't know what you're talking about," Hank said again, like it was his mantra.

"Don't shovel that manure at me," J.J. told him. "I know who you are and I know who you work for. You might think you're making the right move, protecting Warren Ogilvy like this, but you don't know that snake the way I do. He'd sell his own mother down the river if he thought it'd save his skin. His lawyers won't bail you out of this. They'll throw you to the lions. But if you tell us the truth, I'll do my darndest to make sure you get off scot-free. So why don't you wise up and spill the beans?"

"You're making a mistake," Hank said. "I'm just an innocent tourist."

J.J. snapped. He turned so red I thought steam might whistle out of his ears. "Don't play dumb with me! It's bad enough that you destroyed my shark exhibit, but there's a koala's life hanging in the balance here!"

He might have raged on, but Marge placed a hand on his arm and said, "Before you go on, sir, we have a plan to get Mr. Duntz here to talk."

J.J. whirled on Marge. "We do?"

"Teddy does," Mom corrected. "It was all his idea."

Now J.J. turned to me, intrigued. "Do you, now?"

"In fact, we were just about to implement it." Bubba approached Hank, smiling, and launched into the speech we'd all prepared. "Perhaps we've made a mistake here, Mr. Duntz. Perhaps you really are just a tourist. But it's also possible that you're lying. Luckily, this zoo has an animal with the ability to sense lies better than we humans can. Mr. Duntz, meet George."

With that, Mom raised the blinds on the window to the primate holding cell, revealing Furious George, who was still in solitary confinement. George sat behind the bars on his side of the cell, calm as could be, playing with some toys. He didn't even notice us watching him.

Hank grew slightly uneasy, unsure where this was going. "You're jerking my chain," he said. "That monkey can't tell you anything."

Mom sighed with annoyance. "First of all, Mr. Duntz, George isn't a monkey. He's a chimpanzee, which makes him an ape—"

"Same difference," Hank said.

"Actually, there's a great deal of difference," Mom countered. "For starters, apes are far more closely related to humans than to monkeys. In fact, chimps share over ninety-eight percent of their DNA with humans, which means they're more closely related to us than to gorillas. And because of that close relation, they're extremely perceptive to human emotions. Far more than most humans are. And George is the most perceptive one I've ever met. He's incredibly attuned to the subtle behavioral changes people make when they're not telling the truth—and he doesn't like that. He doesn't like that at all."

Hank eyed George warily. "What do you mean, he doesn't like that?"

I almost started laughing and had to step away so Hank wouldn't see me. Although everything Mom had said about chimps sharing DNA with humans was true, the part about being living lie detectors was a lie itself. However, Mom sold it extremely well. Hank, who'd been so tough in front of his fellow humans, was visibly nervous about the chimpanzee.

"Trust is very important to animals," Mom told him. "If George senses he can't trust you, he gets upset."

"Upset?" Hank echoed. "What's he do if he gets upset?"

"Well, there's something else that chimps and humans have in common," Mom replied. "Sadly, we're two of the most violent species of animal on the planet. But you shouldn't have anything to worry about. Like you said, you've been telling the truth, right?"

"That's right," Hank said, although he'd now lost a great deal of his bravado.

"Then I'm sure you and George will get along famously," Mom said. She opened the door to George's cell and waved Hank through it.

Hank hesitated, worried, but then passed into the other room.

George glanced up at his new visitor. I couldn't tell if he recognized Hank or not, but the moment he saw the orange cap on his head, he got furious. He sprang at the bars, screaming and baring his teeth.

Hank nearly leaped out of his own skin. Some of the toughest guys in the world can turn into complete cream puffs around animals. In the same way that Bubba had freaked out near the sharks—or Vance Jessup had panicked on finding the snake in his gym bag—Hank instantly changed when confronted by the angry chimp. He shrieked in fear and scrambled for the door, only to find that Dad had already closed and locked it. Hank jiggled the knob desperately. "Let me out of here!" he whined to Mom. "Your chimp's going psycho!"

"That's his standard response to liars," Mom shouted through the window.

"I haven't even said anything!" Hank cried.

"You said you'd been telling the truth before," Mom said. "Was that a lie?"

Hank's eyes darted toward George. As I'd guessed, he had

no idea that his orange cap was the real trigger for George's anger, but since he was wearing it, George was directing that anger toward him. Even J.J., who hadn't been briefed on the plan, fell for it.

"What's going on here?" the billionaire asked. "Did Hank hurt that chimp?"

"No," Dad explained, keeping his voice low so Hank couldn't hear through the glass. "But someone in an orange cap like that probably did. The thing is, chimps usually don't perceive slight physical differences between humans: Two men look as similar to them as two male chimps look to you. However, some chimps—like George—are very responsive to colors and clothing. Thus, he perceives virtually any man in an orange baseball cap as the one who caused him distress before."

J.J. chuckled, impressed. "So that chimp isn't some living lie detector?"

"No," Dad said. "But Hank doesn't have to know that."

We all looked back through the window. George was trying to throw his toys at Hank, but they all bounced harmlessly off the bars. So George then resorted to throwing something he *knew* would fit through the bars. His own poop.

The first salvo caught Hank in the chest. Now Hank really lost it. "That's poop!" he screamed. "Your freaking monkey's throwing poop at me!"

"He's a *chimp*," Mom corrected. "And yes, they do that when they get agitated." She signaled to Dad to open the door.

Hank raced for it, though before he could make it to safety, George nailed him with something that appeared to have just come out of his digestive tract. It knocked the orange cap right off Hank's head. Hank squealed with disgust and scrambled into the office.

The instant he was gone, George relaxed. He dropped to the floor of his cage and allowed Mom to come right up to the bars. He now chattered to her, pointing toward the door, as though trying to tell her who Hank was.

Meanwhile, in Mom's office, Hank was a gibbering, quivering mess. He reeked of flop sweat and chimp poop. Normally, I might have felt badly about subjecting someone to this, but since this was the very man who'd nearly drowned me in a tank full of sharks that morning, I found the whole thing quite pleasant.

"This was a violation of my rights!" Hank whimpered. "You're not allowed to torture people!"

"We did no such thing," J.J. told him. "All we did was give you a rare one-on-one encounter with one of our animals. Most tourists here would kill for an opportunity like that. In fact, perhaps we should give you another chance. . . ."

"No!" Hank shrieked. He bolted for the office door, but Bubba caught him.

"Aw, come on now, Hank." J.J. grinned, enjoying this. "George there's normally gentle as a kitten. The only time he's ever like this is when someone's not telling the truth."

Even in his terrified state, Hank still struggled to remain tough. "I *have* told you the truth!" he said.

"Well, let's see if George thinks that's true," J.J. said, then nodded to Bubba, who dragged Hank back toward the chimp's cell.

The last of Hank's resolve slipped away. "All right!" he cried. "I admit it! I rigged the tube to blow! But I wasn't trying to hurt anyone, I swear! In fact, I took steps not to. I was watching the entrance to make sure no one was in the tube. You guys just came in the wrong way—and by the time I realized, it was too late!"

Bubba stopped dragging Hank. "Why were you trying to blow the tube at all?"

"To make FunJungle look bad," Hank explained. "To create a disaster that looked like it *could* have killed people, so tourists would think FunJungle was too dangerous to visit."

"Who paid you to do this?" J.J. demanded. "Ogilvy?"

Hank wavered, trying to protect his boss.

Bubba started dragging Hank toward George's cell once again.

Mom came back into her office from the cell. "I hope you like chimp poop," she warned. "I fed George a really big meal last night."

Hank cracked. "Yes, it was Ogilvy! He wants to bankrupt FunJungle!"

"So he paid you to destroy the shark exhibit and steal the koala?" Marge asked.

"No!" Hank exclaimed. "He only asked me to cause *one* disaster. I didn't touch the koala!"

"Oh, please," J.J. snorted. "You expect us to believe that someone else just happened to steal it while you were around?"

"Yes!" Hank cried. "I admit, I *considered* stealing Kazoo. I paid Freddie Malloy to help me figure out what to target and feed me the security codes. The koala was the first thing he suggested. But someone else took him before we could do anything, so we shifted our target!"

All of us in Mom's office exchanged glances, surprised by this revelation.

"You think he's telling the truth?" Marge asked.

"He's already owned up to the shark tank and ratted out Ogilvy," J.J. said. "Why would he keep lying about Kazoo?"

Marge turned back to Hank. "You're saying a stolen koala wasn't good enough for you? You had to go and destroy something else?"

"Yes!" Hank now looked like he was at the end of his rope. "Ogilvy said if the koala was recovered, the whole thing would blow over. He wanted something bigger. Something that'd scare visitors away from FunJungle. I didn't mean to hurt anyone—and I didn't touch the koala! That's the truth, I promise!"

He certainly sounded like he was being honest to me. J.J. seemed to think so too. "All right," he told Bubba. "Don't take him in with George."

"You sure?" Marge asked. "The guy caused you a couple million in damages this morning. We could lock him in with that chimp as long as you'd like."

"That wouldn't be very nice—for the chimp," J.J. said.

Bubba sat Hank back in the chair again. "So you fully admit to sabotaging the shark tank this morning?" he asked.

"Yes," Hank said meekly. He now seemed only a shell of the tough guy who'd sat in that chair minutes before.

"And you admit that both Walter Ogilvy and Freddie Malloy were complicit in this?" J.J. asked.

Hank nodded.

"Lock him up," J.J. ordered.

Marge obediently took Hank by the arm. He didn't even try to fight her as she led him toward the door. In fact he seemed relieved to be getting farther away from George.

"You sure you didn't take that koala?" Marge asked.

Hank shook his head. "I swear it wasn't me."

Bubba turned to me, visibly unhappy about what he had to say. "Sorry, Teddy. It looks like I still need to bring you in."

"What?" Mom cried. "Teddy just handed you Hank! If it hadn't been for him, the shark tube would have blown and no one would have known Ogilvy was behind it!"

"I understand that," Bubba said sadly. "And I'll admit, Teddy might have saved my life today. But that doesn't change the fact that we still have a mountain of evidence against him."

I backed away, stunned this was happening. I'd been so sure I'd figured out who the thief was, it had never occurred to me that I might be wrong. I thought about running again, but I was trapped in the office. Besides, I couldn't run forever.

"This is ridiculous!" Dad protested. He turned to J.J. "Tell these guys Teddy's innocent! Hank's the criminal here. He already confessed to plotting against FunJungle—"

"But not to stealing Kazoo," J.J. said. I noticed he didn't seem nearly as sad about this as Bubba did.

Mom glared at him with disgust. "Are you actually saying that after everything Teddy has done for this park—for *you*—you believe he would have stolen Kazoo?"

"I'm saying that we need to recognize the facts." J.J. gave

Mom a pointed stare. "*All* of us do, no matter how much we don't want to. I thought Ogilvy was behind the koala theft, but he wasn't. Teddy's the only one left who could have possibly done it. And let's face it, the kid has a history of causing trouble around here. So if you want to be upset with someone, maybe it ought to be your son."

Before Mom or Dad could even respond, J.J. walked out, leaving us with Bubba—who looked sort of ashamed—and Marge, who looked like it was the happiest day of her life. "Let's go, Teddy," she told me, grinning from ear to ear. "Seems I was right about you all along."

UNDER ARREST

For the second time that day, I was marched through FunJungle in handcuffs. Once again, Bubba and Marge each held an arm of mine. Meanwhile, Hank the Tank was back in FunJungle security's holding cell. Industrial sabotage was a much bigger crime than the local police were prepared to handle, so J.J. had called some friends in the government and asked them to send federal agents.

Mom and Dad walked alongside Marge, Bubba, and me, although they'd given up on arguing that a mistake had been made, aware the argument would only fall on deaf ears. Now they were merely doing their best to comfort me.

"Don't worry," Mom said. "We'll get you out of this as soon as we can."

"We'll find the real thief," Dad assured me. "And everything will be right again."

"I know," I said, although it probably didn't sound convincing. I knew my parents were lying to me. Or at least they could only hope what they said was true. The fact was, I was in a huge amount of trouble.

Whoever had *really* poached the koala had set me up perfectly. All the evidence pointed to me, while there hadn't been so much as a shred to implicate them. The only hint that someone else was involved at all was the koala hair and poop Marge had found in my room, but I knew the argument that it had been planted there seemed awfully weak. (Who in their right mind would plant koala poop?) With me in hand, the police had no incentive to look for anyone else. That left Mom and Dad to continue investigating, and we were out of leads. The best we had was the tip Marge had received that the koala hair was in my room: I *assumed* that had come from the real thief, but there was no way to know for sure. And Marge refused to share anything more about the tip. She'd only admit that it was a phone call, and that it had been placed the previous afternoon.

All in all, I'd ended up the perfect patsy.

We passed through the front gates into the massive parking lot. There was a cluster of news vans by the park entrance. Pete Thwacker stood in the glare of the Minicam lights, talking to several reporters at once. I caught a few bits of his canned speech between gusts of wind. "We've simply had a technical glitch at Shark Odyssey. . . . I can promise you, it's nothing serious. . . . Nobody was hurt, but the exhibit might have to be shut down temporarily while we make repairs to improve the viewing experience for all our valued guests."

Despite my dour mood, I almost laughed. It was amazing how well Pete could twist the truth with a straight face. Although Tracey had threatened to fire him after the fake koala disaster, I knew she'd never do it. The park needed him too badly.

The police cars were parked a long way from the entrance. Even Marge understood that it was bad for business to have the police right at the front gates, so she'd asked Bubba to park well off to the side. Thankfully, the sleet had finally stopped, but the parking lot was now coated with an inch of cold slush, and bone-chilling winds blasted us as we crossed the wide expanse of asphalt.

"Wait!" someone yelled. "Teddy! Wait!"

Kristi Sullivan was running after us, waving frantically.

Marge tried to ignore her and keep walking, but Bubba stopped. At first I thought this was because Bubba wasn't in any hurry to take me away, but when I saw the excited look on his face, I figured out the real reason: He thought Kristi was cute. "Can I help you?" he asked, trying to sound as suave as possible.

"You're making a big mistake," Kristi told him. "There's no way Teddy stole Kazoo. He would never do anything like that."

"Well, he did," Marge said, though before she could go on, Bubba puffed up his chest and interrupted. "Officer Bubba Stackhouse at your service. What's your name, ma'am?"

"Kristi Sullivan. I'm a keeper in the small mammal house, though I worked with Kazoo until he was taken." Kristi looked to me apologetically. "I'm so sorry, Teddy. I only heard the news just now, when I got to work. I came as fast as I could. . . ."

"Do you have any evidence that someone else took Kazoo?" Bubba asked.

"Of course," Kristi said. "I shared my leads with Marge days ago. Charlie Connor, Freddie Malloy, and Flora Hancock all had motives. . . ."

"That wasn't evidence," Marge huffed. "That was specu- lation. The cold, hard facts say Teddy did this."

"No they don't," I said. "I was framed."

"Oh, not this malarkey again," Marge sighed. "Let's go, Bubba. We've wasted enough time as it is."

"Arresting the wrong person is a waste of time," Kristi countered. "While you've been focused on Teddy, the real thief still has Kazoo. And time is running out. That koala will starve to death soon!"

"He won't if Teddy admits where he's hidden him," Marge snapped, then dragged me away.

Bubba graciously tipped his hat to Kristi, still trying to make a good impression despite the circumstances. "It was a pleasure to meet you, ma'am. Should you come across any concrete evidence that exonerates Teddy here, feel free to contact me directly. . . ."

Kristi ignored him, tailing after me. "Teddy, is there anything I can do?"

"I don't think so," I said. "Thanks for trying, though."

"Yes," Mom said. "It was nice of you to run all the way after us on such a nasty day."

Kristi waved this off. "Oh, it's no big deal. I'm happy to get out of the small mammal house. It stinks in there." She shivered in disgust. "All those rats and bats and stuff. None of them are anywhere near as cute as Kazoo."

Something about this statement struck a nerve with me. I knew Kristi was trying to put my mother at ease, and yet the disgust she'd registered had been real. A thought began to take shape in my mind. I glanced at my father's watch. It was nearly eleven a.m. "Kristi," I asked, "did you say you just got to work *now*?"

Kristi shrugged, not nearly as bothered about being two

hours late as she should have been. "Yeah. But I'll stay later tonight. It doesn't really make a difference. The animals don't seem to care."

We reached the police car, which was covered with a thick layer of sleet. Marge held her hand up to Kristi, stopping her in her tracks. "The time for chitchat is over. Teddy has to go now."

Kristi nodded understanding and waved good-bye to me. "Be strong, Teddy," she said, then wiped away a tear and turned back toward FunJungle.

Bubba opened the police car door, but then stepped away, leaving me with my parents. "You can have a little time to say good-bye," he told us.

Marge rolled her eyes, as if Bubba's decency were a sign of weakness somehow.

I looked into the car. With the windows shrouded in sleet, the backseat was dark and cavelike. Just thinking about getting in made me shudder.

I turned back to my parents, who knelt in the cold slush to hug me good-bye. Mom was crying. Dad looked as sad as I'd ever seen him. And yet, while I should have felt upset or angry, I didn't. Instead my mind was racing. I turned back to Kristi and watched her walking away, in no particular hurry to get back to her job. Suddenly the thought I'd been working on became clear to me.

"Kristi isn't a very good keeper, is she?" I asked.

Mom and Dad blinked at me, surprised I'd chosen this moment to ask that question—but aware I must have had a good reason. "Why do you say that?" Dad asked.

"The animals are all on strict schedules, right?" I asked. "Even the ones in the small mammal house. Although Kristi said the animals don't care if she gets here two hours late, it *does* matter to them, doesn't it?"

"It should," Mom said, intrigued. "The animals might not have to be fed right at nine, but the keepers still need to be here by then to check on them, make sure they're healthy, clean their cages, and things like that. You're right. It doesn't sound like Kristi's paying much attention to her animals."

"This is all very fascinating," Marge said sarcastically, "but as much as I'd like to hear it, we can't sit here all day. Teddy, get in the car." She grabbed my arm and pulled me away.

Mom lashed out and caught my other arm. "Wait," she said.

"I've waited long enough," Marge told her.

"Then another minute won't make a difference, will it?" Mom got right in Marge's face and stared her down. "So unclench for once, Marjorie. This is important."

Marge was so cowed she let go of me and shrank back.

Mom turned back to me, any trace of anger gone. "Now then, Teddy, tell me what you're thinking."

"Well," I began, "I don't think Kristi was paying as much attention to Kazoo as she should have either. She had these huge stacks of fashion magazines on the desk in her office. The only reason for that would be if she was reading on the job, rather than working."

"They might have belonged to one of the other keepers," Bubba suggested, already smitten enough with Kristi to defend her honor.

"Maybe," I admitted, "but Kristi also told me the other day that taking care of the fake koala was even more work than the real one. She said the real Kazoo was easy to take care of, but he shouldn't have been if she was really doing her job. I was in the exhibit with her the night everyone thinks I took the koala. She didn't even check on him. She only changed his water." Bubba started to protest, but I cut him off. "I'm not saying she didn't *like* Kazoo—and I know she learned a lot about koalas and was really good at teaching people about them—but that's not the same thing as taking good care of them, right?"

"Right," Mom and Dad agreed.

"So she didn't take care of Kazoo," Marge groused. "What's the big deal?"

"Koalas don't move much," I explained. "They stay in the same place for hours at a time. Whoever stole Kazoo replaced him with a stuffed animal, and the tourists couldn't even tell the difference. So if Kristi wasn't paying as much attention to Kazoo as she was supposed to . . . maybe she didn't notice that he'd been replaced by a stuffed animal either."

My parents' eyes suddenly lit up with understanding. Dad grinned. "In fact, she might not have noticed for an entire day," he said.

"Meaning what?" Marge asked.

"Teddy didn't steal Kazoo the night he hid in the exhibit," Mom said. "Because Kazoo was stolen the night *before* that."

It took a moment for Marge to comprehend. Then she frowned. "That's ridiculous."

"Is it?" Bubba asked.

"No," Mom told him. "It's completely plausible. The thief took Kazoo and replaced him with the stuffed koala, but Kristi didn't notice. And since Kristi was the only keeper working the next day, there was no one else to catch the mistake."

"Therefore, it was more than twenty-four hours before anyone realized Kazoo was gone," Dad added. "But when you checked the security tapes, you only checked the ones for the night you *thought* Kazoo had been stolen, not for the night before, when he was *really* taken. Which explains why you only saw Teddy, but not the real thief."

Marge shook her head violently. "I don't buy it."

"It wouldn't be hard to check," Dad told her. "Security saves two weeks' worth of footage. We simply need to check the tapes from four nights ago. If Teddy's right, the true thief will be on there."

"Sounds like a wild-goose chase to me," Marge muttered, then reached for me again.

Before she could grab my arm, however, Bubba grabbed hers. "Now hold on," he said. "The last thing I want to do is lock up some kid who doesn't deserve it. There's no harm in making absolutely sure we've got the right person."

Marge shot him a look of betrayal, then pulled her arm free. "Have it your way. But when this all turns out to be a waste of time, don't complain to me." She slammed the door of the police car and led the way back to the park.

Mom and Dad turned to Bubba. "Thanks," Mom said.

"I don't like making mistakes," Bubba told her.

"We better hurry," Dad said. "If Kazoo was taken when Teddy says, then he's been without food for nearly *four* days now, not three."

"Oh no," I said, growing worried. "I hadn't thought of that."

Now that Kazoo's life was in even more danger, there was no time to waste. We all hustled back across the parking lot, through the employee entrance, and toward the administration building.

Pete Thwacker was heading up the front steps as we arrived, his press conference over. Now that the cameras weren't rolling, he was no longer smiling. Instead he was frowning at something on his smartphone.

Mom approached him as we all entered the building. "Pete, I was wondering. Did you have a hand in hiring Kristi Sullivan to work at KoalaVille?"

"I sure did," Pete replied, without looking up from his phone. "She's great, isn't she?"

In the lobby there was a great deal of security. Normally, it would have taken my family several minutes to pass, but because we were with Marge, the guards waved us through.

"Does Kristi have any sort of certification in animal care?" Mom asked.

Pete pursed his lips in thought. "I don't believe so, but honestly, how hard is it to care for a koala? All those things do is sleep. Kristi had something that's a lot harder to come by: stage presence."

"You mean you hired her because she's attractive," Mom said.

Pete shrugged. "Studies show that interacting with attractive women greatly increases our guests' enjoyment."

Mom frowned. "So instead of hiring a qualified keeper, you hired a piece of eye candy."

"Hey, it wasn't only my decision," Pete snapped. "A lot of people weighed in on Kristi. Now, if you'll excuse me, I have yet another crisis to deal with."

"Besides the shark tank?" Marge asked worriedly.

"Yes," Pete sighed. "Not nearly as bad, but still a crisis. Some moron leaked photos of our new tiger cubs to the press." He held up his phone, displaying a picture of them. "They're all over the Internet already. J.J.'s pitching a fit, demanding to know who's responsible."

Suddenly yet another mystery became clear to me. "I'd check out Arthur Koenig," I said. "I overheard him trying to sell them the other day."

Pete turned back to me, stunned. "You did? Why didn't you say anything?"

"I didn't know he was talking about the pictures. I thought he might have been trying to sell Kazoo. But he was definitely doing something illegal—he said he could go to jail—*and* he works in Carnivore Control."

Pete broke into a big grin. He turned to Marge. "Could you go find Arthur . . . ?"

"I've got other fish to fry right now," Marge said. "But I'll send someone else."

An elevator pinged open in the lobby. All of us piled into it except Pete. "Thanks, Teddy!" he said. "If it's really Arthur, I owe you big."

Bubba turned to me and chuckled. "You're a one-man police department, kid."

Marge glowered at me in response.

The elevator doors were just about to shut when Tracey Boyd slipped through them. She regarded us with surprise. "What are all of you doing here?"

"Heading to the security control center," Dad told her, and then explained my theory of how Kazoo had really been stolen one night earlier than anyone realized.

Tracey's jaw dropped as she listened. When we reached our floor, she got off with us instead of continuing on up to her office. "I've got to see this for myself," she said.

Security control was a small room. Two guards sat before a huge bank of monitors, which displayed camera feeds from all over the park. I caught glimpses of the front gates, Hippo River, the SafariLand tram loading station, and two dozen other locations. The guards reacted with surprise when we burst in. There was barely room for all of us inside.

Marge started to say something, but Tracey beat her to it. "I need to see the video from the koala exhibit the night *before* we think Kazoo was stolen," she told the guards.

"The night *before* . . . ?" one guard repeated, confused.

"That's right," Tracey said. "Four nights ago. Bring it up."

"Which cameras?" the other guard asked.

"All of them," Tracey replied.

The guards nodded and quickly typed commands into the system. The computers that controlled all the security footage hummed busily. Within seconds, camera views from the night in question began popping up on the screens, replacing the live feeds. Soon we had all four angles of the door to the koala exhibit's keepers' office, as well as several other feeds showing the various locations in KoalaVille.

"Sync them up, then play them all at once," Tracey ordered. "Starting with closing time."

The guards dutifully obeyed. They synced the video to five o'clock. We watched as Kristi Sullivan herded the last of the tourists out of the exhibit, then went around to the office door. After only a few minutes she emerged again, having taken care of Kazoo for the evening. She zipped her winter jacket, clapped on some earmuffs, and hustled toward the employee parking lot, looking like she was in big hurry to get home.

"Oh my," Mom gasped.

"What?" Dad asked.

"She didn't lock the door," Mom said.

"Back up the tape," Tracey ordered.

The guards did. We watched again, this time in slow motion. Sure enough, Kristi exited the koala exhibit and, in her haste, didn't bother to make sure the door closed behind her. On a normal day the door probably would have swung shut on its own, but a gust of wind caught it and prevented this. Instead the door came to rest lightly against the jamb without completely closing.

"J.J. spent millions on the security for this place," Tracey grumbled. "And yet none of it does any good if some idiot doesn't remember to lock the darn doors."

I was pretty astonished myself. After all the time I'd spent trying to figure out how the thief had so cleverly outwitted the security system, it turned out that they'd simply gotten lucky. First Kristi had left the door open. And then she hadn't noticed the crime had been committed for an entire day.

On the monitors, Kristi hurried off, unaware of the unlocked door.

But someone else was watching. Kristi wasn't even out of sight before a figure stepped out of the merchandise tent, clutching a stuffed koala. We couldn't see the person's face, though. They were wearing a winter jacket with the hood pulled up to shield them from the cold. Whoever it was looked at the stuffed koala they were holding, then at the exhibit, then at the stuffed koala again. Then they approached the keepers' office and tried the door. When it swung open easily, the thief slipped inside.

The thief didn't seem concerned about cameras at all. In fact the idea that there might be security never appeared to occur to them. They were only inside for a few minutes, and then they emerged once again, holding Kazoo, rather than the stuffed koala.

"Holy cow," Bubba said. "Teddy, it looks like you're innocent."

Mom and Dad cried out with joy.

"We told you!" Mom exclaimed to everyone.

Tracey turned to Marge, annoyed. "A twelve-year-old figured this out and you didn't?"

Marge didn't respond. Nor did she make any attempt to apologize for relentlessly trying to pin Kazoo's theft on me. Instead she glared at me angrily, apparently hating me more now than she ever had before.

While I was thrilled to see Marge get dressed down and hugely relieved to be proved innocent, I was still worried about Kazoo. On the security monitors, the koala certainly wasn't happy being taken out into the cold, and he wailed and squirmed wildly. The thief was handling Kazoo roughly in response, which made me think the koala probably hadn't been treated well at all over the last few days.

"Can we find an angle that shows our thief's face?" Tracey asked.

The guards ran through the various camera angles, but despite them all, the thief got lucky again. The jacket hood shielded their face perfectly. There wasn't a single direct view. We couldn't even get a glimpse of hair to determine the color— or for that matter tell whether the thief was a man or a woman.

Everyone else was equally frustrated. "A dozen cameras, and there's not one positioned to get us an ID?" Bubba sighed.

On the monitors, the thief tried to stuff Kazoo into a backpack. The koala fought back with surprising force, clawing with all four of its limbs. The thief responded in kind, angrily smacking the koala, which then sank its teeth into one of the thief's hands. The thief recoiled in pain, though we still couldn't get a view of the face. The thief was so focused on forcing the koala into the pack that their head was constantly angled downward.

"At least Kazoo's really doing a job on the jerk," Dad said.

"That's not surprising," Mom explained. "Koalas look so innocent; people always expect they'll be docile. But they can be extremely aggressive. They have sharp teeth and claws, and if you back them into a corner, they'll do what it takes to defend themselves."

The thief finally managed to overpower Kazoo and cram the poor creature into the backpack. Then, keeping their head down, the thief raced off camera and vanished from view.

"I don't believe it," Bubba groaned. "Not a single clear mug shot in the whole batch."

"Maybe we can still find one." Tracey turned to the guards. "Go back over all that footage frame by frame and see if you can find anything remotely usable. And then check the feeds of every camera between KoalaVille and the main entrance. Our thief must have passed one of them."

"That could take hours," one guard complained.

"I don't care!" Tracey barked. "Just do it! I want to know who took Kazoo!"

"Please," Mom pleaded. "Do what you can. Kazoo has been without food for almost four days. He's running out of time."

"We'll do our best," the guard said. "But there's a chance all this will come up empty. If that thief kept the hood over their face the whole time, we might never know who took Kazoo."

My parents sadly nodded acceptance of this.

"Actually, that's not true," I said. "I know who did it."

Everyone in the room turned to me, stunned.

"Who?" Tracey asked.

"Vance Jessup," I replied.

CAPTURE

Even though I'd proved my innocence, I ended up in the back of a police car. Only now I was a guest rather than a prisoner. Bubba was at the wheel, Marge was riding shotgun, and Mom and Dad were wedged in the backseat on either side of me. Tracey Boyd had demanded that I go along to help ID Vance Jessup. This made Marge even angrier than before. She could barely even look at me. Instead she stared out the windshield, her jaw clenched so tightly I thought her teeth might shatter.

Since Vance was a minor, Bubba was still on the case, as were his fellow juvenile officers, who were following us in a second police car. Bubba had called Principal Dillnut at my middle school, who had confirmed that Vance was there. Once he'd learned of the crime, Mr. Dillnut promised to take

Vance to detention immediately and keep him there until we arrived. Now we were all racing down the road toward town at ninety miles an hour, sirens wailing. It was as much fun as some of the thrill rides at FunJungle.

"Vance's hands and fingers are all bandaged up," I explained as we rocketed along. "I thought it was because he'd been in some fights, but Kazoo obviously did it instead. Vance's hands weren't hurt until *after* Kazoo was stolen."

"There's a thousand ways someone could get their fingers banged up," Marge said grumpily. "That's not enough to convict someone."

"We can check under his bandages when we get there," Dad said. "The bite marks ought to be pretty obvious."

"And what if he claims a dog bit him instead?" Marge asked.

"Then we bring in an expert," Mom said. "I'm sure that any of the zoo vets can tell the difference between a dog bite and a koala bite."

"Plus, there's other evidence against Vance," I told Marge. "Like the tip you got to search my room for koala fur and poop. That had to be from Vance."

"How so?" Marge asked.

"Because of when you got it," I explained. "If someone had *really* wanted to frame me for stealing Kazoo, it would have made sense to call you days ago, right after the theft.

But you didn't get the tip until yesterday afternoon. Vance must have known you didn't have any idea who he was. He was going to get away with the crime. So what's the point of going through so much trouble to plant the evidence in my room and alert the police about it?"

Marge looked at me blankly. This obviously hadn't occurred to her.

"He did it to settle a score with you," Dad concluded.

"Exactly," I agreed. "I embarrassed Vance really badly in school yesterday. He wanted to get even. *That's* why he framed me, not because he was worried about getting caught."

"What'd you do to him?" Bubba asked.

"Dunked him in the Toilet of Doom," I replied; then I thought to add, "It was self-defense."

Bubba laughed out loud. "I can see why he'd be embarrassed, all right." He turned to Marge. "You recorded the call, right? We could try to do a voice match with this Jessup kid. Between that and him having bite marks on his hand, I'd say that's all the evidence we need."

Dad said, "It'd be better if you could just get him to own up to the crime and tell us where the koala is. We need to find Kazoo fast."

"There's just one thing that's missing here," Marge said stubbornly. "A motive. Why'd this kid steal the koala in the first place?"

"Because he's a jerk," I said. "He does mean things all the time. He's the kid who forced me to dump the fake arm in the shark tank the other day. He probably just saw the opportunity to cause trouble and he took it."

Marge shook her head. "Doesn't sound very convincing to me."

Mom said, "You didn't seem nearly this concerned about motive when you tried to arrest Teddy."

"Teddy has a history of causing trouble," Marge countered.

"But he's never stolen anything," Mom shot back. "I'll bet this Vance Jessup has." She looked to Bubba for confirmation.

Bubba nodded. "We've had a few run-ins. But only for little stuff. Shoplifting and such. Nothing like this before."

I considered the crime again. It did seem a little odd for Vance to swipe Kazoo for no good reason. I had the sense that I was missing something, but I couldn't put my finger on it.

My thoughts turned to the koala. If Vance *had* taken it, he hadn't put much thought into the crime. He'd really succeeded by blind luck. It was doubtful that the kid had the slightest idea how to care for an exotic animal. My guess was poor Kazoo had probably suffered greatly in Vance's hands. I wondered if he was even still alive.

We skidded to a stop in front of my middle school. The

second police car parked right behind us. We all piled out and raced up the front walk.

It was lunchtime. The entire school was gathered at the windows of the cafeteria, excitedly watching the arrival of the police.

Before we even made it to the school doors, Mr. Dillnut exited, looking very worried.

"Where's Vance Jessup?" Bubba demanded.

"Er . . . I'm not sure," Mr. Dillnut admitted.

"What?" Bubba shouted. "I thought you put him in detention."

"I did," my principal replied. "But he got the jump on us. He told the proctor he had to go to the bathroom—and instead he must have fled the grounds."

"How long ago?" Marge asked.

Mr. Dillnut tugged at the collar of his shirt uncomfortably. "I'm not sure. Up to fifteen minutes, maybe."

Bubba grimaced. "He could be anywhere in town by now." He turned to the other police officers. "Get over to his house and stake it out in case he shows there."

The policemen raced back to their car and peeled out.

"He's not going back to his house," Marge muttered. "No kid with an ounce of brains would do that."

"That's why the rest of us are gonna comb the town for him," Bubba said. "Maybe we'll get lucky."

I glanced back toward the cafeteria windows. "Maybe we won't have to," I said. "I'll bet Vance's friends know where he's gone." Without waiting for an answer, I ran toward the cafeteria.

Everyone else followed me, but I got there ahead of them. I burst into the cafeteria and instantly spotted TimJim. It wasn't hard to find them, as they were a good six inches taller than almost anyone else in the school. Up until that moment I had always been afraid of them. But I surprised myself— and everyone else—by storming directly toward them. "I need to talk to you!" I demanded.

Xavier rushed into my path, apparently thinking I'd gone insane. "What are you doing?" he asked. "In case you've forgotten, these guys tried to shove your head in a toilet yesterday."

"I haven't forgotten anything," I said, then slipped past him and yelled at TimJim. "Where's Vance keeping the koala?"

Tim and Jim were thrown. They weren't used to kids confronting them like this. Both did their best to play dumb. Given that they *were* dumb, it shouldn't have been that hard, and yet they didn't do a very good job of it. It was a few seconds too long before one of them could figure out what a fake innocent response might be. "What are you talking about?"

"You know exactly what I'm talking about," I said. "Vance stole Kazoo, didn't he?"

"No," they said at once, although it was an obvious lie.

I was about to lay into them again, but before I could, someone behind me shouted, "That's not true and you both know it!"

I spun around to find Violet Grace there. She seemed stunned that the words had come out of her mouth. Everyone in the room suddenly turned to her. Even my parents, Marge, and Bubba regarded her with surprise. She shrank under the collective gaze, looking guilty.

"You knew about this?" I asked.

Violet averted her eyes, embarrassed. "Yes. Vance told me about the koala."

"Why?" I asked.

"Because he stole it for me," Violet said.

Everyone in the cafeteria gasped.

Violet quickly tried to explain. "I didn't ask him to do it! He just did it, thinking I'd be impressed or something."

"Why would Vance be trying to impress you like that?" I asked.

"Because he's had a crush on her since third grade," Xavier said.

Now the entire school turned to Xavier, surprised.

"None of you noticed?" he asked the crowd. "Really? I know he's tried to keep it a secret, but the guy practically drools every time Violet walks by."

Violet blushed, embarrassed by this. "*I* didn't know he liked me. Not until he showed up at my house the other night with the koala." The whole story suddenly came tumbling out of her; after keeping it bottled inside for the past four days, she couldn't contain it anymore. "My parents were out at a school meeting, so I was all alone—and suddenly Vance shows up at the door, saying he has a surprise for me. He totally freaked me out. First of all, he was all cut up and bleeding everywhere. And then he pulls this koala out of his backpack and says he got it for *me*. I thought it was a stuffed animal at first, but then it jumped out and scared the holy heck out of me. I always thought koalas were cute and all, but this one was *mean*. It started running around my house, squealing like a pig, knocking everything over and totally destroying the place. I got up on the couch and told Vance to get it out—but Vance didn't do anything. Instead he sat there, trying to explain that I should *like* him because he brought this crazy thing to my house. He said he was just going to get me some stupid stuffed koala at first, but then he realized he could get me a *real* one, which was like a thousand times cooler. As if I'd ever want this stinky, screeching, freaky thing."

I thought back to the tapes I'd seen of Vance the night he stole Kazoo. He'd originally been holding a stuffed koala— the one he'd intended to give Violet. But then Vance had seen Kristi leave the office door open. And so, on the spur of the moment, he'd decided to bring Violet the real thing instead, thinking he would *really* win her over that way. Then he'd swapped the toy for Kazoo. Only it had all worked out far worse than he'd expected. "I don't think he knew the koala would behave like that," I explained. "He probably thought it would be like a living doll."

"Well, it wasn't," Violet said. "Vance is an idiot. He didn't think anything through. He said he'd gone to Fun-Jungle to scope out the shark tank for some prank and then just swiped Kazoo on a whim."

I groaned, regretting the day I'd suggested the shark tank prank to Xavier even more. Not only had that led to Vance forcing me to pull the prank—but it had also indirectly led to the theft of Kazoo. "Why didn't you tell anyone about this?" I asked Violet.

"Because Vance told me not to," she replied. "I think he really expected that I would just fall in love with him when I saw he'd stolen a koala for me. And he was really upset when I didn't. I mean, like super angry. I told him he'd better take the koala back, and he said he couldn't because then they'd know he stole it. So then I said I was going to call the police—and he said that if I did that, he'd . . ." Violet trailed off, looking scared.

"Did he threaten you?" Mom asked.

Violet nodded, fighting back tears, then looked to me

again. "I *tried* to reach out to you anyhow, though. I gave you my phone number. . . ."

I grimaced, feeling like a fool. Under normal circumstances I *would* have called Violet. (Even if I'd suspected she was only using me to get to Summer.) However, a lot of other things had happened that day. The truth was, I'd forgotten Violet had given me her number at all.

But Vance hadn't, I realized. He'd been watching us through the cafeteria window. He'd *seen* Violet give me her number—and it had made him think I was a threat. Maybe he thought Violet was tipping me off about him and the koala. Or maybe he thought she was showing interest in me rather than him. Whatever the case, he decided to get rid of me. He had just learned I was a suspect in the koala's theft— so he snuck into our home and planted evidence in my room to frame me. He hadn't done it as revenge for embarrassing him, as I'd originally suspected. He'd done it to keep me away from Violet.

"Do you have any idea where Vance is keeping Kazoo?" I asked her. "It's important. He's dying."

Violet shook her head sadly. "Vance took the koala from my house that night, and I never saw it again. I was hoping he would take it back to FunJungle, but when he didn't, I . . . I was too afraid to ask. And if I called the cops, he'd know I was the one who turned him in." She shifted her attention toward TimJim angrily. "But they'd know. Vance tells them *everything*."

We all looked toward TimJim, only to find that while Violet had been distracting all of our attention, they'd been sidling toward the door. Now they made a break for it.

Bubba and Marge raced after them, but the boys had too big a head start. They were at the door before the police could take three steps.

As TimJim opened the door, though, Ethan Sokol and Dash Alexander tackled them. The football players broadsided them so hard I could hear the wind getting knocked out of them from across the room. The twins ended up flat on their backs, the jocks pinning them to the floor.

"Tell us where the koala is," Dash warned, "or we pound both of you into dog food."

"Even you two meatheads aren't strong enough to do that," Tim shot back.

"Oh, it won't be just Dash and me," Ethan told him. "It'll be *all* of us." He pointed toward the cafeteria.

The entire student body nodded agreement. If there was one thing that could unite every single person in our school, it was saving a koala from Vance Jessup. Even a few of the cafeteria ladies joined the crowd.

TimJim gulped in fear.

"His uncle has a garage in town!" Jim blurted out. "Jessup

Automotive! He's been keeping the koala there!"

I turned back to my parents and the police. Bubba Stackhouse gave me the thumbs-up sign—this was the info he needed—and then waved for me to come quickly. I started toward him, but Violet caught my arm.

"I'm so sorry," she told me. "I should have told someone sooner. If that koala's dead, I'll never forgive myself."

"It's not your fault," I said. "Trust me, I know how intimidating Vance Jessup can be."

Violet smiled, then released my arm. "Go get him," she said.

I grinned back, then raced out of the cafeteria. The entire student body followed me. Jessup Automotive wasn't that far from school, and this was the most exciting thing that had ever happened in town. No one wanted to miss it. They swarmed past Mr. Dillnut, ignoring his demands that everyone get back to class.

"This is not a holiday!" he yelled impotently at the crowd. "This is an unexcused absence for all of you!"

Bubba, Marge, Mom, Dad, and I all piled back into the police car. We peeled out of the parking lot.

Despite the urgency of the situation, I noticed both my parents were grinning at me.

"What's wrong?" I asked.

"Nothing," Mom said cheerfully. "It just seems you've made a lot of friends."

"Who was that cute girl who gave you her phone number?" Dad asked.

I could feel my ears turning red. "Nobody," I lied.

"She sure looked like somebody to me." Dad looked at Mom, and they both stifled a laugh, as though this was all hilarious.

I tried to change the subject. "Here's what I don't understand: Why would Vance steal Kazoo just to impress a girl? How could he possibly think that would work?"

"It wouldn't be the first time a man has done something incredibly stupid to get the attention of a woman," Dad told me. "In fact, I'll bet there isn't a man out there who hasn't made a fool of himself for love." He looked back at Mom, and they both smiled again.

"I still don't get it," I said.

"You will someday," Dad told me. "Maybe even sooner than you think."

It didn't take long to cover the few blocks to the garage, especially since the police car could tear through town at well over the speed limit. Jessup Automotive sat at the end of Main Street, right on the edge of the small commercial district. It was an old-fashioned garage and gas station that had recently gone out of business. The windows were boarded up. Behind it was a large yard surrounded by a chain-link fence. The yard was a maze of storage sheds and broken-down cars that had been pilfered for spare parts over the years.

Bubba braked to a stop by the gas pumps. He and Marge leaped out of the car, though when my parents and I tried to follow, they turned on us.

"Stay here," Bubba told me. "It could be dangerous back there."

"But . . . ," I began.

"When we find the kid, we'll bring him out here for you to ID," Marge said. "Now just sit tight and keep your nose out of our business for once."

I tried to protest, but Mom signaled to me to let it go.

Marge and Bubba slunk toward the boarded-up garage with their guns raised, like they were infiltrating a nest of professional assassins instead of going after a teenage boy with a stolen koala. They both seemed very excited to have an actual mission for once.

"Idiots," Mom muttered. "They'll probably end up shooting each other."

Bubba banged on the garage door. "Vance Jessup! We know you're in there! Come out with the koala!"

There was no answer.

My parents and I climbed out of the police car—it was too cramped and stuffy to wait inside—but we heeded Marge's warning and didn't try to follow her. Instead we waited by the gas pumps.

Behind us, people had begun to emerge from the businesses on Main Street, intrigued by the police activity. They filed out of the real estate office and the furniture store and the diner. One man came out of the barbershop halfway through a shave, his face still covered with lather.

The garage door was open. Bubba and Marge slipped inside.

A noise began to grow in the distance, a great murmur of voices. I glanced down Main Street. Several blocks away, a horde of students charged around the corner. It was my whole school, racing to see Vance's capture.

A weird, piercing screech suddenly came from the junkyard. It sounded like a large bird being strangled.

"That's a koala!" Mom exclaimed.

I'd never heard Kazoo make a sound before. But then I'd never seen him in distress.

Vance Jessup burst out of a storage shed and raced through the junky cars, wearing a backpack from which the angry koala noises emanated. Since the police were blocking any exit through the garage, he ran for the chain-link fence instead.

"He's out here!" Dad called to the police, while Mom yelled, "He's getting away!"

We heard Bubba and Marge scrambling somewhere back in the junkyard, but Vance had gotten a huge jump on them.

He quickly scaled the fence and leaped to the ground. Now the only thing standing between him and escape was me and my parents.

Before we even knew we were doing it, we were running to stop him. Mom and Dad flanked him on both sides, while I ended up facing him head on.

Vance froze, looking from one of us to the next, unsure what to do. He no longer seemed tough and menacing to me. Instead he seemed like a scared, desperate kid. There were a lot of new scratches on him, including a slash of claw marks across his face.

Kazoo was thrashing about in the backpack, screeching and howling.

"There's no point in running," Dad told Vance. "There's nowhere you can go."

"All we want is Kazoo," Mom said, trying to sound as soothing as possible. "His life is in danger. Just hand him over and we'll tell the police you cooperated."

Vance relaxed for a moment, as though ready to give himself up.

But then Marge and Bubba burst out of the garage and charged toward him. "Get him!" Marge howled.

Vance bolted. As I was the smallest and weakest of the people boxing him in, he came right at me. Dad and Mom grabbed for him, but he dodged them.

Without really thinking about it, I planted myself in his path. "Stop!" I yelled.

"Move it, loser!" Vance yelled back.

Although it only took Vance a second to reach me, a hundred thoughts went through my head. I considered getting out of the way, but decided against it. Every moment still counted for the koala. So I stood my ground, even though Vance was much bigger than me and coming on like a freight train. My father's advice about how to deal with bullies came back to me. Just pop him in the nose, he'd said. I'd never hit anyone in my life, but when I thought about all the things Vance had done to me—harassing me and threatening me with swirlies and framing me for a crime he'd committed— not to mention all the mean things he'd done to Xavier and dozens of other kids, and how he'd even threatened to hurt Violet if she told the police what he'd done, and how he'd been so rough with Kazoo when he'd stolen the koala and probably had been even rougher over the past few days . . . the next thing I knew, my hand had tightened into a fist, and it was swinging right toward Vance's face.

I connected harder than I expected because Vance was running right at me. He could have gone around, but his inner bully had kicked in. He wasn't merely trying to get away. He was trying to flatten me in the process. I don't think it ever occurred to him that I might try to fight back.

I caught Vance right on the chin, so hard that his teeth clacked. His head snapped back and he wobbled on his heels. For a moment he stared at me in shock, as though unable to believe that I'd punched him. And then he pitched forward, passing out on the ground at my feet.

Mom and Dad stared at him for a moment. Then Dad turned to Mom and grinned. "I told you that would work," he said.

Mom sighed, but then stole a glance at me, and I could see that despite her best intentions she was actually proud of what I'd done. She quickly turned her attention to Kazoo.

Luckily, Vance had collapsed face-first, so he hadn't landed on the koala, which was still thrashing about in the backpack.

"It's all right, Kazoo," Mom cooed softly. "You're safe now. We're here to help."

To my surprise, Kazoo calmed quickly, soothed by Mom's voice. Mom unfastened the clasps on the pack, and the koala poked his head out.

He wasn't in good shape. He'd lost a lot of weight in the last few days. His hair was matted and dirty, and a few patches had fallen out. He shivered in the cold. It seemed he'd used the last of his energy trying to fight his way out of the backpack. Now he simply collapsed on his side. He didn't even try to fight as Mom picked him up and wrapped him in her jacket.

"Is he going to be all right?" I asked.

"Yes," Mom said. "Thanks to you."

Dad put an arm around my shoulders. When Mom's back was turned, he winked and whispered, "Great punch, kiddo. Trust me, that guy's never gonna bother you again."

Marge and Bubba arrived, gasping for breath after their brief run. Marge looked like she was about to lay into me for getting involved in police business, but before she could, Mom said, "We need to get Kazoo to the animal hospital at FunJungle as fast as possible."

"Of course," Bubba agreed. Then he turned to Marge and threw her his keys. "Take my car. I'll stay here with Vance. Get the Fitzroys and the koala back to FunJungle, pronto."

Marge wasn't happy about being ordered to chauffeur us, but even she knew it was pointless to argue. "All right," she grumbled.

"Come on," Mom said to me, motioning toward the police car.

"I don't need to go back to school?" I asked.

"I think you've earned a day off," Dad said.

As we headed for the car, my fellow students arrived in force. They all swarmed around us, expressing concern for Kazoo and gaping at Vance Jessup.

"We saw you deck Vance!" Xavier crowed. "That was amazing!"

Lots of other kids echoed this. Dozens who had never even bothered to introduce themselves to me now shook my hand and patted me on the back.

I pushed through them all toward the police car. "I have to go," I told Xavier. "See you Monday?"

"You bet," he grinned.

As I reached the car, Violet Grace emerged from the crowd. "How's Kazoo?" she asked.

"He'll be all right," I told her.

Violet sighed with relief, then glanced at Vance's prone body. "Do you still have my phone number?" she asked.

I paused, halfway into the police car. "Yes."

The cheerleader gave me a shy smile. "Then call me sometime," she said.

Epilogue

ONE LAST SURPRISE

KoalaVille came down even faster than it had gone up.

Doc Deakin, the head vet at FunJungle, had done a miraculous job of quickly nursing Kazoo back to health, but that was of little comfort to the Australians. They had already been furious about the koala's theft. When the entire story was revealed— that FunJungle hadn't properly installed the security cameras in the exhibit, that a keeper hadn't locked the door, and worst of all that no one had noticed the koala's disappearance for more than a day—FunJungle's contract to display Kazoo was immediately revoked. Within twenty-four hours a team of official "koala ambassadors" arrived to take Kazoo back home to Australia. To J.J. McCracken's dismay, they still charged him the full five million dollars he'd agreed to for six months of koala rental.

And so, on a chilly, slate-gray day only a week after Kazoo had been recovered, my parents and I stood on the hill above KoalaVille, watching a demolition crew flatten the koala exhibit as quickly as possible.

"It's not a bad exhibit space," I said as the bulldozers churned toward it. "Couldn't they have put another animal in it?"

"Of course," Mom said. "But everyone would still think of it as Kazoo's old home—for a while, at least. And J.J. McCracken doesn't want that."

"The longer KoalaVille stands, the longer it reminds people of Kazoo," Dad added. "And Kazoo is a pretty big failure for FunJungle."

I nodded understanding. Under Pete Thwacker's direction, anything with Kazoo on it had been removed from FunJungle as quickly as possible. Banners had been taken down. Park maps were reprinted. The bazaar was packed up and, under the auspices of charity, thousands of Kazoo dolls, T-shirts, and other merchandise were shipped off to the developing world and distributed to poor people who didn't have enough toys, clothes, or koala-themed snow globes.

Luckily for FunJungle, at least the Kazoo story had a happy ending: The koala hadn't died. And while the press had a field day with the theft, they—and the public—never learned about the *real* disaster that had occurred that week: the sabotage of Shark Odyssey. Pete Thwacker had done an incredible job keeping a lid on the story, and perhaps more importantly, not a single shark had been hurt. However, it would be months before the tank could open again. All the sharks had been moved to a different facility while the tank was drained and the glass tube was rebuilt. Meanwhile, park engineers were dreaming up a few new bells and whistles that could be added to bolster the story that Shark Odyssey was merely closed "to enhance the viewing experience."

In the meantime, Hank the Tank was in custody—as was Freddie Malloy, who the police had caught at the San Antonio airport, trying to board a plane to Mexico. J.J. McCracken was now quietly pressing charges against Walter Ogilvy and the Nautilus Corporation. Ogilvy was actually suing back, claiming that placing Hank in a room with an angry, poo-throwing chimpanzee was illegal coercion, and therefore his confession had been given under duress. Since no one had apparently ever used a chimpanzee to extract a confession before, it was probably going to be a long time before the case was settled. "It might even go all the way to the Supreme Court," Dad had joked. "Hank the Tank versus Furious George and his flying feces."

As my parents and I watched, KoalaVille collapsed like a house of cards under the bulldozer. Within seconds, Kazoo's home was gone.

Seeing this bothered me more than I'd thought it would.

I turned away—and noticed someone else had come to watch the demolition.

Kristi Sullivan stood by herself uphill from us. The view was much better where we were, but Kristi had been avoiding my family. Or maybe it was just me. Mom said Kristi was still terribly embarrassed about her role in Kazoo's theft— and how all her mistakes had ended up implicating me. Now she seemed like she was on the verge of tears.

"Is Kristi going to be fired?" I asked.

"No." Mom sounded annoyed. "Though, thankfully, she's not going to be a keeper anymore. Instead Pete Thwacker transferred her to public relations. He claims she has some attributes that would make her a strong asset in dealing with the press."

"What's that mean?" I asked.

"That she's pretty," Dad explained.

Mom frowned at the very thought of this. "If that girl had been doing her job, Kazoo would never have been stolen in the first place. If that koala had died, it would have been her fault as much as Vance's. Any other zoo would have sacked her. But here they give her a promotion."

I looked toward Kristi again and caught her watching me. She quickly turned away, not wanting to meet my gaze. Then she pulled the hood of her parka over her head and hurried away.

Although Mom was obviously angry at Kristi, I didn't feel

that way toward her. Yes, she'd messed up, but she hadn't done anything wrong on purpose. I was still more upset with Marge, who'd been so determined to arrest me that she'd never bothered looking for the real thief. To my relief, Tracey Boyd also shared this opinion. In fact she was livid at Marge for botching the investigation. Marge wasn't going to be fired either, but she was getting demoted to shoplifting patrol while someone with actual crime-fighting experience was brought in to run park security.

Meanwhile Arthur Koenig *had* been fired. I'd been right: He was the one who had stolen—and then sold—the photos of the tiger cubs. This was a violation of his contract, and so FunJungle didn't even have to give him two weeks' notice. Security just showed up at his office and forcibly removed him from the park.

Most importantly, Vance Jessup had also gotten the punishment he deserved: twelve months in a juvenile detention facility. Which meant he wouldn't be bothering me again for a long time.

With Vance gone, TimJim had stopped bullying me—and everyone else—as well. Maybe they were just nicer without Vance around. Or maybe they'd been shamed after getting trounced by Dashiell and Ethan. Or maybe they were simply trying to be on their best behavior; Bubba Stackhouse was still figuring out if he could arrest them as accomplices in the koala theft, since they hadn't told the police about it.

All in all, school had become significantly better since I'd solved the crime and helped catch Vance Jessup. Maybe that was why I wasn't angry at Kristi Sullivan; while she'd unwittingly gotten me tangled up in the whole Kazoo business, I'd ultimately benefited from it. Lots of kids wanted to be friends with me now—and since Xavier was my friend, they wanted to hang out with him, too. Dashiell and Ethan were encouraging me to try out for the school soccer team in the spring. And Violet Grace now seemed to be interested in *me*, rather than just my connection to Summer McCracken.

At Dad's urging, I'd called Violet. ("When the head cheerleader asks you to call her, you call her," he'd advised.) But I didn't just do it because she was cute and popular. She was also really nice and turned out to be much less superficial than I'd originally thought. I'd been nervous on the call at first, but it had gone pretty well. At one point I'd mentioned that I could give her a private tour of FunJungle, and she'd jumped at the chance. She was going to come do it the next Sunday. I didn't really think of it as a date, but Xavier did. I think he was more excited than I was.

Truthfully, even though I liked Violet, the idea of a date with her—or whatever it was—felt a little bit wrong. Like I was cheating on Summer, somehow. Which was crazy, of course. Summer and I were only friends, she was going to school two thousand miles away, and she could be annoyingly distant at times. She hadn't even called me after Kazoo had been recovered. She'd only sent texts. A lot of texts, but still, it wasn't a substitute for talking. Plus, her own father didn't seem to care much for me. Yes, he acted friendly to my face, but over the past few weeks he'd threatened my parents' jobs and allowed me to be arrested—and yet, once I'd been proved innocent, he hadn't even thanked me for my help, let alone apologized. I'd come to realize that J.J. McCracken was far more slippery than I'd thought, and sometimes I even caught myself wondering how much Summer was like him.

While I was standing there, watching the bulldozers with my parents, my phone rang. It was Summer. Any doubts I'd had about her immediately melted away. I answered as quickly as I could. "Hey! How are you?"

"I should be asking *you* that," she said. "You've been through a lot more than me lately."

"I'm fine," I said. "Want to video chat?"

"Nah," she replied. "I've got a better idea. Turn around."

I did. To my surprise, Summer was standing only twenty feet behind me. She was wearing a pink parka and a big smile. Her usual bodyguards stood a few steps behind her.

I couldn't believe she was actually there. I kept staring dumbly, as though maybe she were simply a mirage.

Dad gave me a nudge with his arm. "What are you still hanging around here with us for?" he asked. "Go say hi."

I tucked my phone in my pocket and trotted over to Summer. "What are you doing here?"

"I live here," Summer teased. "Did you forget already?"

"I mean, why aren't you still at boarding school? Isn't there still a week until winter break?"

"I took all my exams early," Summer said, like this was no big deal. "I wanted to come home sooner. I wasn't enjoying school all that much."

"Really?" I asked. "I thought you liked it there."

Summer shrugged. "It's nice and all, but it's kind of dull. This place is a lot more exciting. Hippo murders. Koala kidnappings. Who knows what will happen next?" Summer lowered her eyes. "Plus, there were some things I missed here."

I wasn't sure, but it looked like behind her curtain of blond hair Summer was blushing. Before I even knew I was doing it, I said, "I missed you, too."

Summer turned even redder, but she looked up and smiled again. "My dad will probably flip, but . . . I was thinking of asking him if I could go to school *here* next semester."

Despite all the excitement I'd had lately—being framed for the koala theft and getting caught in the shark tube and punching out Vance Jessup—my heart now beat faster than it had for anything else the previous week. Suddenly I understood Dad's comment from a few days before—about how someday there'd be a girl I'd do anything to get the attention of, no matter how stupid it was.

"That'd be awesome," I said.

Kazoo is not the only koala in danger!

In fact, all koalas are in serious trouble. Sadly, these adorable creatures are heading toward extinction. The primary reason for this is habitat loss. Koalas can live only in eucalyptus forests—and those forests are being torn down all over Australia.

Koalas used to be hunted for their fur. Today, they die from malnutrition, from being hit by cars, and from being mauled by pet dogs—at a rate of thousands every year. Australia's wild koala population has dwindled from millions to a few hundred thousand.

Unless koala habitat is protected, soon the only place to see koalas may be in a zoo. And your grandkids might not be able to see them anywhere but a museum.

But this fight isn't over yet! The koalas can still be saved! To find out what you, your friends, and your school can do to help them, visit the Australian Koala Foundation online at savethekoala.com.

And if you're interested in helping protect other animals and critical habitats all around the world as well, check out the websites of these wonderful organizations.

World Wildlife Fund: worldwildlife.org

The Nature Conservancy: nature.org

Center for Biological Diversity: biologicaldiversity.org

Thanks!

Stuart Gibbs

Don't miss *Big Game*, the next
FunJungle book from
Stuart Gibbs!

Kazoo is not the only koala in danger!

In fact, all koalas are in serious trouble. Sadly, these adorable creatures are heading toward extinction. The primary reason for this is habitat loss. Koalas can live only in eucalyptus forests—and those forests are being torn down all over Australia.

Koalas used to be hunted for their fur. Today, they die from malnutrition, from being hit by cars, and from being mauled by pet dogs—at a rate of thousands every year. Australia's wild koala population has dwindled from millions to a few hundred thousand.

Unless koala habitat is protected, soon the only place to see koalas may be in a zoo. And your grandkids might not be able to see them anywhere but a museum.

But this fight isn't over yet! The koalas can still be saved! To find out what you, your friends, and your school can do to help them, visit the Australian Koala Foundation online at savethekoala.com.

And if you're interested in helping protect other animals and critical habitats all around the world as well, check out the websites of these wonderful organizations.

World Wildlife Fund: worldwildlife.org

The Nature Conservancy: nature.org

Center for Biological Diversity: biologicaldiversity.org

Thanks!

Stuart Gibbs

"I live here," Summer teased. "Did you forget already?"

"I mean, why aren't you still at boarding school? Isn't there still a week until winter break?"

"I took all my exams early," Summer said, like this was no big deal. "I wanted to come home sooner. I wasn't enjoying school all that much."

"Really?" I asked. "I thought you liked it there."

Summer shrugged. "It's nice and all, but it's kind of dull. This place is a lot more exciting. Hippo murders. Koala kidnappings. Who knows what will happen next?" Summer lowered her eyes. "Plus, there were some things I missed here."

I wasn't sure, but it looked like behind her curtain of blond hair Summer was blushing. Before I even knew I was doing it, I said, "I missed you, too."

Summer turned even redder, but she looked up and smiled again. "My dad will probably flip, but . . . I was thinking of asking him if I could go to school *here* next semester."

Despite all the excitement I'd had lately—being framed for the koala theft and getting caught in the shark tube and punching out Vance Jessup—my heart now beat faster than it had for anything else the previous week. Suddenly I understood Dad's comment from a few days before—about how someday there'd be a girl I'd do anything to get the attention of, no matter how stupid it was.

"That'd be awesome," I said.

THE STAMPEDE

I was helping walk the elephants when the first shot was fired at Rhonda Rhino.

It was a little after seven o'clock on a February morning. We had to walk the elephants early, because it couldn't be done during normal theme-park hours. The elephants were walked *through* the park, and tourists would just get in the way.

In the wild, elephants walk a lot. They've been known to cover more than fifty miles in a day, although the average is around twenty. They're built for walking (they're the only animal with four knees), but even at a massive, state-of-the-art place like FunJungle Wild Animal Park, they couldn't build an exhibit big enough to let them roam that far. So, in the interest of keeping them fit and happy, the staff walked the elephants in the morning, the same way normal people walked their dogs—only, the pooper-scoopers were a lot bigger.

I wasn't really supposed to be walking the elephants because I was only twelve years old. Any animal that weighs eight tons and is capable of lifting a small car can be dangerous. But since I was the only kid who lived at FunJungle, I'd gotten to know lots of the keepers well, so they cut me some slack—as long as I kept a safe distance and one of my parents came with me.

That wasn't a big deal. My father was always happy to bring me. As a professional wildlife photographer, he didn't mind getting up early; that was the best time to take pictures of animals in the wild. Plus, being with the elephants reminded him of life back in Africa. My mother was a famous primatologist, and before my folks had been hired by FunJungle, we'd spent ten years in a tent camp in the Congo while Mom studied chimpanzees. We'd all loved it, but a war had forced us to give up that life. Living in a trailer park behind the world's biggest zoo was probably as close to the African experience as we could get, but it still wasn't quite the same.

For starters, it was really cold that morning. The temperature in the Congo had rarely dropped below seventy degrees, while winters in central Texas could be bone-chilling. I had never even owned a sweater in Africa; Now I was wrapped in a ski jacket with three layers underneath. Our breath clouded the air in front of us, while steam rose off the elephants' warm bodies.

The elephants didn't seem bothered by the cold, though. The whole herd was walking, twelve elephants ranging in age from sixty to three. Eleanor, the matriarch, was in the lead, while the younger mothers and their offspring followed. (The park's only breeding male, Tembo, had to be kept apart and did his walks late at night.)

It took five keepers to control the elephants. Two flanked the herd on either side, gently directing them along Adventure Road, the park's main concourse. The keepers were all armed with brooms with the bristles wrapped in towels, which looked kind of like giant Q-tips. These were used to gently prod the elephants along, or to nudge them back into line should they veer off and try to eat an expensive piece of landscaping.

Bonnie Melton, the head keeper, brought up the rear. Bonnie had forty years of experience in zoos and knew more about elephants than almost anyone on earth. She was wrinkled as a prune—caring for elephants meant you spent a lot of time in the sun—but she had the enthusiasm of a high school kid. While none of her subordinate keepers seemed pleased to be working so early, Bonnie was chipper as could be, even though she had an industrial-size pooper-scooper slung over her shoulder.

"How's school going, Teddy?" she asked me, as we led the herd past the front gates.

"Pretty good," I replied.

"You making friends okay?"

"Yeah, I guess."

"You guess?" Dad repeated, then put an arm around me proudly. "Ever since Teddy knocked out the local bully, he's the most popular kid in school."

Despite the freezing temperatures, I could feel my face grow warm with embarrassment. "No, I'm not, Dad."

"The head cheerleader came over for a date," Dad told Bonnie.

"It wasn't a date," I corrected. "She only wanted to see FunJungle behind the scenes."

"Sounds like a date to me," Bonnie said, stifling a smile.

I tried to change the subject. "If anyone's the most popular kid in my school, it's Summer McCracken."

Bonnie nodded knowingly. "She would be."

Summer McCracken was the daughter of J.J. McCracken, the local billionaire who'd sunk a good deal of his fortune into building FunJungle. Summer was only a year older than me, and she was the first friend I'd made at FunJungle. Until recently, she'd attended prep school on the East Coast, but she'd asked to come home—so now she was the newest student at Lyndon B. Johnson Middle School.

"Is that why she transferred from that fancy-schmancy school?" Bonnie asked. "So she could be belle of the ball here?"

I shrugged. "Summer said life was more exciting here."

Bonnie laughed. "Here? We're thirty miles from the nearest city." She suddenly turned and yelled, "Kwame! Don't eat that!"

Kwame, a four-year-old elephant, sheepishly unwound his trunk from an oleander bush like a kid who'd been caught with his hand in the cookie jar.

"There *has* been some excitement here," Dad pointed out. "A murdered hippo. A stolen koala. An escaped tiger. Those kinds of things don't happen too often at prep school."

At that moment, Eleanor Elephant lifted her tail and deposited a large pile of poop on the concourse.

"Oh yeah," Bonnie said. "This place is a thrill a minute." Then she hoisted the pooper-scooper off her shoulder and hurried off to clean up after Eleanor.

According to Summer, poop had always been J.J. McCracken's biggest concern about letting the elephants walk around the park in the morning. "Oh sure, he'll *say* he's worried about safety," she'd told me, "but really, it's the poo. He's terrified the keepers will somehow overlook a big old elephant poop one morning and that some unsuspecting guest will step in it."

I could understand J.J.'s concern. Elephants make nearly two hundred pounds of poop a day—as well as enough pee to fill a bathtub. A janitorial team armed with industrial-strength cleansers had to follow the elephant parade around the park every morning. To that end, J.J. had looked for an alternative way to exercise the elephants—and had even considered building jumbo-size treadmills at one point. Nothing had panned out, though, so for the time being, the elephants were still walking.

"I'll bet that cheerleader *thought* it was a date," Dad said.

I turned away from the elephants and looked at him, surprised. "What?"

"She spent almost three hours with you," Dad told me. "I don't think she would have done that unless she liked you."

"Or she likes animals."

"What's her name again?" Dad asked. "Daisy?"

"Violet," I corrected. "Violet Grace."

"You should ask Violet to the movies sometime."

"No." I looked back toward Bonnie. I would rather have watched a person clean up elephant poop than have this conversation.

Dad wouldn't let it go, though. I got the sense this was a talk he'd been wanting to have for a long time. "Why not?

She's the head cheerleader and she likes you. Back when I was in middle school, I dreamed that would happen to me."

"I just don't want to ask her—that's all." Normally, I didn't like the idea of lying to my father, but at the same time, I didn't feel like telling him the real reason I didn't want to ask Violet out.

However, Dad was savvier than I realized. "Is this about Summer?" he asked.

I turned back to him, surprised. But before I could answer—or figure out how *not* to answer—Athmani Okeke came along.

Athmani was a wildlife security specialist from Kruger National Park in South Africa, where he'd worked to protect the animals from poachers. FunJungle had been open only six months, but already its hippo mascot had been murdered and a popular koala had been stolen, so J.J. McCracken had decided his animal security needed to be greatly improved. He'd hired Athmani as a consultant right after New Year's, and Athmani had been working so feverishly since then, he'd barely left the property. He was wearing a camouflage uniform from Kruger, because he still hadn't made it to town to buy any new clothes yet.

"Good morning, gentlemen!" he called, waving to both of us. Athmani spoke with a lilt in his voice, the way many native Africans did, which made his words sound a bit like a song. His skin was so dark that the whites of his eyes seemed to glow against it. "What brings you out here so early this morning?"

"Getting a little exercise." Dad shook Athmani's hand. "How about yourself?"

"I'm making sure my elephants are safe." Athmani held up his hand to me for a fist bump. Fist bumps were new to him, and he seemed to find them amusing.

I knocked my knuckles against his. "Do you think they're in danger?"

"Well, they're not while I'm around." Athmani grinned, but it didn't last long. "To be honest, I'm not crazy about them walking around the park like this. Lots of things could go wrong."

"We've got them under control," Bonnie said, trotting back over. Her pooper-scooper was considerably heavier and smellier now, though neither she nor Athmani seemed bothered by the stink. Their years around the elephants had made them immune. "And they love the exercise. They can't just sit in their exhibit all day."

Athmani frowned. "I'm not that crazy about their exhibit either. I have concerns about security in that part of the park."

"Like what?" I asked.

Before Athmani could answer me, a rifle shot rang out.

It sounded like it was coming from close by, loud and clear, shattering the morning quiet.

I know what a rifle sounds like. There are lots of hunters in that part of Texas. Our trailer sat right on the edge of the woods, and I'd heard plenty of rifle shots from there.

But I'd never heard one this close to FunJungle before.

Dad, Bonnie, and the rest of the keepers instantly went on alert. So did all the animals. By now we were close to Monkey Mountain, and the air was suddenly filled with startled whoops and cries from the primates. Elsewhere, birds squawked, zebras brayed, and big cats roared.

But the elephants responded most dramatically of all.

It's not a myth that elephants never forget. They have tremendous memories, particularly of emotional moments. Eleanor had been born in the wild and orphaned by poachers. When the rifle sounded nearby, she panicked. She trumpeted loudly and ran, leading her herd toward safety. The other elephants dutifully followed. They veered away from their keepers, off Adventure Road, stampeding in the opposite direction from the gunshot.

Unfortunately, Dad and I were right in their path.

"Look out!" Dad yelled, as though maybe I hadn't noticed twelve elephants bearing down on me and trumpeting at the top of their lungs. He grabbed my arm to drag me away, though I was already moving.

An elephant can run twenty-five miles an hour. Dad and I dove out of the way just in time. The herd thundered past us, then plowed right through some decorative landscaping. A group of topiary animals was flattened into mulch within seconds. One of the bigger females sideswiped a large oak tree, which toppled as though it had been hit by a truck, crushing a souvenir kiosk.

"Eleanor, relax!" Bonnie shouted, but her words were drowned out by the ruckus the elephants were making. Bonnie and the other keepers ran after the herd, but keeping up with it was hopeless. The elephants were too fast, and to make matters worse, they—like most animals—responded to fear by emptying their bladders.

The evolutionary reason animals (and in many cases, humans) do this is that it's hard to run with a full bladder. Plus, all that pee and poop weighs quite a lot—especially when you're an elephant—and when you're fleeing for your life, every last bit of weight you can leave behind helps. Within seconds, the ground was a minefield of elephant poo, with an ocean of pee around it. Understandably, the keepers were in no hurry to run through it.

Ahead of them, the panicked elephants stampeded onward—even though the Gorilla Grill, one of the most popular restaurants at FunJungle, sat right in their way. In the wild, there's not much that elephants can't plow through, except for the occasional baobab tree, so when they're on the run, they tend to go in a straight line, flattening anything in their path.

The restaurant was no match for them. The front of it was floor-to-ceiling windows. The herd smashed right through them, shattering the glass and splintering the support beams, then stormed through the dining area, crushing tables and chairs as though they were made of paper. They crashed through the far wall, trampled the outdoor furniture, and raced off toward Monkey Mountain.

I picked myself up off the ground and surveyed the wreckage. The restaurant was totaled. The service counter had been pounded into toothpicks. The grills had been upended and jets of flame flared from where the gas lines had snapped. Geysers of soda erupted from the previous site of the soft-drink dispenser. Then, with a shriek of rending wood, the roof caved in.

Bonnie and the other keepers kept after the herd, desperately yelling commands at them as though they were Labrador retrievers. "Stop! Stay! Bad elephants! Bad elephants!"

My father and Athmani both looked extremely concerned—although they weren't watching the elephants. In fact, neither seemed to notice the restaurant had collapsed. They were staring off in the opposite direction, where the rifle shot had come from. Both started running that way.

"Wait!" I called, chasing after them. "Shouldn't we help with the elephants?"

"Bonnie will get them under control," Dad told me. "Right now I'm more worried about whoever fired that shot."

"You don't think it was only a hunter?"

"No," Dad said. "Whoever fired that gun was too close to FunJungle. I don't think they were going after deer or rabbits."

"You mean . . . ?" I began.

"Yes." Dad looked back at me, and I could see the worry in his eyes. "I think someone just tried to kill one of our animals."